The Back Door Man

Dave Buschi

Copyright © 2011, 2017 by Dave Buschi
Cover design by Carl Graves

ISBN: 978-0-9839150-3-4

For Kristi

Prologue

ON the tarmac were their private jets. The men had flown in from around the globe: London, Zurich, Seattle, Moscow, New York and Beijing. Only a few details remained to be discussed.

"When?"

"Tuesday."

"And this man—this James Kolinsky—is the one?"

"Yes. It's all been arranged."

"Lock it tight. This will be dissected for years to come. We can't have any holes."

"Understood."

"The family too, of course."

"Of course."

One of the men signaled and three girls, each bought on the black market and trained in the art of seductive entertaining, entered the room carrying trays. Champagne was poured and the girls bowed demurely and left the room. The man with the shock of white hair lifted his flute. "Gentlemen."

The men raised their glasses.

"I toast to our success. Three days from now each of us will be sixty-billion-dollar men."

Here, here! Salud! Prost! Gan bei!

1

Tuesday

IT was too early in the morning for there to be crowds. James Kolinsky had seen one at an ATM on the way over here, and now this.

"What's going on?" a woman said.

"Someone said they're locked."

James stayed on the fringe and listened to the anxious chatter. People were just standing around. For a brief moment, he caught his own reflection in a bank of windows. His shirt was too wrinkled. It had passed the sniff test when he'd pulled it from his closet an hour ago, but he'd obviously not seen how bad it looked in the light. So much for trying to get a third wear out of it before dry cleaning. As for his hair, that too was looking a little wooly; he was going to need to pull out the shears soon and give it a trim.

"Everyone please!"

There was a man up front holding up his hands. James had to crane his neck to see that it was Security. The man told the crowd the office was closed and for everyone to go home.

James absorbed this change in routine along with everyone else. People just stood there at first, some in shock. The man repeated the announcement and ignored any questions, of which there were several. Some folks were quite demonstrative.

Not James, though, he took it in stride. At least on the surface. He was the sort that internalized everything. On the exterior he might look unaffected, but that in no way was reflective of what was really going on inside his head. Because right now, under his affable freshly-shaved face, worry and stress had burst right out the gates.

James followed the second wave of folks back to the parking deck. The elevators were filling up, so he took the stairwell. He got out of breath walking up the steps to the fifth level. He'd gotten so out of shape, he realized. There was a time he could have run up these steps without getting winded. It was like middle age had crept up on him overnight. Not unlike the tire—the one around his middle. One day it was just there. He hadn't liked it, but he'd accepted it along with everything else.

Absently, feeling the bubbling onset of mild panic from what had just happened, he looked over the edge of the deck. *Computer Tek*, otherwise known as *ComTek,* had a pretty campus with stately buildings sheathed in bronze glass. With the people gone, James could see Security stationed at other entry points. A lone woman in a pantsuit was talking with Security; she soon walked away shaking her head.

It would have been nice to have an explanation. No such luck, though. Instead, he had to imagine *what ifs*, and unfortunately, he was very good in that department.

A few paces away, a colleague was getting in his car. He and James exchanged some words. Neither voiced it, but it was there unsaid. ComTek had had an endless string of bad quarters. The stock was trading at an eight-year low. It didn't take a genius to know, particularly with the economy as it was, that now was not the time to be looking for a job.

"Well... see you tomorrow. Let's hope," the man said with a nervous laugh.

"Yeah, see you then." James forced a smile. As his colleague drove off, he immediately started wondering: what if ComTek had closed its doors for good? Companies weren't hiring anywhere. Even in the tech sector, which was better than most industries, jobs were scarce. And there were hundreds of software and systems engineers in the office. They'd all be competing for the same jobs. He'd have to move his family to find anything that paid even close to what he was making now, and that's if he was lucky.

He was the bread winner. His family depended on him. They'd eat through their savings, and with the cost of health coverage...

Easy boss—he was doing it again. Jumping ahead of things. They'd just closed the doors; no need to assume the worst. The company wasn't in that dire straits; least not yet, as far as he knew.

He took his eyes from the dash and started his car. With a residual wince, he remembered he needed gas before his trek home. He'd pushed it just coming here.

The closest gas station—and only one around for miles—was just outside the ComTek campus, two traffic lights away. That was just a short hop, and he had plenty of gas to make it that far. Unfortunately, once he got there, there was a slight complication. The pump wouldn't take his card.

Now that was annoying.

He walked into the store. The cashier was dealing with another customer.

"—had fucking cash, think I'd be using plastic?"

"My apologies." The cashier bowed his head. "Not working."

"Fuck!" The customer stormed out.

James stood there bemused. "Credit cards aren't working?"

7

The cashier shook his head. James didn't even need to check; like usual, he had no money in his wallet. He walked outside.

This wasn't good.

He tried to think where he could get some cash. The nearest ATM was several minutes away and James recalled seeing that ridiculous line as he'd driven by it on the way to work. That would take forever. And since it wasn't his bank, he'd get dinged with those BS fees. They robbed you blind. Two bucks to use it and two bucks from his own bank. It was criminal when you added it up. Four bucks to take out forty; ten percent. What a freakin' racket.

If he could help it he didn't want to just throw that money away. Better to think of another option. Perhaps a convenience or grocery store? They usually let you get cash when making a purchase. But he couldn't think of any that were close. This area was an old industrial district, now called tech alley. It had a few fast food joints and sit down restaurants, but that was about it.

He'd have to get on the highway. And with his gas situation that was definitely a no go. At a loss, he considered just driving. Which of course was another bad option...

Wait a second. He suddenly remembered he'd started cookie collections for Katie's Brownie troupe... *and that money was at the office.*

The office. Which was shut down.

Foiled, he worked it through his head. He just needed to get in and out. If he took the back way in, used the back door, it could work and it would save him some aggravation... also a little money... not to mention get him home sooner...

All good things. By the time he got to his car he was already ninety percent there. He chewed on his remaining reservations as he started his car; *it'll only take a few minutes…* He pulled out into the street and headed to ComTek.

HE bypassed the campus entrance by taking the service road and parked by a grove of trees. He walked the short distance to the service dock. At the service door, he pulled out an encryption card and typed in a four digit code.

The door clicked open. He went up some stairs and opened the door to his floor. This area of the building was known as 'Cubeville'. If you didn't know your way around, it was easy to get lost. The place was an unending maze of full-height cubicles. It didn't have any windows or discerning features to orient you. Part of that was intentional. Even signage was limited at ComTek, due to the company's emphasis on security.

As he went by doors that looked like all the others, he heard voices. He froze. That might be Security.

Shit.

Not wanting to have to explain himself, he ducked behind a cubicle.

"…incompetence. I know what I said. It was supposed to happen at noon."

James recognized the voice. *That was the COO. What was he doing here?*

Panic overtook him. 'Pink slip' Portino was not a man whose attention he wanted to catch. This would not look good if he was discovered hiding behind a cubicle wall.

James looked around and wondered what to do.

2

HE didn't have to wonder long. There was a faint ting of an elevator. The voices of Portino and the other man went away. James took a deep breath once he realized they were gone. He hadn't known what he was going to say if Portino had found him.

That was just a little too close for comfort. He suddenly questioned his bright idea of coming here. *Well... it was too late now.* He was already knee-deep in it, might as well get this over with.

He went to his work area. His was a crammed, but orderly workspace. He'd personalized his cube with mementos and photos. Two framed diplomas, one his mathematics degree, the other his masters, were under his shelving unit. Once upon a time, those degrees had been sources of pride. Lately though, he'd considered taking them down. It wasn't quite as he'd imagined it. In his mind he'd always thought they'd have a nobler setting than being hung on a flimsy cubicle partition.

He unlocked his desk drawer and retrieved the money from the envelope. He paused. His monitor was in sleep mode. He hadn't turned off his computer last night in order to run a static code analysis on a binary executable, which was a time-consuming operation.

It'll only take a second. He took a seat and clicked his mouse. His computer took several seconds, but once it came to life, a window popped up that indicated the program he'd run last night had completed successfully. He closed the window and logged onto the system with his password to access the Web.

He confirmed his personal interface security wall was still active—an add-on feature he'd downloaded to screen his keyboard strokes—and quickly typed in his bank's IP address. It was a habit of his. Engrained in him due to the nature of his job. Something he did every day.

The fact that his debit card hadn't worked at the gas station, irrespective of what the attendant said, worried him. He typed in his user passwords. It seemed to take longer than normal, but finally, after what was almost a full minute, his account information pulled up.

The balances for his and Sue's joint checking and savings account displayed on the screen. Sometimes when he was having a bad day, he'd look at those two numbers and feel cautiously optimistic. Their frugality had allowed them to bank a sizeable savings. It wasn't huge—and least not by rich people's standards—but it was growing, slowly and surely each month.

They scrimped and made do with less, but they were working towards something. The house they lived in was modest and while getting a mortgage on it at the time had been a stretch, his salary had grown incrementally in those years. Staying put in that house with their low interest rate and having finally paid off their credit cards and student loans had allowed them to be in a position to save.

It hadn't always been that way. It had taken them a long time to get to that point. James could still remember the 300 square foot flat they used to live in, and when their savings was what remained on their cards before they got maxed. They'd come far from those ramen noodle days. It was nice to be in a position where they didn't have to worry about money every day.

He blinked as he looked at the numbers. A sudden chill came over him. What normally should be a healthy five digit savings balance, was now zero.

$0.00.

He looked at his checking balance. Instead of having about two thousand dollars in it, it showed a negative number. Feeling like the floor beneath him had just opened, he clicked on the transactions page. He looked at the transactions. The names, which said where the purchases were made, were all over the board: *Berlin, VT; Tucson, AZ; Dade County, FL.* There were other purchases that appeared to be international transactions: *Espana; Ukraine.*

James clicked to open the details of when the purchases were made. All of them were done in the last 24 hours. Their status was listed as *pending*.

This wasn't happening...

In a state of shock, he clicked his mouse. He had to go several pages back to see transactions he recognized. His positive balance was quickly eroded by transactions he hadn't made. Multiple transfers from his savings into his checking account were also shown. Those transfers were quickly drained by more debits. He went to the tabs at top.

He had to notify the bank.

He scanned for the number to call. He had to stop the pending transactions; tell them they weren't his and for them to stop payment immediately before they were permanently debited from his account.

As he scanned the Home page for the telephone number to call, or a tab to take him there, his screen froze. His computer had locked up. He couldn't get the cursor to move. He wanted to scream. He pressed *Ctrl Alt Delete.*

Nothing happened.

No. No, no, no...

He pressed the keys like a man possessed. Finally, the cursor broke free and darted across the screen. The web page still wasn't responding. After several tries with his blood pressure spiking with each error message, he was able to close the web browser down. He restarted and frantically typed in the bank's IP address again.

He waited. Waited.

A *timed out* message appeared on the screen. He pounded his fist on his desk and yelled in frustration.

He clicked his mouse. His vision was getting blurry from his unblinking concentration. He typed in the bank's IP address again. It wasn't responding. A busy message appeared: *Please try again; the website you are trying to access is currently experiencing very high volume.*

Goddamnit!

"Hello, is someone here?"

The voice almost didn't register. James broke his manic focus from his screen.

"Hello?" The voice again; male. It was coming from across the room. In horror, James realized that was probably Security.

He stayed in his seat and looked at his screen. He tried moving his mouse. He typed on his keyboard. In disbelief, he looked at his hands.

What was he doing? He took his hands from the keyboard. He looked around, expecting to see someone behind him, but no one was there.

"This building is closed. You are trespassing by being here."

The voice this time was amplified. The man was approaching.

Oh my God. He had to get out of here.

He ducked down. His glowing monitor was going to give him away. He quickly reached up and turned off his screen.

He looked out of his cubicle. There was no one either way. The voice had come from the left, or had it?

Not sure, but knowing he couldn't stay where he was, he went right, keeping bent down. This direction, unfortunately, took him further from the stairs, not towards them. He moved as quickly as he could in his bent state, taking a series of turns in the cubicle maze.

He heard a sound and immediately froze. The sound was close. It was the crackle of a radio. A man's voice, so close it gave him goosebumps, started speaking into his walkie-talkie.

It sounded like he was just over the cubicle wall. If the man turned the corner, James would be in full view. James backtracked, holding his breath, praying his shoes didn't squeak to give him away.

His mind raced. He was cut off. If the man kept coming, James was toast. The man would find him and with Portino here it was only a matter of the man bringing it to Portino's attention, which he certainly would.

Desperate, James considered running. Running as fast as he could. He realized that was insane; he had to do something else, but what? As his eyes scanned frantically for an answer, he thought of the cubicle space he'd just passed. It was at the end of a dead-end aisle.

Heading back that way, he went into the cubicle. He could still hear the man's walkie-talkie crackling. James took a deep breath and pressed the button to turn on the computer. The computer emitted its low *whirr* noise and began to boot up. The monitor blinked to life. James quickly left the cubicle. Moving as fast as he dared, he went three cubicles down and inside it for cover.

He crouched and listened. He couldn't hear the computer from this far away, but he heard the man's footfalls. The man seemed to be moving quickly. He must have heard the noise.

James took another breath. Okay… now.

He looked out into the aisle. There was the man with his back to him. He was holding something in his hand that almost looked like a gun.

Jesus.

It was a gun.

Fear threatened to overwhelm him. With supreme effort, James refocused. He knew there would not be a better time; he had to do it now. *Now!* He left the cubicle and quickly darted down the aisle and took a right. He didn't risk looking back. Wanting to run, but knowing his footfalls would be heard, he went in a fast walk.

He turned down another aisle. He glanced back. The man wasn't following.

He went past a series of cubicles and kept going. The door to the stairwell was just ahead. He went faster now, almost running. The door got closer.

Closer.

"Stop!"

Oh shit.

The man had seen him. For a split-second, James considered stopping, but it was as if his legs wouldn't obey and kept moving. He reached the door and yanked it open. Before he knew what he was doing, he'd darted inside the emergency stairwell and was going down the stairs.

3

SHIT, shit, shit.

He ran down the steps. He went past the third level… the second…

That man had a gun!

He reached the ground floor landing. He almost stumbled as his hand missed the rail on a cutback. A long fire escape corridor lay ahead of him.

What was Security doing carrying guns?

The man was behind him. He heard footfalls and the sound of voices. There was more than one of them. The voices were coming from down the corridor, as well as from the stairwell above. *Oh my gosh, this was not good.*

Not good…

He went under the lee of the stairs and opened a door that said 'not an exit' and ran down an internal corridor, which took him deeper into the complex. As he turned a corner, he heard a yell behind him.

There was a tee in the corridor. He took a left. Ahead would be an exit, but it would take him by a Security station. Making a split-decision, he yanked open a door on his right and entered a mantrap. The door that shut behind him would trigger an alarm if he tried to open it again. James fumbled for his passkey.

This section of the complex was off-limits to most employees. James's job gave him special access. He inserted his passkey into the slot and pressed his palm against the biometric scanner. He knew that a digital record would be made of him entering this space. He couldn't worry about that now.

A green LED blinked and the door clicked open. James quickly went inside. He was in a room that spilled into a larger space. An insistent hum was coming from row after row of server racks, all of which were interconnected with wires and conduit. This was Central IQ. ComTek's brain.

James moved away from the door. Security would not have access to this area. In moments the man chasing him would look into the vestibule and see that James was not in it. The list of individuals granted access to this area was less than thirty in number. James was almost as good as caught, if the man had seen him go through the door.

James looked on the wall next to the door. There was a flat screen monitor with a split screen. One image was of the mantrap and the other was a view inside the corridor. James watched as Security ran past the door and disappeared from view.

Phew. He hadn't been seen. This area linked up to two other exits. He could get out of here now.

Or maybe not.

He paused as his head began to string together the loose pieces. It wasn't quite that simple. Not by a long shot.

With painful clarity he saw the pickle he'd put himself into. His lack of judgment in coming to the office, which was becoming more stupid with each passing moment, was about to be compounded twice. First, he'd run from Security. A decision, which now seemed absolutely absurd. He should have tried to explain himself. But now, if he just left, he'd be leaving behind a digital record that would leave no doubt how this would end.

He'd be fired.

Eleven years of working for the same company was about to end badly and abruptly. Gone would go his references. He might even get blackballed from working in information security again.

If he turned himself in now the consequences weren't much better. His running had set off a cascading implication of wrongdoing. Not only had he secretly entered the building, but by entering this space he'd entered a red zone and compromised security.

Even if he fabricated some legitimate-sounding story for being here—his integrity and judgment would be under a cloud. He'd never be entrusted with sensitive assignments again.

His options were growing more limited by the second. If he had any hope of getting himself out of this lose-lose situation he'd have to plow ahead into more awful territory. He took a deep breath, hardly believing he was even considering it.

There were maybe three individuals in the company who might be able to attempt it. He'd theorized about it countless times. A major part of his job was to assess the holes; the weaknesses in the multi-layered security net that protected ComTek's most vital assets. Those exercises were usually hypothetical role-playing scenarios, which his seven-person tiger team analyzed. Each hypothetical breach had resulted in a new series of protocols being implemented.

ComTek had some of the most sophisticated information security features of any company in the country; its Security IQ was on par with systems that protected interests of national defense. Never though, not once, even in a bad nightmare, did he think he'd ever be put in this position. The thought of it was enough to make him want to throw up, but he grimly realized it was the only option available to him where the end result was him keeping his job.

The solution was daunting but doable. *He hoped.*

He had to erase his digital footsteps. He had to alter the memory matrix, including what the cameras would have captured. 99.9 percent of the time that was something easier said than done. But if there was any silver lining to this numskull predicament, it was in its timing. Several days ago he'd discovered an anomaly; a glitch in the system that could give him an opening to exploit.

He opened a panel on the nearest wall. He typed in a six digit access number and switched the toggles that would take the latent systems off-line. This was standard procedure for doing diagnostics on the remote systems and would temporarily interfere with any security inquiries.

All log-ins and passkey user data would be unavailable. It was an anomaly that James had discovered last week, and rather than delegating to someone on his team, had handled himself by creating a security patch. The static code analysis he'd been running on his computer last night, in fact, had been an exercise to assess the patch's effectiveness.

Fortunately, he hadn't put the patch in place, yet.

James sat down at the closest terminal and quickly went to work. His running had left him caked in sweat. He felt a chill from the air conditioning. It was much cooler in this space than it was in other areas of the complex. Temperature and humidity in here were regulated at a consistent 69/50. That took some doing as the servers put off a tremendous amount of heat. Over three hundred tons of cooling was needed to condition this space.

The place was supplied with continuous, uninterruptible power. Strict environmental management systems were in place, which in addition to the air conditioning and humidity control, were able to detect moisture intrusions. No drinks were allowed in this area, not even water bottles with spill-proof caps. A warning light on the wall was detecting James's own body moisture right now. If excessive moisture was detected an audible alarm would go off.

James knew he wouldn't trigger the alarm just with his sweat. Nevertheless, that light wasn't doing much to help his concentration.

James sometimes spent a greater part of his day in this controlled, managed environment. Like the floor where his cubicle was, there weren't any windows in this space. A person was cut off from the world in here. The hum, which became background noise after a while, stayed with you, even when you left.

James looked up and took in the distributed cluster architecture around him. The majority of this space wasn't even used for ComTek's essential operations, but was leased by outside companies.

ComTek's most profitable division was secure data storage. In this gargantuan space, and in another larger off-site facility called a "hot site", were enough servers and storage clusters to archive 200 exabytes of data. A daunting mind-blowing capacity that could only be truly appreciated by looking at the roster of clients that utilized ComTek's services.

Google, Microsoft and Facebook all leased "space" from ComTek. Next to banking institutions and the credit-card industry, they were three of ComTek's most profitable clients.

James knew he needed to do this quickly. While he felt confident that Security hadn't seen him, or at least hadn't gotten a visual of his face, there would be a digital record of him in the system due to him using his passkey. There was also his biometric signature. Cameras would have captured some of his movements. There were cameras situated throughout the complex. That camera footage, which he knew firsthand was never looked at, would now be scrutinized. They would just need to pull up the last ten minutes and he'd be captured on four of those cameras.

ComTek's overarching security breadth was also its Achilles' heel. It would take forty-two employees, each watching six screens, in order to monitor in real time all the camera footage. An impossible task obviously, considering each Security detail was comprised of a dozen individuals. To say nothing of the fact that none of those individuals were savvy with technology.

That was being kind. Just last week:

"Damn thing don't work."

Not surprising, considering it wasn't plugged in.

Regardless of Security's shortcomings, it didn't take a rocket scientist to operate *Phalanx's* interface features. It was a simple procedure to pull up the screens and play back footage. James gauged he had only minutes to get done what he needed to get done before they pulled up footage of him and made a positive ID. Once that hurdle was accomplished there were only fourteen more security features to access and address.

Piece of cake. James felt positively ill.

Twenty-two minutes later, he still didn't feel any better. But he was out. And he'd scrubbed his tracks clean.

He picked the most remote egress point to exit Building C. The camera that captured this location would still be playing an endless loop for another three minutes so his exit should go unnoticed. James was sweating again; he'd never really stopped, not even with the chill of the air conditioning. He couldn't believe what he'd just done.

James had never run a red light. He was a rule follower. Even when he drove home on some nights when it was 1 AM and there was a red light at that ridiculous intersection near his house that took forever, he always waited. He waited for that darn light to turn green, even though he was tired, wanted to get home, and knew beyond a doubt that there were no police around and no way for him to get caught.

He followed rules. Always.

What had happened to him?

James's head was swimming. He felt like he was having an out of body experience where he was dead and looking down at a body he no longer recognized.

He had to remind himself to pay attention. This wasn't over, and wouldn't be until he was safely in his car, which would soon have gas to take him home.

He moved quickly. Security was concentrated in another part of the complex looking for the intruder. They hadn't called the authorities. James knew the protocol. Calling the authorities was the last on a long list of options, only to be done in the direst of emergencies. It would take the building burning and a verbal mandate from the CEO or Portino for that call to be made.

ComTek prided itself on its fail-safe security measures. Almost all of which were overrated. Portino was partially to thank for that—the man's vigilant cost-cutting in the last two years had left the company a shell of its former self.

If word got out that an intruder had attempted to break into the complex and hadn't been apprehended, then ComTek's depressed stock would take an even deeper nosedive. It would be catastrophic. Companies used ComTek for storing their most vital data and paid handsomely for that service.

James had gone through all the scenarios of what consequences would ensue for his actions. He knew what tomorrow would bring. Tomorrow would be business as usual. No one would know this had ever happened. At least no one in the public sector. The information would be confined to a handful of individuals, just like the last few times.

Like the time that the cleaning service had accidentally thrown in the trash data tapes that contained personal information on over one million Citibank customers. Or the time that it was discovered that the backup systems on the Siemens' account hadn't been working for six months. The list had others. James had seen it, owing to the wide scope of his job. He saw more things than the top brass would ever like him to know.

James kept to the median that tracked next to the woods. He skirted the parking lot, not taking any chances. This area was designated as overflow parking for service vehicles and was rarely used. Surprisingly, there were six vehicles scattered in the lot.

As he took a path that led into the woods, James glanced at one of the cars parked by a generator. It was a white Cadillac Escalade with tinted windows. He knew the car's owner: Nick Paulson.

What was that jerk doing here?

He didn't dwell on that thought for long. There was still the bank he needed to deal with. He took out his Blackberry. A few minutes ago he'd inputted the bank's number into his address book. He'd gotten the number from the back of his debit card, where he should have looked in the first place.

He pulled up the number on his screen and placed the call. He had to stop those payments from being deducted before the bank drained all his and Sue's savings! Once that was done he'd cancel their cards and put a hold on their account.

His adrenaline had been going forever and he felt nauseous. This day was way too exhausting.

4

NICK Paulson, thirty-three, tall and handsome in a movie star sort of way, was cursing James Kolinsky's name.

That fuckin' dickhead. I thought he fixed this.

For the last half-hour he'd been trying to determine who had accessed Building C. Portino had made it very clear they needed to identify and locate the intruder.

Paulson thought it a waste of time, but like a good soldier he was humoring the boss. This was an unneeded distraction. The person had been spotted in Cubeville, of all places. What was the big concern? They'd steal a few pencils from someone's desk?

Paulson had gone over all the digital capture. Half the footage was worthless. The resolution was ridiculous; two boxes were completely out of focus, a third was a granulated static mess, and a fourth was offline. All of these problems were supposed to have been fixed months ago.

Paulson was tired of reviewing sloppy work. In the two years he'd been here—it felt longer than that—he'd identified more problems in more divisions than any of his worthless cohorts.

He was surprised, however, at Kolinsky dropping the ball on updating the *Phalanx* system. That was Kolinsky's team responsibility. It wasn't like that man to be careless; he prided himself on his attention to detail and professionalism.

Professionalism, Paulson almost laughed. Kolinsky had used that exact word, Paulson knew, when asked to critique himself during his last performance review. As if that was what got you ahead. The guy was clueless.

Paulson snickered, recalling the conversation that he'd seen on video.

"How does three percent sound?"

James had nodded and said meekly *"whatever is fair".*

"Like a lemming," Portino had said, who was watching the video along with him. "He deserves this for being such a putz. We selected well."

Kolinsky. The man had absolutely no idea how to play the game.

Not the case for Paulson. When that had been his gig he'd had it wired. He knew exactly how to advance quickly. First off, never dicker around at a place with no growth potential. In nine years he'd had seven jobs. Each job hop he'd upped his salary north of fifteen percent. Kolinsky, compared to his younger colleagues, was a fossil around here; he'd been at ComTek longer than most higher ups, taking the spoon-fed two or three percent annual raises each time.

Paulson knew all the details. He'd done his homework. The man had never once asked for a bigger slice, even with all his contributions. And not once had he come close to campaigning for a promotion.

The guy was a certified idiot. One of those lifers who was going to be a lowly manager till the day he died. Idiot didn't even know that some of the people that reported to him were making more than he was.

You want to get promoted? Fuckin' get some balls. Paulson had always been willing to walk away.

You want to keep me? Make it worth my while. And walk the talk. Paulson projected supreme confidence, even when he was in over his head. His image was polished. Forget the nerd or slob look most his cohorts adopted; Paulson was all about designer clothes, tailored shoes, and acerbic wit. His was the whole package. Kolinsky had never polished his shoes in his life—he looked like a bum, complete down to the perma-stubble on his face. And he wondered why he lost out when it came time for promotions?

Third on that list, but most importantly: it was *all* about relationships. Paulson was an ace in that department. He didn't waste his time with the lowlifes (which in his view was anyone under Director level), like Kolinsky did, that just sent a subtle message to upper management that you belonged with the riff-raff. Paulson long ago had adopted the right attitude. Made it known that he belonged with the big players. Could speak their language.

With the foodies he talked about the best restaurants in town. With the risk nuts he talked about skydiving and racing his Viper at the track. With the cigar and wine aficionados he could rattle off the best years for Opal or the finest smokes he'd ever had.

That's what got you ahead. Relationships forged by common connections. Of course, it didn't hurt that he was brilliant, and that wasn't just him saying that. Paulson knew he was the perfect prototype. Companies salivated for guys like him and paid top dollar to get them—as they had time and time again. Just look at how he read on paper.

Stanford undergrad. Grad school at Harvard. He'd cut his chops as an analyst at Goldman Sachs before his stint at Silicon Valley. He'd worked abroad for several high-tech firms, which broadened his impressive repertoire, and also gave him his chummy British accent. An affectation he adopted on those choice occasions when he was putting on the charm. If he only knew what he knew now when he was back in school.

Paulson fantasized about it often. It was his one big regret. He'd left a few too many begging for it without closing the deal. But he hadn't had enough time. Christ sakes, how many skirts could a man fuck anyway? Not enough, for damn sure.

All of that, of course, was soon to be rectified.

Paulson flexed his fingers and cracked his knuckles. It was time to get this done, so he could move on to his new life.

Paradigms changed. He'd soon more than make up for lost time. This drudgery he'd signed up for was about to be old news. No longer would he be doing demeaning kiss-ass bullshit. Soon he would be free to do whatever the fuck he wanted for the rest of his fucking life.

"I want this person identified," Portino said. "I don't like loose ends."

"No problem," Paulson had said. "Consider it done."

5

JAMES was in a rundown area. He gripped his leather satchel and tried to look as casual as he could muster. There was little chance he could be successful pulling that off with everything going on. He was a mess.

His car was blocks away. He'd locked the doors, checked them twice and hoped for the best. It wouldn't surprise him if it was on concrete blocks by now. He'd taken everything of value out of it, which wasn't much.

He looked at his Blackberry hoping that the battery would show some flicker of life. After being routed through the bank's automated teller system three times, each time being dropped, he'd tried to call his wife again. Something was up with his reception; even connections to his home line were cut off before he could talk. His voice was hoarse from yelling in frustration.

All of this while having to go through the agony of finding the gas station closed. The same gas station he'd tried the first time. A random shooting had occurred, of all the crazy things. A policeman had been there. The gas attendant was answering a bunch of questions. James was told to move along; the gas station was closed.

James walked past some derelict buildings, keeping his eyes peeled for a pay phone. In the back of his mind he wondered if they even made pay phones anymore. With the exception of airports he never saw them. People relied on cell phones and PDAs nowadays.

Why, in hindsight, had he driven this direction? He only had himself to blame. After finding the gas station closed, he'd driven around trying to find another gas station, and this is where he ended up. In no-man's land. It didn't even look like the city of Raleigh he knew. He saw boarded-up businesses; peeling posters on rotting fences; garbage strewn on sidewalks.

His back had a sharp pain from having to push his car the last few feet, so that it would be against the curb. He hoped he hadn't pulled his back out; just what he needed, to mess up his alignment. That would take weeks to fix with his chiropractor. He'd left his car next to the remnants of a parking meter. The meter itself had been shorn off and there was just a rusting metal post.

The curb at one time had been painted, indicating it might have been a no-parking zone, but the paint was peeled so badly that it was barely noticeable. There weren't any signs to indicate whether it was a parking zone or not. He didn't know which was worse: to be towed to some junkyard in this area where it'd be stripped clean for parts, or to have his car stolen outright—not that he had any choice in the matter.

He'd never run out of gas. Ever.

James could feel eyes on him. A fried chicken establishment called "B&Ls" with bars on the windows had several sketchy-looking gents loitering in front. The place wasn't open, yet. What were those fellas doing? James walked by feeling like a big juicy drumstick holding a bag full of dough.

If only they knew he was broke. His entire savings was wiped out, probably, by this point. *Pending.* That word was seared into his brain. How long, he wondered, before those transactions were permanently debited from his and Sue's joint account? Twenty-four hours? When had the clock started ticking? Last night? Some of those transactions were posted yesterday, which probably meant twenty-four hours were about to lapse.

His head was in a fog thinking of the ruin of it all. He grasped at the straw of an idea that their account was FDIC insured. But what did that mean? Did the bank cover losses like theirs? That seemed unlikely; FDIC was more to cover the prospect of a bank going under, not a customer who failed to notify them they were a victim of identity theft. And then there was the bigger question: was the theft isolated to just the bank? What about his and Sue's 401(k)s? If they'd stolen his identity, could they have accessed their retirement accounts?

He almost felt like crying. All these questions, and he didn't have one answer. And there was nothing he could do about it, at least not until he got some gas. He was powerless... robbed... destitute... no gas... no car... no transportation. He wallowed in self-pity. Up ahead, he saw some more folks. They were gathered in front of a mom and pop grocery. His eyes, glassy and wet, strayed to what was next to a telephone pole in front of the grocery.

It was a pay phone.

He felt a flicker of hope.

The pay phone was one of those old open ones with just a bikini cover to keep out the rain. As he got closer, he could see the metal cord hung limp without a receiver. A metal binder that at one time would have held a phone book was now bent and battered like it had been beaten with a brick. The black box that was the phone terminal was destroyed. Someone had tried to pry open the metal panel that gave access to the coin depository.

James gnashed his teeth and looked over at the grocery. Reluctant, but warming to the idea considering his limited options, he wondered if the store clerk would let him borrow the store's phone? Or maybe one of its customers had a cell phone he could use? He looked for a likely prospect.

There were several people with bundles in their arms. Each was walking quickly away. A few were scampering to get inside, past the people coming out. They weren't using the door to get in. They were going through what James realized was an opening where there once had been glass storefront.

James, feeling obtuse that he hadn't noticed it till now, realized what was going on. *These people were stealing.*

A woman holding a little girl's hand was scurrying away with a jumbo bag of diapers. Another man was trying to cradle what looked to be cans of food. He was bumped and the cans spilled from his arms and clattered on the sidewalk. A fight ensued. People grabbed the cans and ran.

James looked on in partial disbelief.

A man with nothing in his arms was staring at him; his eyes flicked to James's satchel. *Just great... as if he hadn't been robbed enough.*

James skirted the small mob scene and found a stretch of open sidewalk. He picked up his pace, and glanced back to see if anyone was following. People were running in all directions, carrying stuff they'd taken. The man that had been looking at him was nowhere to be seen.

James slowed his walk and went past dilapidated buildings, a weed covered parking lot, and a closed pawn shop. He heard the plaintive sound of sirens in the distance.

Finally, the sound of sane civilization. Police were coming to the scene to restore order. But the sirens faded until he couldn't hear them anymore.

James wondered what was going on. First the shooting at the gas station and now looting in broad daylight? Crazy. What was the probability? A part of him wondered if these occurrences were common around here.

He passed an alleyway, and noticed halfway down it there was a girl and two men. The girl was clutching something in her arms. Her eyes, the size

31

of saucers, looked at James. The men's craven faces turned and looked at him.

James looked away. Whatever they were doing was none of his business; he had enough problems of his own. Keep walking.

"Please."

It was the girl. She was either talking to the men or sending out a plea to James for help. James paused. *Just keep walking.* Don't get involved, you don't have time for this.

Please.

The woman's voice tugged, grabbed and wouldn't let go.

Please.

He looked back. Dammit. He stopped.

Don't, he told himself. But his legs were already taking him back to the alley.

6

PAULSON had about wrapped it up, but there was something nagging him. He went over it again: The intruder had entered through a service entry at the rear of Building C. It was a low-tech entry. The keycard lock rendered a partial, which meant it had been offline all night. That sometimes occurred when some idiot propped the door open for deliveries, which in this situation didn't seem to be the case—no blockage was discovered at the door.

From there the intruder appeared to have used one of the emergency stairwells to get to the fourth level. Again, no keycard was used. Cameras had picked up the intruder entering—it was only a partial back shot, but it was clear enough to determine the intruder appeared to be male and had dark hair. From the blue stripe on the wall of the stairwell Paulson was able to determine the person was just under six foot in height. The man was wearing a white collared business shirt.

Security had given their spiel, which was backed up by the camera footage. Coincidentally, all camera shots that would put this to bed and render a positive ID were either partially disabled or the images captured were of such poor resolution that they were worthless. Sixteen minutes after the stairwell entry, the intruder went past the Security station on the lower level. The station, of course, had not been manned. The intruder had then presumably used the front door to make his exit.

The fucking front door!

All in all, from what he could ascertain, there were seven perimeter protocol lapses by Security. *Seven!* Those worthless flesh bags were worse than the Keystone Cops.

Paulson had determined that no restricted areas were breached. Or at least no entries registered on the sensors. The intruder appeared to have taken nothing. A computer was turned on in a low security area, but no log-in was done, and no data appeared to have been taken.

All of which, seemed sketchy. Why would someone go to the fourth level? There was nothing there, but cubicles and staff offices.

Security had inventoried all the cars parked in the deck. There were only a few, and all the owners were accounted for. Paulson had pulled up his eye in the sky. His SUV Cadillac was outfitted with a LoJack. In his wallet was a card the dealership had given him. On it was his VIN, as well as his pass code.

It was pretty slick. He just went to the LoJack website; plugged in the numbers and in moments, *wa-la,* an aerial shot pulled up his car. It was Big Brother. Forget the stuff you saw in the movies, the technology available today totally kicked ass. Just with a couple clicks he could track exactly where he had been, the speed his vehicle had gone, and any other detail, including street names of where he'd parked.

The site didn't pull up old aerial footage like Google or Flash Earth. No. The LoJack site pulled up live footage. *Live.* Every time he used the site, he got a hard on. The frames were refreshed every couple of seconds. He could count the cars next to his. There was a red and blue one parked to the left of his.

The technology was so damn effective; it seemed it had to be illegal. He'd showed it to Portino when he first bought his ride. The man hadn't been impressed—which of course was annoying, until he'd found out that most Mercedes came with LoJack; it was standard on the premium models.

34

Portino had checked out the site before. In fact, it was his idea when they were doing some of their work to tag LoJacks on all of Kolinsky's team.

While that had taken some doing—having to get the VINs, register them under aliases, go through all the circuitous bullshit, including getting the RFIDs inserted—once it was done, it was an easy way to keep tabs on them. Particularly since all of his work had to occur after hours. What a pain in the ass that had been. Especially that stiff Kolinsky. The man was a workaholic Monday through Friday—some nights he didn't leave till around nine or ten. For about three weeks Paulson felt like he was working the night shift.

Paulson chewed on his toothpick. This was getting ridiculous. He had uncovered nothing. Two hours wasted, and all he had to show was some lousy pixilated camera footage of some fuzzy person running. Damn that Kolinsky, if his team had fixed that interface problem with the digital stream like they were supposed to, he'd have ID'd the intruder by now.

Instead...

Paulson paused. Something clicked in his head. *If not for the cameras...*

A sinking feeling came over him. Paulson went back to the LoJack site. He pulled up the VINs and pass codes for Kolinsky's team. One by one, he inputted the numbers.

Several minutes later, he walked into Portino's office.

"Rex, we have a problem."

7

IT was a boneheaded idea, but better than nothing. James held his Blackberry out in front of him. He'd plugged the earplug to the side of it, and the cord was trailing from his satchel. He pointed the Blackberry at the two men who were holding the girl.

"Step away from her."

One man was holding her neck in a choke hold. The other was in front, in the process of lifting up her dress. The men turned. The simple action of them turning sent a frisson of electricity through James.

"You don't want to do this," James said. "Leave her alone."

One of the men held a knife. It was a stub thing, just a few inches long. It almost looked like a paring knife that one would use to skin an apple or potato. "This ain't none of your business."

The other looked menacingly at James. "How 'bout you cut him, see if 'at make him wanna stick 'round?"

James pushed the side button of his Blackberry several times.

"I've called the police. You should leave now," James said. "Before you do something you regret."

"What you talkin' about?" the man with the knife said. "Give 'at thing to me."

"I'm recording you," James said. "I'm sending these images real time in streaming format to the nearest police precinct. You don't want to take this any further. It'll just go bad for you."

Both the men frowned. The man behind the woman let go of her neck. They stared at James's Blackberry.

"Tha's just a phone."

"He's got somethin' in the bag," the man with the knife said, his eyes narrowing. "See 'at cord?"

James took a step back. "It's not too late. You can stop now and just go. You don't want to make this worse for you."

"Get 'at bag, James."

For a second, James thought the guy was speaking to him—how in the world did he know his name? He then realized the man with the knife must also be named James. The man took a step forward and the other man screamed.

It was so discordant that James blinked. When his eyes opened, he saw the girl moving in a blur. She had something in her hand. Now it was the man with the knife's turn to scream. He dropped the knife. The man clawed at his eyes.

It all happened so fast. Both men were screaming. The girl was spraying something. A sharp stench assaulted James's nostrils.

The girl grabbed something from the ground and ran towards him. "Go!" she said.

It took a split-second to register. James watched her run by him. Then he was following, his cord trailing from his satchel, flopping like a whip, as they both raced down the sidewalk.

8

THEY ran for several blocks. The men they'd left with pepper spray in their eyes were probably still back in the alley, groping at their eyes or looking for water to douse the pain. James was sitting on what once had been a porch. Ivy had taken over and covered most of the boards and what remained of the windows.

The girl hadn't said a word, not since the alley when she'd said "Go".

"You okay?" James said.

The girl's lips tightened. She looked young. James would have guessed she was eighteen or nineteen, but she could have been younger. Her cocoa skin was smooth and had a shiny sheen that looked wet. Her hair was unkempt and looked like it hadn't been washed for days. The dress she was wearing was thin, almost threadbare. She'd pulled together where it had torn as best she could. Her arms were crossed and her body was bunched like a little girl's.

The bag she'd been carrying was next to her. It was a shiny black tote that was full of various odd items. He made out a stick of deodorant, a phone, some bundled clothes and what looked to be a teddy bear buried in the middle.

The teddy bear surprised him. He suddenly felt very sad.

"How old are you?"

She looked at him sharply, those vacant eyes suddenly burnishing with life. "Old enough." Her voice was like a lash.

"I'm sorry," James said, "I didn't mean…" He didn't know what to say.

"My name is James. I don't live around here. My car ran out of gas." He felt like he needed to say more. "I'm married and have two daughters. I'm an engineer. I work at ComTek."

"Good for you." She took her eyes from him, as if suddenly judging him harmless.

His own words had sounded odd; irrelevant. The girl was looking at the street. He suddenly thought of his own daughters and wished he was home right now hugging both of them.

"Do you live around here?"

"Mmm," she said.

"Was that a yes?"

She turned sharply. "I don't owe you nothin'."

"Of course not. I'm just glad you're okay."

The girl chewed on her lip.

"What was that you were holdin'?"

"My phone?"

"Yeah, you were fooling with that—right?"

James nodded. "It's a good thing you had that spray."

"Mmm, thought I was out. I'm surprised it worked."

She said it so matter-of-factly; like it wasn't the first time she'd had to use the spray. James didn't dwell on her response. He felt a surge of empathy that almost overwhelmed him—*this poor girl had almost been raped, and she was acting like it was a common day occurrence.*

"Would you mind if I borrowed your phone?" he said, needing to change the subject.

"I'm out of minutes."

"I've got some money. I'll pay for the overage. It'll just be a short call. I won't be more than two minutes."

"You don't understand," she said. "It don't work. I used up my minutes. I ain't got Verizon, I've got NuCall. *Pay as you go. Don't sweat it.*"

Her last words might have been an ad tagline, not that James had ever heard of *New Call* before.

"You out too?"

"What do you mean?"

"Your phone? You out of minutes?"

"No, it's my battery. It's dead." James fidgeted. "Listen, I need to know if you're going to be okay? Because I don't think I am."

She laughed and he hadn't been trying to be funny. She smirked. "You're a fish out of water? Ain't ya?"

James shook his head. "I'm just not used to this. This day has been a little strange."

"Tell me. Everybody's gone plumb crazy. Those two that tried to jump me? I don't know what they were thinking. Acting like it was Christmas or something."

James looked down. "Do you have a family? Someplace you can go?"

"Yeah." Her answer was abrupt and James was afraid he'd insulted her. She softened her tone. "I got a family. I live with my grandma and my kid, 'bout seven blocks from here." She stood up. "You okay?"

"Sure." James looked at her. It was amazing. She was concerned for *his* welfare. He stood up. "I didn't get your name."

"Taneesha Burke."

"Well Taneesha, thank you for saving me."

Her forehead bunched.

He explained. "If you hadn't had that spray, I might be in a lot worse shape."

Her face, which was really quite pretty, broke into a smile. James smiled back. "Well, I'm going to get going. Do you think you can point me in the direction of the nearest gas station?"

One of her eyebrows arched. "Where you think you at, James?" She seemed to think for a second. "Car around here?"

James nodded.

"Well, c'mon."

She hopped down the steps and James had to hustle to keep up.

ON top was barbed wired. Beyond, was a junkyard. Taneesha had a strip of garden hose in her hand, which she'd taken from the side of an abandoned house.

"Watch for the dog," she said.

"Dog?"

She pulled at the fence and James could see it had an opening where some of the links had been cut. "You first," she said.

"Did you say dog?" James's feet were rooted. A terrible fear of dismemberment by Doberman came over him.

"We're fine," Taneesha said. "C'mon, slide in."

"You sure this is the way to a gas station?" James said. "Is this a shortcut?"

She laughed. "You're funny. C'mon."

James surveyed the area past the fence, looking for any type of movement. Not seeing any, he squeezed through the opening. He held it for her as she squeezed through behind him. They walked past some rusty relics that were once cars.

"Not these," Taneesha said.

She walked spry of step, as James scrambled to keep up. His eyes darted everywhere. Behind every car he expected some mangy junkyard dog to come barreling out. The only thing that kept him from running back towards the fence was Taneesha's upbeat demeanor.

She seemed to have almost completely recovered from what had happened with the men. James admired her resilience and verve. It was a good sign, he hoped.

As she stepped over some debris, James noticed that Taneesha's legs were very graceful and toned. It wasn't like him to notice such things. But Taneesha was hard not to notice. He suddenly realized she was a very pretty young girl.

He felt guilty having that thought—particularly considering the ordeal she'd just gone through—and almost tripped. He needed to pay attention to where he was walking. There were all sorts of debris on the ground. Taneesha bent down and picked up an old plastic bottle. She tossed it aside. A moment later she spied a large plastic container and picked it up.

James kept looking for the dog. He figured he'd hear it first.

Taneesha yelped gleefully.

"These weren't here last time. C'mon." She picked her way over some old railroad ties.

It didn't seem to James they were getting anywhere. He looked for a fence to indicate the other side of the junkyard, but all he saw was an endless field. "Where are we going?"

"This'll do," Taneesha said. "I hate this part. You do it." She handed him the hose she'd cut. "Don't get it on us," Taneesha said, as she unscrewed the car's gas cap.

"We're going to siphon gas?"

"Yep." Taneesha handed him the plastic cube container. The label on it said 'fresh spring water'. "How do I do this?" James said, looking at the hose.

"Wipe it first," Taneesha said, as she put the other end in the gas tank. "To get it going, give it a good pull. But be careful. You gotta move quick. Jam that end in the jug and try not to get it on us." She stepped back.

James wiped off the end of the hose; gave it a quick yank and jammed it in the mouth of the water container.

Taneesha laughed. "You big dummy. Give it to me." She grabbed it and gave the hose another wipe. She put her mouth to it, gave it a hard suck and jammed the hose into the container as gas started to spill out.

James watched in wonderment. He knew what he was seeing was caused by differences in pressure and gravity. Still, seeing the gas come out made him feel like a kid in sixth grade science lab. "Cool."

Taneesha filled up the container and crimped the hose. "Take this." She handed him the container. "It's heavy."

James took it. Taneesha extracted the hose. She removed the other end and closed the gas cap. She looked around, then walked over and picked up what appeared to be the remnants of some shirt. She tore off a strip and handed it to James. "That's to plug it up." Her forehead pinched. "Uh oh."

"What?"

She bit her lip and looked at him apologetically. "I hear the dog."

9

THE man took a drag on his unfiltered cigarette as he looked out the window. The nubs of his fingers were stained yellowish black.

"Look at this," Peter said, as he flicked his ashes out. "You only find this where they live."

Smoke fumed from his nostrils. "See that garbage. What is that, a kitchen sink? It's like one big garbage can. These people... I bet if you put 'em in a cage without any toilet and left them for days, unlike civilized sorts who'd use the corner, they'd just shit on the floor and step in it." He took another drag. "Let me see that picture again."

His partner, Denis, handed him a print. It was a digital photograph from the torso up. Peter had read the jacket. Like usual, there wasn't much, just a few details: age and other particulars. The one difference in this case was there was a RFID tag on the guy. That was a first.

Their Muscovite friends usually kept it simple. They didn't bother using such fancy methods. It made Peter curious. The marker was in the car, but still, he wondered if this was a straight deal, or something that had been passed around.

Not that it mattered. A deal was a deal and their friends didn't pay them to ask questions. They were just supposed to get the job done, and put a rush on it.

They didn't get many of those. Cost extra.

Peter handed the picture back. Denis had his laptop open. The car they were tracking hadn't moved. Peter wondered why a white guy would be down in this neighborhood. Maybe he was a dealer. If he was, he'd obviously ticked off the wrong people.

Peter took another drag and tossed his cigarette out the window. "This ain't normal." They'd passed three public disturbances and a building that was burning. Even for this area that was unusual. "How close are we?"

Denis held up a finger, which meant they were close. Three blocks later Peter saw it. It was a late model Jap car that was parked along the curb.

"That it?"

Denis nodded.

"It's attracted roaches." Peter parked two car lengths behind and lit another cigarette. "Tuck that under the seat."

They both opened their doors and walked towards the car. Three teens in long white sleeveless tees that covered their bare asses stopped what they were doing and looked at them.

"What's up?" Peter said.

The three didn't run, which told Peter either these kids were stupid, or they had good instincts and knew Denis and he weren't cops. Peter's money was on them being stupid.

"You guys having car problems?"

The three stole glances at each other.

"Don't stop on my behalf," Peter said. "We'll just be here a minute." He nodded at Denis who held up the photograph.

"Seen him?" Peter said.

None of them responded.

"You three look like you bit into prunes. C'mon think. It can't be that hard. Might do you some good. *To think.*"

The teen closest to Peter was the first to make a move. He went to pull the gun that Peter knew was under his shirt.

"Bad decision," Peter said. He looked at his partner whose gun was already drawn. "See my partner? Gives him an excuse. He's not open-minded like myself. So let's try this again. Where's the guy owns this car?"

"Fuck you, bitch," said the teen.

"You're not listening," said Peter. "Denis, make him listen."

Denis shot him in the leg. The kid went down screaming. Peter looked at the other two whose mouths had dropped open. "How 'bout you two?"

"I don't know nothin'," said one of them, his voice high and scared. The other shook his head vigorously.

Peter sighed. And for a moment he thought this was going to be easy.

These three were obviously worthless. He looked around. There was no one else in sight. Just the five of them now by this car.

He looked at Denis and nodded.

"Clean it up."

10

AFTER they left the junkyard they had a laugh. The dog that showed up had been old and toothless with a teddy bear demeanor. Taneesha had rubbed the dog's ears.

James walked with Taneesha until it came time for her to turn off. He offered to walk her home, but she insisted she was fine.

James hesitated. He wanted to help her somehow, but didn't want to insult her. She seemed to read his mind. "I'm good."

He nodded. "I know. I enjoyed meeting you, Taneesha."

She smiled and said goodbye. As he walked to his car, he felt hopeful about her situation, as well as his own as crazy as that seemed. The plastic container held two gallons of gas. That should be enough to get him home. Once home he could take care of the bank stuff.

That optimism changed when he saw the three youths. As he debated what to do, a black sedan had driven up. Two men had gotten out. The men each had close-cropped hair and were wearing sports coats despite it being warm. The tall one had a deep red tan. The squatty one had the neck of a man that lifted weights.

James thought for sure they were undercover police officers. He'd just about stepped from his cover when something inside him told him to wait.

He wasn't close enough to hear what was being said. The squatty one held something out that looked like a piece of paper. A few words were exchanged and then he shot one of the youths.

Jesus!

James tucked from sight. There were more gunshots. A few minutes later, he surveyed the aftermath. The youths were on the pavement. As for the two men and their car, they were gone.

James came to terms with what had just happened. He'd witnessed three murders. Half in a state of shock, he approached his car.

Fighting the heebie-jeebies and avoiding the pools of blood, he walked past the bodies. They were definitely dead. His car still had its wheels, minus the hubcaps. There was a jack near the back wheel, which hadn't been set. With his foot, he nudged it away. It didn't look to be his.

His car door was open. He set down his satchel, gas and went to his car and flipped open the trunk. Inside his trunk was a plastic bag. The bag held two pints of oil, a funnel, and an almost empty roll of paper towels. His car was always burning too much oil and he kept the pints for emergencies. Using the funnel, he poured the gas from the container into his tank.

That done, he set the container down, then thought better of it and picked it back up along with the rag that had been its stopper. The container would have his fingerprints on it. With this murder scene, he didn't want to leave any trace that he'd been here. He was going to report what had happened, of course. He just hadn't figured out how he was going to do so. A part of him was afraid the cops would think him a suspect. It seemed crazy, but why wouldn't they? It was his car and the dead boys had been breaking into it. It was just his word that two random men had done the shooting.

James looked around. No one else had witnessed what he'd seen. He gathered up his hubcaps that were on the ground and put them in his trunk, along with the empty container and rag.

He wiped his hands with some paper towels, picked up his satchel and looked to see if there was anything else lying around. Not seeing anything, he closed his trunk. A minute later, he looked in the rearview mirror, put his turn signal on and pulled out into the street.

11

"...OF Texas has declared a state of martial law. This is live footage we're seeing. Sandra is on the scene. Sandra can you hear us? Yes, yes! I'm here outside a Safeway in upscale Brookwood. These people have been going in and out for the last half hour."

Blam, Blam!!!

"Oh my God, Oh my God...those were gunshots. Sandra, can you hear us? Sandra? Pull the cameras, pull the cameras! She fell down, was she shot? I didn't see... I don't think so. We've lost the feed. That was horrible. Is she okay? Get her back! Can you get her back?"

Sue, forty-two years old with comely features and dirty blonde hair streaked with a few invisible grays, called the girls in. She didn't want them outside, not even in the backyard, not with what she was seeing on TV.

"Girls, go play in your rooms."

Katie and Hannah started to head upstairs when they stopped in their tracks.

"Why does that man on TV have a gun, Mommy?"

Sue clicked the TV off. "It's make-believe, honey."

"*Mommy.*" Her youngest daughter, Hannah, gave her a scolding look. "You know it's not good to tell fibs. That was the News. That's not pretend; that's really happening. Why did that man have a gun?"

Looking at her daughter, Sue winced and felt a pang of tenderness at the same time. The fact her daughter knew what a gun was wasn't good—she could thank the neighbor's kid for that—the real amazement was it wasn't that terribly long ago that Hannah was speaking single monosyllabic words. Now here she was, not yet four years old, and she was speaking like a little adult.

"You're right honey. Mommy should never tell fibs. That man had a gun to protect his store."

"Why does he want to protect his store?" Hannah's pretty little mouth pinched serious.

"Because, you know when we go to the store and have to pay for things at the register?"

Hannah nodded. "Uh huh."

"Well, that man had a gun because there were people who weren't going to pay and he was just trying to make sure they did."

"But isn't a gun bad?"

"It is, most of the time."

"So he's a bad man?"

"Not exactly," Sue said. She knew these questions could go on forever. She knelt down and gave her a hug. "Have I told you today how much I love you?"

"*Mommy.*"

"Yes."

"What have I said about hugs?"

Sue let go of her daughter. "Sorry."

Hannah scampered off to join her big sister who was already upstairs. Sue smiled and bit her lip. Her daughters were so different from each other. Her oldest, Katie, loved hugs when she was the same age. Hannah, on the other hand, was ultra-independent and didn't go for the touchy feely stuff. She reminded Sue of herself when she was younger, while Katie was more like James.

Katie liked structure and things to be a certain way. Katie's side of the room was all in order, with dolls lined up and pillows perfectly placed. Hannah's side, in contrast, was ordered chaos; she loved to let it spill into Katie's space, which of course led to yelps of "MOM".

Sue lingered at the foot of the steps, waiting for the inevitable scream. When it didn't come, she sighed and went into the kitchen. She couldn't shake it, she felt emotional and stressed. All morning she'd been worried about James. He'd called twice, but she hadn't been able to hear anything he'd said. He should be home; it had been long enough; traffic couldn't be that bad. Most businesses were shut down with what was going on.

When Allyson's mom called to cancel the birthday party they were supposed to attend, Sue had turned on the news. James had also called around that time. His voice, the little she heard of it, had sounded strained. She'd tried to call him back, but only got his voicemail.

When James's second call came and was immediately disconnected she couldn't help but thinking the worst. One of her most deep-rooted fears was that their daughters would grow up and not know their daddy. Sue didn't want them to relive her own childhood. Her own father had been a stranger to her. Even now that he was retired and lived less than an hour away, they didn't see each other.

Which was fine as far as Sue was concerned. She preferred it that way. But she didn't want that life for her daughters. If she could have, she'd have wrapped a bubble around their house to keep Katie and Hannah safe. Luckily, she and James saw eye to eye on how they wanted to bring up their girls. They'd done everything they could to insulate their daughters from the realities out there.

The girls were limited to what they could watch on TV. Only an hour a day and the shows were carefully vetted. Hannah was all about *Speed Racer*, which of course, she couldn't watch. The show was too violent.

Car crashes at every turn, the characters hitting each other—it was unbelievable really. Sue had bought the video at James's urging. He was a big fan of the TV show when he was growing up.

When they began watching it with their daughters, they'd cringed seeing its content and turned it off. Sue wanted to throw it away, but James had convinced her to keep it. *"Hannah will be old enough in a year or so. I loved Speed Racer, saw it all the time, and didn't grow up violent."* Which was true. James was a complete softie. You wouldn't think he had a violent bone in his body. If she didn't know him like she did, she never would have believed he'd boxed and gone to school on a wrestling scholarship, owing to having been a high school All-American.

The phone rang and interrupted Sue from her thoughts.

It was Ellen from the Neighborhood Association. There was going to be an emergency meeting in one of the cul-de-sacs. Sue had barely put the phone down when it rang again. This time it was Enrique.

Enrique worked with James. He'd been over for dinner once. His family lived abroad. James, as his manager, had taken him under his wing. He seemed to be a good kid and the girls had enjoyed meeting him. It was unusual for him to call.

"He's not home, yet?" Enrique said. He sounded worried.

Sue said no, and Enrique let her know that ComTek had closed this morning. "If you can, please have him call me. It's very important."

Sue said she would and put the phone down. She stood there in a partial daze. She couldn't help it; panic began to set in. Something must have happened to James. This wasn't like him. He called every day to let her know what time he'd be coming home.

She reminded herself that he had called; so that meant at least he hadn't had a horrible accident. Maybe he was just having car trouble, which was bad since she couldn't go to help him if she didn't know where he was.

But still, car trouble was better than other alternatives.

Sue was still standing there, when the phone rang again. The caller ID read: 'wireless caller', which was what it read when James called from his cell phone. She picked up the phone quickly.

"James!"

There was a pause. "Sue?"

She didn't recognize the voice. "Who is this?"

"Sue, it's Dad, are you okay?"

"I'm fine."

"You sure? I'm worried about you and the girls with what's going on."

Sue snapped back an answer. She was annoyed that he suddenly would care about her and the girls now. She hung up shortly, emotions rising. She dialed James's number and got his voicemail again.

She wanted to scream, but Katie beat her to it. "MOM!"

Sue pulled it together and went upstairs to play referee.

12

JAMES stared at his gas gauge. He was at a dead stop. In front of him was an endless row of vehicles, none of which were moving. There must be an accident or obstruction ahead.

He had absolutely no idea where he was. Presumably, he was still a long way from home; he wasn't even sure he was going the right way. He hadn't seen an Interstate or exit he recognized. Now stuck here, he was going to run out of gas, yet again, in some no-man's land.

The delivery truck in front of him hadn't budged one inch. In the lane next to him, up two cars, a man had stepped from his car. James could see others in his rearview mirror that had done the same. Someone was pointing into the sky.

James looked out his window and saw planes. Lots of planes. They seemed to be circling.

He stared at them. He counted over a dozen and could see dots, which hinted of more. They were jumbo jets, passenger planes; thousands of people circling, stuck in their own sort of hell.

James glanced at the gaping hole on his dash where his radio used to be. Those kids had pried it out—something he hadn't noticed till he'd left. He'd first panicked seeing his radio gone. He knew that meant it was back at the scene of the crime. He thought of driving back, but he wasn't even sure how to get back.

And even if he could, he wasn't sure he wanted to see them again. Dead. In those pools of blood. Those poor kids.

He still couldn't believe it. He felt in a daze, everything hazy. He'd passed strange sights. Buildings burning, groups of people milling around. And now these airplanes in the sky.

What he wouldn't do to know what was going on. He looked at the tinted windows of the car next to him. They were the opaque kind where you couldn't see anything inside. He motioned for the driver to put his window down. Either the driver didn't see him, or was ignoring him.

His gaze went back to the planes. He thought of his wife and girls and wished he was home right now. The truck in front of him moved an entire foot and stopped.

He cursed and surprised himself with his own voice. He was going to go crazy sitting here. He picked up some of the papers that had spilled from his glove compartment box. It didn't make any sense to tidy his car, but if he didn't do something he was going to explode. Any moment he expected to hear the tell-tale knocking sound from his engine before it just conked out.

He put the papers back in the glove box. Something was sticking out from under his passenger seat. It was a cord of some sort. He pulled it out and realized what it was. It was the charging cord for his Blackberry.

It took a moment for it to register.

His charging cord!

He quickly grabbed his Blackberry. He fumbled with it and plugged the cord into its side. He inserted the charger end into his car's charging port.

Now he just had to wait.

That shouldn't be a problem.

A sedan went by on the shoulder. It was followed by another car. James looked in his rearview mirror. He could see other cars were getting the same idea. He looked at the stopped truck in front of him that was going nowhere. He knew it was breaking the rules and was probably a traffic violation, but at this point he didn't care. He turned his wheel and eased onto the shoulder.

There was no need to press on the gas. It was creep speed only, stop and go. The shoulder got roomier further ahead. James drove over chunks of rubber. An entire tire from some semi-trailer was littered all over the shoulder. Its shredded remnants scraped his undercarriage.

Cringing, he expected to blow a tire or have his muffler shorn off. He drove over what looked to be a highway sign and further on what looked to be part of a pick-up truck's liner bed. Ahead, a white garbage bag, still full of garbage, was trailing from under a car, leaving a trail of refuse.

He glanced down at his fuel gauge. The needle was into empty. In that split second a Bronco that was stuck behind a semi-trailer made a move for it. James was almost clipped as it surged onto the shoulder. The Bronco hit something. It bounced a few times, but didn't stop. James looked for what it had hit, but only saw gravel and asphalt. The driver of the semi-trailer blew his horn. He realized the Bronco must have clipped the semi-trailer as it pulled out.

He could almost smell the desperation in the air, mixed with the rank stench of vehicle exhaust and miserable heat. He was sticky with old sweat and dehydrated. He didn't dare use his A/C so as to conserve gas. His windows were down, but only seemed to bring in waves of carbon monoxide and heat. James felt weak and dizzy. His mouth was parched. What he wouldn't do for a sip of water.

As he passed a mile marker, a red light on his dashboard blinked. It was his fuel warning light.

Oh shit.

He kept going, his view taken up by the Bronco's wide body. A bumper sticker that said 'Jesus loves you' was on its spare wheel cover.

The Bronco stopped. After what seemed forever it began to move again. He saw an exit sign, which said a mile to go, and hope, though brief, surged inside him. It wasn't an exit he knew, but it didn't matter. Just so long as he didn't conk out on this shoulder.

James followed the Bronco. Drivers were honking. People two lanes over who were stuck, unable to make a move for the shoulder, were out of their cars, or in their cars trying to merge. James saw what looked like black smoke billowing up into the sky.

He kept going. His fingers clenched on his steering wheel. The smoke seemed to be from further ahead.

The Bronco began to pull slightly over. The shoulder was opening up. A red car elbowed its way in, then another car. It almost clipped him. James narrowed-up his distance. Anything more than half a car's length was asking for others to surge out in front of him.

The red warning light on his dashboard seemed to shout at him. He knew he was on borrowed time. When it came on earlier, it took about fifteen minutes before his car just died. Knowing it was ridiculous, but still thinking it, he blamed the manufacturers of his car. What type of warning was fifteen minutes? As if fifteen minutes could get you anywhere.

Several cars were pulling off. James followed, driving over gravel and grass. Then he was on asphalt again and realized it was an exit lane.

Please...

The cars slowed and then stopped. *Oh shit, not again.*

A minute later they were moving again. James held his breath. Their speed, which was only a snail's crawl, picked up some. His speedometer went from zero to five. He had to tap the gas pedal to keep up.

James passed a broken down car with steam fuming from its hood. That was going to be him any second now. He prayed there was an open gas station up ahead. He was doing ten miles an hour now, which upped to fifteen. The exit lane merged onto a two lane road. There was an accident that had bottlenecked the road to the left, explaining why they were merging now without having to stop.

James didn't recognize the area. It was another part of the city he'd never been in. There were construction barricades along the shoulder. He could see an enormous structure off to the left, which appeared to be a prison. It was about eight stories tall and its windows were just narrow slits. James scanned for a gas station and thought he saw one ahead.

The traffic light turned red and James had to stop. He considered running the light, but put that thought aside. There were bound to be police around here. Last thing he needed was to get a ticket. He'd run out of gas just waiting for them to write him up.

An urge he'd been ignoring came to the forefront. He needed to go the bathroom badly. What next? Hives? He felt like screaming in frustration.

Trying to concentrate on something other than his bladder, he focused on his surroundings. There seemed to be lots of people on either side of the road. Some were walking, while others were running. A good number of them seemed to be wearing the same outfits; jumpsuits of some sort.

James looked back at the prison. Was that a wail of a siren? He looked at the men in orange jumpsuits.

His car door was yanked open.

"Out! *Mamon!*"

James looked up. He saw a man with a shaved head, pockmarked face and black gristly goatee. Before he knew what was happening, the man grabbed his arm. James was pulled from his car. He didn't try to resist. His foot caught as he stumbled out.

The man, whose face was contorted into a masque of diabolical rage, yelled at him again. Whatever he said was unintelligible. James stepped back. The man jumped in his car. Not even bothering to close the door, the man stomped his foot on the gas. James's car shot through the red light. There was a flash and a crash as another car hit the back of James's Nissan and ricocheted off.

It was as if time warped and went from fast to slow. James watched, unable to move, as the car that hit his flew by. It slammed into a concrete barrier with a resounding boom! The car's airbags deployed instantly.

In his peripheral vision, James saw his old beater of a Nissan do a three-sixty. It spun like a top and came to a stop. A moment later, his car was moving again. Its back wheels kicked up gravel as it headed down the road. It went a ways and then started to slow.

Stunned and shaken, James looked at the occupant in the car that had hit the concrete barrier. The front of the car was caved in like an accordion. Black smoke was spilling out.

James walked closer. There was a woman inside. The airbag had deflated some and the woman's head was flopped forward, her long hair splayed on the bag. Her neck was limp. She appeared to be unconscious.

The smell of gas assaulted his nostrils. Gas was spilling from the car. The windshield was shattered into a million spidery cracks.

James looked fearfully at the gas. It was a larger puddle now with rivulets that went off in several directions. He looked around, but no one was stepping forward to help her. He stood there, indecisive. The front of the car—or what was left of it—was on fire. Sparks were popping from live wires.

James rapped the side window, but she didn't budge. He tried the door. It was badly bent in. He pulled as hard as he could, but it was either locked or stuck. It wasn't budging. There was no back door as the car was a coupe. The side windows were still intact.

"Miss!" He rapped the window again, hard.

He couldn't tell if she was breathing or not. Her face was bleeding.

James yanked on the door handle again, but with no luck. He looked around and saw a mass of people and cars. No one was stepping forward to help.

Shit.

He went through the gas and around the car to get to the other door. He had to get the woman out.

The front of the car was in flames. James heard a shout, but ignored it. He slipped and caught himself on the car. He continued forward; his eyes laser-focused on the door handle.

He got to the handle and pulled. The handle clicked and the door cracked open. He had to yank it. The sound of metal shrieked. It opened partially. He looked at the flames. He looked at the woman slouched over her seat belt. *Oh my God.* He realized he was going to have to go in the car and undo her seat belt and pull her out.

The flames were licking the windshield and putting off tremendous heat. The dash was pushed in from the crash. James yelled at her, but she didn't move. She was definitely unconscious.

Fuck.

He went inside the car and felt a sharp pain, which he ignored. He had to climb over the passenger seat to get to her seat belt. He pushed the red button, but the seat belt stayed fast. He pushed it again and yanked. It came free. He could see flames all over the crumpled hood.

They seemed alive. They were hot. It was like an oven. The flames were blackening the cracked windshield and popping noises were going off.

He yelled at the girl and her eyes opened. He grabbed her, pushed aside the deflated airbag and her seatbelt. He got hold of an arm and her clothes. He pulled. There was no way to be gentle. In the back of his mind he knew if she was hurt, he might be harming her—possibly even paralyzing her—by moving her. But if he didn't get her out, she was going to die. In fact, if they both didn't get out, they were going to die.

He pulled as hard as he could. She was dead weight. She bumped and slid over the seats. It felt like he was on fire. He coughed from the smoke; his eyes stung, but he didn't dare stop. He got a better grip and put one arm around her waist. He pulled her from the car.

His feet found purchase on the asphalt. He stepped backward, half dragging her, half carrying her. He almost slipped on gravel, but caught himself. His feet kept moving. In front of him, flames had engulfed the seats. He hacked and coughed, but didn't let go of the girl.

He was thirty feet away when the flames licked the gas on the ground. It was instantaneous. James and the woman he was carrying were thrown backward. As he fell, a concussion flash of heat and flames went over them. James heard the roar. Felt the heat singeing his face. It was above him like a tidal wave of fiery air.

Then his head hit something and all went black.

13

THE bickering wasn't dying down. Sue didn't want her girls to hear this. She took hold of their little hands.

"Police aren't going to help us."

The voice wasn't raised. It wasn't trying to drown the others out who were talking over each other, struggling to be heard. The fifty or so people in attendance seemed to simmer for a moment. Ellen Marigold, President of the neighborhood association, a prim and proper woman in her early sixties, raised her hands in the air.

"Quiet, please. Who said that?"

The people standing next to the man took a step back. Darren wasn't a man that spoke much. He wasn't one for these types of meetings either. In his twenty-three years living in the neighborhood this was only the third meeting he'd attended. He was reclusive; long retired. He preferred things quiet.

"We're on our own with this." The crow's feet near his eyes were deep. His back was hunched.

"What do you mean the police won't help us?" said someone from the back.

"How can they not help us?" someone else said. "We pay our taxes. We deserve protection."

"What about the National Guard?"

"Hold on! Please, hold on," Ellen said. "We need to speak one at a time." She glanced at Darren's name tag. "Darren, do you have something to share?"

Darren's face set. He didn't like the attention, but he was man enough to know he'd brought it on by speaking up. "TV's not telling us. It's the Nigerians. Another station says it's the Chinese. They don't know. We're not going to find out for a while. That's how it works.

"As for the police—they got families themselves. The few that are out there have too much on their hands. They're not going to help. You know that. All we can do is sit tight. Lock our doors and ride it out."

Darren was done. He'd said his piece. The others were quiet for a moment. Then others chimed in. It soon got back to bickering.

"What about food? I'm out of milk. What happens when we run out of food?"

"What does that have to do with anything?"

"Shut up! Listen to Frank."

Someone else yelled and Sue led her girls away. The voices died down behind them. Walking alongside her, Katie and Hannah were quiet. Sue realized she should have driven to the meeting. This was too long of a walk for the girls.

"Mommy, can you carry me?"

"Sure, baby."

Sue picked up Hannah. She was still thinking of a conversation she'd overhead at the meeting.

"This has been coming for a while."

"What do you mean?"

"Two statistics about our city: $185,000 and $6,000. Do you know what those two numbers are?

"No? I'll tell you. The top twenty percent of households and the bottom twenty percent. That's what they earn."

"Really?"

"Really. What does that tell you?"

"That a lot of people make a lot more money than me."

"Me too. But that's not the point."

"I see your point. Are you sure about that bottom twenty percent? You can't live on $6,000."

"Less than six thousand. And I'm sure."

"That's crazy. Twenty percent—that's..."

"One hundred thousand people," they said together at the same time.

Each neighbor looked at the other in surprise. "That's good. So you see the numbers I'm talking about."

SUE checked her cell phone again to make sure the ringer was on.

"Mommy, you okay?" Hannah said.

"Why do you ask, baby?"

"'Cause, I'm scared."

"Mommy, where's Daddy?" Katie said.

"He hasn't gotten home from work, yet. Baby, can I set you down for a moment?"

Hannah gripped her harder. "No!"

"Okay, okay." Sue felt like crying, but held it in. She knew she needed to be strong. Where was James?

14

"CAN you hear me?" The voice sounded distant.

It was a man, older. Behind him, sky.

James pushed himself up. He was on grass, not asphalt now. Confused, he looked around. There were vehicles and people off to the side. A stone's throw away was the car that had exploded. It was still burning, petering out black smoke.

"What happened?"

"You hit your head. How do you feel?"

James rubbed the back of his head and felt something sticky. It was blood. Whatever he'd hit had cut him.

"I looked at it. I think you're okay."

"Are you a doctor?"

"No, but I was a medic once... I'd get that checked."

James looked around. He felt out of it. Disoriented. "Is the girl okay?"

"She's fine. You did a very brave thing."

"Where is she?"

"Over there." He pointed towards a group of people near some cars.

"I checked on her. She's alright, but I should probably get back to her."

James nodded. The man walked away with a limp. James looked at himself. His pants were grimy with dirt and what looked to be grease. He pushed himself to a stand and winced. A sharp pain came from his ankle.

He took his weight off it and sat back down. He checked to see what it was. His ankle was swollen, but didn't seem to be cut. He realized when the escaped con had pulled him from his car his ankle must have twisted when it got caught.

He stood up again and tested it. It appeared to be a sprain. It could take his weight, but hurt.

James stood there. The scene was surreal. The car was a burning shell and no one was trying to put it out. People were just staring at the smoke. Cars were in a long line, one after the other. No one was trying to drive past the wreck.

James looked up the road. It was mostly empty. He could see a few people walking, but that was it. Up a ways, not far off, was a car that was sitting in the middle of the road. It was white. It took him a second until he realized that was *his* car.

He stood there and looked around again.

Then he started limping.

WHEN he reached his car, he found it empty. The driver's door was wide open. His ankle hurt.

He took a seat and surveyed inside. The man hadn't taken anything from it. Even his Blackberry was still there, plugged to its charging cord.

James picked it up and powered it on. The battery icon showed a very small charge. He had messages. Seven of them.

James looked at the numbers that had called. He didn't waste power listening to the messages. His wife had called three times. Enrique, from work, had called twice? The other two numbers he didn't recognize.

James pushed 'talk' to call his wife back. The phone began to ring. As it rang, James looked around trying to figure out where he was.

15

SUE heard the phone ringing inside. She fumbled with the keys, got the girls in, and closed the door. By the time she got to the phone, she was too late. The person had gone into voicemail.

She pulled up caller ID. It said 'Wireless number'. Hope surged. That could be James!

"Mommy," said Hannah.

"In a minute, honey." Sue touched speed dial to retrieve the messages.

"Mommy, the door's open," said Katie.

"Hold on." Sue cradled the phone to her ear. *You have three messages*, said voicemail.

"Mommy." Hannah pulled at Sue's shirt.

Katie screamed from the other room.

Sue paused and took the phone from her ear. She looked down at Hannah, the usual source for Katie to scream. Her eyes swept the kitchen and noticed the back pantry door was wide open.

"Katie?" Sue said.

"Mommy!" Hannah grabbed Sue's leg.

Sue picked her up. "Katie answer me." Sue walked into the next room.

Her heart dropped. There were three men standing there. Three men she didn't know.

16

JAMES cursed his stupidity. He'd just left Sue a worthless message. He should have checked where he was before dialing.

He looked at his car. It was crumpled at the point of impact and the bumper was shorn off, leaving exposed Styrofoam. He tried to open the trunk, but it was bent too much to budge.

His options weren't good. He considered trying to push his car off the road, but with his ankle swollen and back aching, he didn't see how he'd get that done. Just walking this short distance to his car was hard enough. His ankle was obviously sprained. He needed to elevate and ice it.

James made sure he had everything he needed from his car, left a note, and gingerly limped down the road. He didn't like leaving his car, but didn't have a choice in the matter. There was no one around to help push it to the side.

The bathroom urge came over him again; it was a wonder his bladder hadn't exploded. He saw an abandoned gas station and went behind it. That taken care of, he took stock of his situation.

His car was wrecked and abandoned. He was filthy, alone, lost, and with no easy means to get back to his family or to find out if they were even okay. With the exception of the few dollars in his pocket, he was flat broke. Every penny of his filched in some identity theft nightmare.

He looked up into the sky and could see planes circling, ominously, as if he was carrion and they were the vultures. He had no idea what was going on, but from the look of things it wasn't good. It could be a terrorist attack or something just as bad.

He questioned his decision to walk away from the accident. He still couldn't believe he'd gone into a burning car. Gingerly, he touched the back of his head. He looked for signs and saw one ahead, but it lacked a cross-street.

Great.

That's all he had to go on. He found a spot to sit down and took out his Blackberry. He couldn't walk anymore.

17

THE men moved through the house. They locked the doors. They were dressed in dark clothes and wore gloves. The one with tattoos up his neck stopped in front of the fireplace and picked a framed photo off the mantle. He asked where her husband was. He had a heavy Slavic accent and broad features with deep-set eyes. Sue said he would be home soon. She told him to take anything he wanted, but just to please go.

The man ignored her and left the room. Sue's focus was on her girls and keeping them safe. But she also feared what might happen to James if he came home.

"Mommy, I'm scared," Katie whispered.

Sue hugged her. "I know honey, but it's going to be okay. This will all be okay."

The tattooed man came back into the room. "Artem, upstairs. Vasily, get started. You know what to do."

Hannah whimpered and Katie dug her face into Sue's side. "Please," Sue said. "My purse is in the kitchen. I have some money in there. Take it and please go."

The man ignored her. He had some clothes in his hand. He walked past them and into the kitchen. Sue glanced at the mirror above the mantle and could see his reflection. He stopped in the kitchen and looked around. If he was looking for her purse, it should be right in front of him on the counter. What was he doing?

He didn't reach for her purse, but instead pulled off his shirt. His back was heavily muscled and tattooed like his neck. He undid his pants and let them drop to the floor. His bare behind was stark white. Sue caught a hideous pointy glimpse as he turned around. At that exact moment, the man looked up and saw Sue in the mirror. He flashed a lupine smile and Sue quickly looked away.

A moment later the man walked in wearing James's khakis and one of his button-down shirts. The clothes were loose on him, but otherwise fit. He plopped himself down on the recliner. He looked over and grinned.

Sue's stomach curdled. The man snorted a laugh, turned on the TV and began to flip through channels.

18

ENRIQUE, impatient to tell him something, had gone on as James's phone started to beep. What he was saying didn't make any sense. Something about *AngelGuard* and how this could come back to them.

James shook his head, not making sense of it. He checked his watch. He wondered if he'd given the right address for the used car dealership across the street. Looking at the digits from here, he realized the 3 might be a 5. It looked like a three, but he couldn't be sure.

Great, what if he gave the wrong address?

A man came out of the dealership. James hadn't thought it was open. Two more men came out and the three of them had a discussion and went over to an older model sedan.

One of the men pulled something out. The other two backed away and then took off running. The man that remained just watched. As they peeled from sight, he looked at the ground as if looking for something and then turned and…

Blam!

James stared, alarmed by what he was seeing. *Blam! Blam!*

The man had just shot the windows out of an unoccupied car? What the hell was this, the Wild West? First there was the shooting at the gas station, the grocery store being looted, then Taneesha, the teens who were shot at his car, the jail break…

Jesus. The whole world seemed to be going crazy. With a new rising fear, James noticed that the man with the gun was looking across the street at him.

At that moment there was the sound of crunching gravel. James turned to see a sports car coming towards him. It was Enrique! He was in his old Mazda RX-8. The car pulled alongside him and James opened the passenger door and got in. "Let's go."

"Everything cool?"

"I'm fine, but you may want to go."

"What was that noise? Sounded like gunshots."

"That's why you may want to go."

19

RUNNING on adrenaline and fear, Sue rummaged through her purse quickly. She barely slipped the key in her pocket when the man walked in to check on her.

"What's taking so long?" the man said with a caustic tone. Accusation and anger was in his eyes.

"I had to run the water for it to get cold."

The man frowned and surveyed the running faucet and rest of the kitchen. His eyes settled on the chopping block and kitchen knives. Sue had considered those, but with the three of them she knew that would just get her and the girls killed.

One way or another, however, she was getting her girls through this. She focused on that goal and put everything else aside. These men were not going to harm them.

"Hurry up." The man stood there and watched her fill the cups. She finished and turned off the faucet.

She glanced at his clothes on the floor; the ones he'd had on before he took her husband's. The man noticed her glance.

"Hold it," he said.

Sue froze.

"Put down the cups."

She did.

His eyes bored into her. "Lift up the shirt."

"No." She looked at him defiantly.

He grabbed her. It was so sudden and fast that she didn't have time to react or resist. He got her by the wrists. His grip was like a steel vise. With one hand he yanked up her shirt.

He gave a long leering look, taking in her slim waist, bra, and full breasts. He smirked lasciviously and let go.

Sue sucked in a breath and pulled her shirt back down. With dismay, she realized she'd been powerless in his grip—like a rag doll. He was so strong it was frightening.

He sneered. "That wasn't so difficult, was it?"

She picked up the cups. He looked at her cravenly. She squeezed by him to get to the other room. He didn't let her pass easily, but forced her to brush up against him. The fleeting contact with him almost made her vomit.

He laughed.

She rejoined her girls in the den. They were being watched by the man named Vasily. He looked at her with only coldness. No help was coming from him, she realized.

"Mommy," Hannah said. Her face was red and puffy from crying.

"What is it baby?"

"I need to pee pee."

Sue nodded and girdled herself. She looked at their captors. "I need to take my girls to the bathroom."

She expected the man with tattoos to refuse her request, but instead he just shrugged. "Vasily, go with them."

The man nodded. Sue led her girls down the hallway and the man followed.

At the end of the hallway were two doors. One was the bathroom. The other opened to the garage. She knew it was locked, but the key in her pocket would open its deadbolt. They were so close, yet so far. Her mind churned, trying to think how she could create an opportunity to unlock that door.

Not wanting to delay and telecast her intentions, she opened the bathroom door and let her girls in.

"I've got to close the door."

The man frowned and shook his head.

"They need privacy."

The man just stood there.

"Please?" she said.

The man grunted and took a step back. Sue closed the door and nodded to Hannah. "It's okay, honey."

"I can't."

It took coaxing to get Hannah onto the potty. She reminded her daughter of the time on the plane and how she was such a big girl then. "It's just like that time. You can do this, baby."

Hannah's eyes were wet and she bravely looked up.

"I love you, baby. You can do this."

Inwardly, Sue was crying. With relief, Hannah finally went.

"Baby, I'm so proud of you."

Sue looked at Katie. "Do you need to go?"

Katie shook her head.

"You sure?"

"I'm okay, Mommy." Katie's bottom lip trembled.

Sue made a decision. She made it then. She felt the key in her pocket and glanced towards the door.

She might not get another chance like this. "Girls," she said softly, "I want you to keep close. Do you understand?"

Her girls nodded. They looked so adult. She was so proud of them.

She quietly locked the bathroom door and opened the cabinet beneath the sink. Inside was extra toilet paper, tissues, a plastic plunger and a scented candle. The plunger was the flimsy kind, whose handle was just hollow plastic. None of it could help her.

She bit her lip and closed the cabinet. She looked around quickly. Her eyes settled on the mirror on the wall. It was mounted with screws; she remembered the hassle of putting it up. She glanced at her reflection. The face that looked back at her was full of determination.

At that moment, the door handle moved.

The man was trying to get in.

20

BEYOND the barricades, police were struggling to maintain order. A man with a megaphone was urging everyone to remain calm.

"I know," Enrique said, as he drove at a crawl. He'd taken off his baseball cap. His black hair was matted down into a Caesar coif. With the exception of his faint European accent, he came across as your typical twenty-something-year-old you'd see at a bus stop with iPod plugs reading a gaming magazine.

"How else do you explain it?" Enrique said.

The crowd outside the bank was getting worse. They drove past a news van. Enrique had filled him in on what was happening. Throughout the city were other demonstrations. The Governor had declared a State of Emergency and called in the National Guard. The President was scheduled to make an address in the next hour or so.

"Payment servers," Enrique said. "And from there it rippled."

James was absorbing it all. This crisis that ballooned in less than a day began with payment servers. Payment servers. Most people didn't even know what they were. But people knew credit cards. Without payment servers credit cards were just plastic. Useless plastic. Payment servers were the workhorses that did the heavy lifting.

James's job made him more informed than most when it came to such things. He was familiar with the POS process. When a credit card was swiped, the data that routed over public telephone networks utilized payment servers to decode a portion of encoded information. The process parsed numbers into manageable buckets. Those buckets were encrypted and only when they linked appropriately and were unlocked with the right value, or 'cryptographic key', would money flow in and out of accounts.

Those series of fail-safes allowed commerce to flow seamlessly, simultaneously protecting the customer and ensuring a vendor they would get paid. A credit card took seconds to use, all thanks to payment servers, crunching data and giving the green light.

And right now that process wasn't working. And that was only the half of it. Widespread reports were coming in of people who'd had their savings wiped out overnight. The glitch that was somehow disrupting credit card transactions was backwashing into banking networks.

James wasn't alone. *Thousands, perhaps millions, had lost all their money.* The magnitude was hard to fathom.

The Gold Standard was long gone. Paper money was almost obsolete. The majority of purchases today were done using debit or credit cards. Wealth was digitized; warehoused in database servers. Servers were the modern-day vaults for people's cash.

And that information had been compromised.

With credit cards not working, businesses—the few that were still open—were only accepting cash. In some cases, people were bartering to buy gas and food. Businesses everywhere were locking up and hiring gunmen to protect their wares.

It kind of explained everything James had seen so far. The looting, the shootings… people weren't taking it so well. Unable to get gas, food and other basics they were resorting to other means, including violence, to get what they needed. How quickly a civilized society came apart at the seams.

Enrique was animated. "You're talking infiltration of silo focused systems, multichannel delivery networks, dual factor authentication, scrambled PIN pads, randomly generated passwords. Think about it? That can't be done unless you have direct access to protected data storage. And what person or company has access on that scale?"

It was crazy what Enrique was implying.

James was still processing what Enrique had relayed just a few minutes ago. At work Enrique had noticed a few 'signatures', those faint binary traces that usually indicated someone was snooping on a system. In the beginning, Enrique thought he was just being paranoid.

After putting in his own spyware—a big no no, which flouted corporate policy—Enrique had discovered that someone was using his log-in. Several key bundles were accessed. Key bundles were the three cryptographic keys that were used with a Triple Data Encryption Algorithm. Alone they were worthless, but if someone knew what they were doing, knew the protocol and the systems, key bundles could enable a person to access secure areas of the network.

"Why didn't you tell me about this earlier?" James said.

"I'm telling you now."

Enrique watched a crowd of people cross the street. His voice lowered, becoming almost reflective. "Do you remember that rogue trader that French bank blamed for losing over seven billion dollars? The one that made all those stock trades for months during the middle of the night without the bank knowing it?"

"What does that have to do with this?"

"It was a few years ago, but if you remember that man always claimed he was innocent."

Enrique went on another tangent. He mentioned the company *AngelGuard* had gone through the roof in trading. It was the one bright note on Wall Street before the market's precipitous drop. In overseas trading AngelGuard was up a thousand percent. "One thousand percent,"

Enrique said, as if James hadn't heard him the first time.

James knew the history: ComTek had almost bought the company a few years back. AngelGuard specialized in Internet security.

"Word got out."

Every financial arm that utilized AngelGuard had not been infected. All other networks were down, even those protected by Symantec, the leader in Internet security.

"This thing is viral. But even the worse viruses never spread this fast."

Enrique paused, and looked at him. "What's ComTek's biggest account?"

"I guess that would be Wells Fargo or BOA."

"You got it. And you could name a couple other big banks with those. We've got them all."

Things were opening up around them. Demonstrators were thinning out, moving en masse.

"That rogue trader? What if he *was* innocent?" Enrique said. "That always made more sense to me. He didn't benefit from any of those trades he made. Why would someone do that? They wouldn't. I'll tell you what I think. I think he was set up to be the fall guy."

Enrique pressed on the gas. "Who's going to be the fall guy in this crisis? Believe me they're going to find 'em. And when they unravel this and fix this mess, they'll back door this to whoever was responsible."

Enrique shifted to second. "That stuff at work gives me a bad feeling." He looked at James. "So what's it going to be? Your house still? Or can we swing by The Vault so I can show you?"

21

"*OTVA li!* Open the door."

The door shook as the man attempted to force it. Sue yelled for him to stop and unlocked it. The man barged in and looked at Sue menacingly. "Why did you lock it?"

"You're scaring them. We'll be right out."

His voice rose: "Why did you lock it?"

"For privacy. Give us a second."

"No! Come out now." He grabbed Sue by the arm. She was pulled roughly from the bathroom and pushed forward. She and the girls were ushered upstairs.

He corralled them into the spare bedroom. "Be silent. If you say a word, I *keel* them."

He grabbed the covers off the bed. He threw the covers on the floor and shoved them tight against the base of the door with his foot. He glowered at them.

"Stay quiet." He drew a knife for added emphasis. "If you say anything…"

Katie screamed. Sue clamped her hand over her mouth.

"Again, and I *keel* her." The man grimaced. "Do you understand?"

Sue nodded. The man's knife gleamed cruelly. His face was grimly set. Sue had no doubt he meant what he said. She whispered to her girls, urging them to be quiet.

The doorbell rang.

Then nothing.

Only silence.

Sue was holding Katie and Hannah close. Katie's hair was against her cheek. Hannah was pressed against her chest, her little body trembling.

The doorbell rang again, twice in quick succession. More silence and then footsteps. *Someone was coming up the stairs!*

There was pounding on the door and words were exchanged. Their captor opened the door. In the hallway were the other two. One of them had a roll of duct tape in his hand.

"Who screamed?" His eyes were ablaze.

"Please," Sue said.

The man lashed out with the back of his hand. Katie screamed. The force of the slap knocked Sue down. Her head rung. She tasted blood in her mouth.

She forced herself to stand. Her vision was blurry. She pulled her girls to her; then stood in front of them.

The men started speaking to each other in Russian.

Sue stood tall, defiance in every fiber of her being. "You will not hurt them."

"Shut up. We will do whatever we want." The man with tattoos pulled out a length of duct tape. "Put your hands behind your back."

"What are you going to do?"

"Vasily! Artem!"

The two grabbed her. Sue struggled, but it was no use. The men quickly overpowered her. Sue stopped resisting. "You don't need to tape me."

The man with tattoos ignored her. He bound her wrists with tape.

"Mommy!" Hannah cried.

"It's going to be okay, baby," Sue said. *"Please."* She implored her captors to show mercy. They answered her pleas by throwing her on the bed and duct-taping her ankles.

Katie screamed. Sue wept as the men began to tape her girls.

22

BOB Pulaski started his truck. The engine rumbled to life. It was a beater of a Dodge, a full-fledged antique, but still ran just fine. His big leathery hands gripped the knobby wheel. He looked across the street at his daughter's home.

It was only the second time he'd seen where she lived. He'd come by once before, but Suzy (he knew she went by Sue now) had made it very clear he wasn't welcome. That had hurt, but he couldn't blame her. He'd not been the best dad.

All through her childhood he'd been gone. In her early years, it was because of the war. Vietnam. He was drafted and served two tours. When he returned he'd gone back to what he knew, working with his hands to support his family. He'd gotten into oil catting and soon was working on rigs, where he was gone for months at a time. His job took a toll on his marriage. From the get go, it never stood a chance. Sue's mom had stuck with it way too long, but eventually it wore her out. When she served him divorce papers, he wasn't surprised.

He was a loner by nature and never truly embraced the husband/father role. Roughnecks weren't good at making pretty. They weren't used to domestic settings—sitting at a table with china and silverware, going to church with the family. Their lives were twelve-hour shifts day-in and day-out working on rigs in the middle of the ocean. Even when he was put in charge of rigs, his life wasn't much different. He was constantly away.

He fought his share of demons. Back in the war, he'd seen stuff in the bush he wished he hadn't. For years he tried to drown those images seared into his consciousness with Jack and Johnny. Not that that ever worked. His drinking binges just made things worse. He'd never hit Sue's mom, but when he was on the bottle he'd heaped more than his share of abuse. He'd said things he later regretted and done stuff he wasn't proud of.

Back then he was a young buck and plenty stupid. What he wouldn't do to turn back time, so he could patch things up and prevent the worst two mistakes in his life: letting his wife and daughter slip away. The only two good and pure things he'd ever had.

He was proud of his daughter. Even though he wasn't there for her when she was growing up, her mother, bless her, made sure he knew about the highlights. He'd saved all the letters she ever wrote. Somehow she always knew where to send those letters, no matter where on the map he was.

His little daughter had been on the Homecoming Court her junior and senior year. She'd gone to college on a full academic scholarship. Suzy got those smarts from her mom.

Bob had done fine in school, and if not for lack of funds might have gone to college, but Suzy was in an entirely different league. She was scary smart, even as a little girl. He remembered her reciting back to him an entire kid's book when she was only three. He'd read the book to her a few times, and she'd taken the book from his hands and read it to him, flipping the pages and reading. For a second he thought she was actually reading the words—*at three years old!* But she'd just memorized it by hearing him read those few times.

He could remember that like it was yesterday. He was so proud of his girl. He wanted to tell everyone and had to anyone who'd listen.

Taking a breath, trying to hold that thought as it began to slip away, he looked at his daughter's house.

She had a good husband in James. He loved her and deep down seemed to be a good man. He and James didn't have much in common, but that was alright. James had gone out of his way to make him feel welcome when he'd stopped by that one time. He'd shown him his granddaughters and had introduced him as 'Grandpa'. Hearing that name for himself had made a tear well in his eye.

Katie and *Hannah*, like their mom, were beautiful. Bright saucers for eyes and angelic faces that Michelangelo himself couldn't improve upon. No doubt they were with their loving parents now. Bob didn't see any cars in the driveway. No one had answered the door when he'd walked down that driveway and rung the bell. He crossed his fingers, hoping they'd gone someplace safe.

It was scary what was going on. The whole world was turned upside down. He'd come over to make sure they were okay. Seeing things on TV had pushed him past that stuck point—that Hoover Dam inside him that kept him back. When he'd called Suzy on the phone, she'd sounded odd, like she was upset. It could have just been from hearing his voice. 'Dear old dad' most likely wasn't what came to mind.

He took in the domestic setting across the street one more time. The pretty house and yard. A cat, presumably theirs, went up the front steps and stopped at the stoop. He hadn't met their cat, but Hannah had said they had a cat. He remembered her cute little voice. She wasn't shy, even meeting him for the first time. He couldn't get over it. She had only been two-and-a-half and there she was speaking like a big kid.

Hannah had told him he had to meet 'Tigerlily'. He never got a chance, though. Suzy had pretty much ushered him out of the house when she'd come home.

He sighed. What he wouldn't do to start all over. To have the time back he'd lost with his daughter. To be the dad he should have been. He loved her more than anything and now that he had nothing but time, she didn't want to have anything to do with him.

He took his truck out of Park and set it for Drive. He was about to pull into the street when he suddenly paused. The cat at the stoop was crying. He could hear her plaintive wail even from here. My, he thought, she was a bawler.

Tigerlily. That name was way too dainty for her. With those lungs, they should have named her 'Bawler'. He watched the cat pirouette on the front stoop before she arched her back, settled down and took a seat where she could survey the yard. She was a proud thing, judging by the way she sat. Erect and observant.

Bob winked at her and pulled out into the street. The cat watched him drive away. A grown man with a tear streaking down his cheek.

23

IT was hard to breathe with tape over her mouth. As bad as it was for her, she was thinking of her girls. Their nasal passages weren't as developed. *How could these monsters tape their mouths?* They might suffocate.

Sue struggled on the bed, trying to see them. Hannah looked scared. Katie's skin tone didn't look good. *Oh my God.* Sue realized that Katie wasn't getting enough oxygen. She dealt with sinuses a lot and didn't breathe out of her nose very well. The doctor during a recent checkup had said it was possible she had a condition known as a deviated septum, which meant there was some obstruction in one of the nasal passages. It could make it hard to breathe when the sinuses got inflamed. Just yesterday Katie had said her nose hurt.

Oh please, let Katie be getting enough air.

Sue looked at Katie, trying to get eye contact. Katie looked listless.

Please... baby, look at me.

Their captors had left the door open. Sue heard their voices. The men were speaking Russian. Sue tried to move her hands. She had some play. She'd kept her wrists slightly apart as they'd wrapped them.

Katie looked bad. Her skin tone was a bluish pallor.

Sue strained and tried to reach her front pocket. The key was in there. If she could reach it she might be able to use it to cut through the tape.

She tried, stretching as far as she could, but the pocket was too far. Contorted as she was, she started to cramp. She let up and looked around the room. There was a desk near the bed. She remembered that its drawer contained pens and a letter opener. The men had stopped talking. She looked up as one of them peered in the room.

He must be able to see that Katie was in bad shape. Please let him do something.

Show a thread of humanity. Pull off the tape!

Sue started to squirm, trying to get his attention. She tried to speak through the tape, but it was only a guttural mumble. The man frowned. His face hardened and his eyes narrowed. He shut the door.

Sue wasted no time. She slithered towards the edge of the bed. She put her legs over. Making sure not to lose her balance and flop off, she found the ground. She scooted towards the end of the bed, which was closest to the desk.

As she did so, a wave of dizziness came over her. She stopped moving and forced herself to slow her breathing and take deep breaths through her nose. Her lungs were screaming, and she panicked until she realized she was getting air.

She took slow deep breaths and scooted the rest of the way. The desk was close now. She was at the very end of the bed. This was the toughest part. She had to stand without falling and move the last foot or so to the desk. If she fell, the noise would bring the men into the room. From their actions, Sue was certain they had no intention of letting them live.

She managed to stand. With her ankles taped together, it was like balancing on a post. Her hands, taped behind her back, felt for the desk. She started to wobble. For a fearful split-second, she thought she was going to topple, but somehow got a finger hold on the desk and steadied herself.

There… the drawer pull.

Sliding to the side, so as to give room for the drawer to slide out, she pulled the drawer out. Her fingers felt inside, touching the pens and other items. She felt something cold. *The letter opener!*

Very carefully she pulled it out and pushed the drawer back in. She kept her backside close to the desk to balance herself. Her fingers fumbled with the opener and it dropped with a metallic thud.

Her heart skipped.

She looked at the door.

No one came in.

She felt for the opener again. It had landed on the desk and she was able to retrieve it. Manipulating her fingers, she got a grip on its handle. After several attempts she managed to move its point towards the tape. Operating solely on feel, she worked the point against the tape. Her fingers kept cramping and she had to take periodic breaks.

She looked at Katie and Hannah the entire time. Katie wasn't moving. Hannah shifted once. She couldn't see their faces.

Please God, let them be breathing.

She kept going, ignoring the cramps. The opener had punctured the tape and she could feel it making a difference.

She created more punctures. With each new one she pulled and flexed her wrists. The tape was loosening. She redoubled her efforts. She tried again and again. Straining hard after another cut, she pulled and got one hand free!

She wasted no time. With her hands free, she pulled the tape from her mouth and frantically cut the tape from her ankles. Once unbound, she quickly went to Katie first and pulled the tape from her mouth. She pulled the tape from Hannah next.

Hannah's little body heaved. *Breathe!* Katie gasped and Hannah sucked in air. Sue watched as their little chests filled and exhaled. She whispered encouragement to them. She quickly cut the tape from their ankles and wrists.

Tears were streaming down her cheeks. Her girls were breathing! They were alive!

She hugged them both. Hannah cried.

Sue touched her mouth and whispered, "We have to be quiet."

Katie looked pale, but she was breathing. Sue cupped her silky hair and smiled through her tears. "I'm going to get us out."

Hannah gripped her and wouldn't let go.

"Baby, I'm going to open the window."

Quietly, she lifted the window sash and then the storm window. She used the letter opener to cut through the screen and pushed the screen away.

The dormer looked out onto the front yard. A steep roof led to a twenty-foot drop off. There were bushes down there, which she couldn't see from this vantage point. She could only see the edge of the roof and the gutter, which she was fairly certain wouldn't hold her weight; possibly not even the girls.

Taking a breath, she looked at her girls.

"This is what we're going to do."

She told them the plan.

24

0 0 1 1 0 T 0 H 0 0 0 0 E 0 0 1 1 0 0 1 1 1 0 V 0 0 A 0 1 U 1 L T 1 0 1 1

THE small monument sign had only a numbered address. No company name. Nothing to indicate what sort of structure might lie ahead.

A separate sign, which said 'Private Property / No Admittance', was further down the lane. Enrique flashed a card and the barrier went up and allowed them to pass. The buildings up ahead were two-story. To the laymen eye, the "hot site" looked like an unassuming office park.

That was intentional.

There was a chain-link fence, which ran around the several-acre perimeter. It was ten foot high. 'No trespassing' signs were posted along it.

About twenty-five yards past the fence was a landscape berm. That little swell of earth cleverly disguised a series of concentric concrete rings. Each concrete ring went around the entire office park. There were three of them with diminishing radii.

From a casual glance they almost looked like curbs, except instead of asphalt around them there was patchy scrub grass. Each curb varied in height and width. The largest was two foot tall and of equal thickness. Taken together, they weren't much of a barrier. A person could easily step over them.

A vehicle, however, would have a harder time. In fact, each curb would stop almost any vehicle in their tracks. The curbs were actually grade beams, which went deep into the ground. The first went down eight feet below the surface. The next went down twelve and the last went down eighteen. Short of a monster truck, no vehicle was getting over those curbs.

However, the concentric rings weren't intended as vehicle deterrents. Their main purpose was to protect from earthquakes. Specifically, the destructive seismic waves that rippled across the surface when an earthquake happened.

Not that this was an earthquake zone. But better to be prepared; least that was the rationale. If an earthquake were to occur, those concentric rings, each tuned to a different frequency range due their differing sizes, would form a shield around the two-story buildings at their center. In theory, the rings would perform like a rock in a river's rapids. Seismic waves of an earthquake would flow around the two-story buildings, leaving them unharmed in their wake.

A rather expensive means of insurance. Particularly since the science was untested and unproven. Theoretically it had been tested in labs, and was on the cutting edge of the best way to protect structures from earthquakes. It borrowed from similar principles that stealth bombers used, when absorbing and deflecting radio waves. It had to do with vibrations and wavelengths and how lateral energy flowed across surfaces.

Three concentric rings, all visible, like tips of icebergs.

Beneath the soil were two more rings that couldn't be seen. The fourth was just below the surface and nearer to the buildings. It was made entirely of recycled tires. Rubber, for diffusing vibrations. The last ring was buried a little deeper. It was made of plastic—recycled plastic—from millions of water bottles.

These five rings were all arranged around five, non-descript, low-slung buildings. Each made of ochre-colored brick with windows of dark tinted glass. Nothing special about them. Very ordinary. Looked like countless office parks seen in suburbs everywhere.

With one or two exceptions.

The roofs of the buildings were actually huge solar arrays. Together they could generate 1.9 megawatts. That was enough to power 2,000 homes.

Impressive. But only a smidgeon of the power this place actually required.

The windows of the buildings were another peculiarity. They were opaque spandrel glass. Couldn't really tell just by looking at them—they looked like normal glass. They were for appearances only. No one could see through them, in or out.

Above those windows were louvers. From a distance they looked like brise soleils. They tracked continuously around each of the buildings.

The louvers were for air circulation. The buildings, more just shells, housed hundreds of absorption chillers, all utilizing cutting-edge technology. They ran at night when power costs were less expensive. They tied into on-site thermal storage facilities so that cooling could be provided during the day.

Lots of cooling.

Again, none of this was visible. The place to the naked eye looked like any unassuming office park. Outside of Raleigh there were plenty such office complexes that had similar looking structures.

There weren't any vehicles in the parking lot. That was unusual, James thought. There were always vehicles in the lot.

They pulled up to one of the buildings and emptied from Enrique's car. There was a niche next to the double doors, which from a few feet away almost looked like an ATM terminal. In the niche there was a keypad and a place to put one's hand. It was a biometric scanner. James pressed his hand against the reader and typed in a passcode. A moment later, the doors clicked open.

They entered a small lobby. There were no pictures on the walls and no rugs on the floor, just concrete. Bare concrete.

The only adornment at all was a white line on the floor. A camera captured their entry. In front of them was a desk where Security normally sat. It was empty. James frowned. He'd wanted to follow standard protocol. With no one here that was going to prove difficult to do.

They went through a mantrap, which looked like a vestibule, except for the metal bars and bulletproof glass. There was another scanner, this time for retinal identification. James placed his forehead against an ivory-colored cushioned pad and let the red eye oscillate across his face.

Seconds later, the door clicked open. James and Enrique walked down a corridor and entered the DECON chamber.

The DECON chamber was split into two areas. One for women and one for men. The men's area looked like a locker room. A very sterile locker room.

From a large locker they each retrieved some disposable scrubs, sat on the benches and stripped down. They slipped into the scrubs and adjusted them to fit. They put their shoes back on. They put booties over their shoes and stored their pants and shirts in the lockers.

It was all routine. In James's case, he'd done this at least a hundred times since this place had been built. He didn't even view it as strange anymore. It was like wearing a hard hat at a construction site, or a tie to the office.

"Ready?" James said.

"Yep," said Enrique.

They went through the airlock.

25

BEHIND them the doors hermetically sealed. There was a short corridor ahead, which ended with a pair of stainless-steel elevator doors. Even now they could hear the vibrations coming from below.

Appearances and sizes were misleading. From the outside the place had appeared to be an office park. It wasn't. And as for size, "The Vault" was considerably larger than it appeared. That was due to the fact that the majority of the hot site was below ground.

They entered the elevator. Enrique pressed the button for one of the lower levels. "How's your ankle?"

"Fine." James was keeping his weight off it as best he could.

As they descended, the vibrations intensified; unseen equipment emitting a constant hum. Everything in this facility was fully automated. Very little was required from the operators, aside from the need to verify systems were performing correctly. Ever since the Siemens' fiasco, where the backup servers hadn't been working for months, an enhanced series of fail-safes had been implemented to prevent similar failures.

The businesses and corporations that relied on The Vault were too lengthy to mention. Today a crisis had done a tsunami on the financial community. Tomorrow they would all be knocking on the door of The Vault to bail them out. Except this time the bailout wouldn't be the Fed with money like a few years ago, but ComTek with their data.

All their data... from the names of the accounts to the amounts, and everything in-between.

The Vault's primary function was the protection of data. It served as the last bastion of defense for many of its clients. Large companies, for the most part, still utilized their own data recovery systems. But since the latest breakthroughs in compression technology and deduplication, where almost unlimited amounts of data could be sent in seconds from anywhere in the country, many companies in the last two years had either shifted to using ComTek in lieu of their old systems or were using them as a redundant system. The cost was negligible, when considering the low cost per terabyte and the credits insurance companies typically gave for having two independent disaster recovery systems.

The Vault continuously backed-up and protected distributed data from thousands of locations. The encryption process that The Vault utilized was state-of-the-art. Even if a server blade were to leave the facility, the data it contained was useless without the cryptographic keys that unlocked the data. Those keys were protected through an intricate matrix that only the client controlled. Clients didn't need to worry about their data being vulnerable. All information contained in The Vault was impregnable even to the most sophisticated algorithmic attacks.

The Vault was so nicknamed for good reason. This place was for serious data storage. A tier-5 facility. The only of its kind. It didn't get more serious than this.

The lift came to a stop.

A moment later the doors opened. They exited into a shiny sterile environment and walked past humming equipment to the *Fishbowl*. The room had glass walls on all four sides. As they entered, the two-inch thick glass door—actually it wasn't glass, but rather a composite material similar to PYREX®—sealed behind them and the insistent hum from the servers was replaced with silence.

Enrique took a seat at one of the terminals. Above them was a bank of monitors that showed dozens of views from the surveillance cameras. It was eerie being the only two people in the facility. Even on Christmas Day this place normally had a small cadre of personnel and Security.

"Let's make this quick." James wanted to get to his family. Already, he was questioning his decision to come here.

Enrique moved the mouse and typed on the keyboard. "It's going to take a few minutes."

A sharp pain came from James's ankle and he grimaced.

Son of a.

"I'll be back. I'm going to the Break Room to get some ice."

26

SUE wedged herself between the wall and dresser and pushed with her legs. The dresser fell in front of the door with a crash. Sue knew it would only hold the men for a moment. She joined her girls in the closet and pulled the bi-fold closet door shut. Through the slats she peered into the room. She heard the men yelling.

She touched her girls. "It's okay. I'm here."

The closet they were in had the scent of cedar. Winter coats and other garments were hung on the rod above them. Their house was built thirty years ago and had plenty of quirks. This closet was one of them. It served double duty. As a space-saving measure, the closet was designed so that it opened onto two rooms: the room they'd just left and the adjacent room that was once a bedroom, but now served as James's office.

Sue and her girls crawled through the coats. They could hear the men banging on the door.

"Now, Mommy?" Katie said.

"We need to wait."

Sue looked through the slats into the office. She saw James's computer. It was turned on for some reason. He usually left it turned off. To the right of it, she could see the door. It was already open.

There was the sound of wood splintering and Sue took the opportunity to pull the bi-fold door open. She maneuvered back through the coats so she could look into the room they'd just left. The dresser was shaking. The wood trim around the door was hanging off the wall. They'd succeeded at breaking the door jamb and she knew it would just be a matter of seconds before they pushed the dresser out of the way.

She crawled back and joined her girls. "Okay."

She nudged Hannah and Katie forward.

There was a loud wrenching sound and then a crash. By the sound of it, the dresser had fallen from its side. The three of them left the closet and Sue went to the open door. She took a chance and peeked out into the hallway. She caught a glimpse of the men entering the room they'd just left. She looked back at her girls.

"I'll be right behind you," she whispered.

"Mommy?" Hannah's lip trembled.

"It's okay, baby. I'll be right behind you."

Her girls went through the door and headed down the stairs. Sue followed behind. They reached the landing. There was a propane tank that for some reason was propped against the wall. They squeezed past it, headed down the last few steps to the hallway and made a beeline for the garage door.

Upstairs, the men were yelling.

Katie and Hannah reached the door. Sue fumbled with the key. She got the door open and locked it behind them. She knew that would only slow them down for a moment. But that was all she and her girls needed.

Her girls were by the minivan. Sue went to the workbench area. They kept spare keys to both cars in a jelly jar that was hidden behind James's tool box.

Sue pulled the tool box aside and looked for the jelly jar.

It wasn't there.

27

JAMES finished slurping down his second bottle of water, and then limped back towards the Fishbowl with an ice pack. He looked at his watch. Enrique better have something to show him. If not, they were leaving, conspiracy evidence or not. He'd turned the TV on in the Break Room and had been horrified by what he saw.

An airplane collision had occurred half an hour ago and debris had rained down on a suburb only five miles from his house. Air Traffic Control was scrambling to route planes without use of the computerized systems they normally relied on. An FAA spokesman declined to comment further, other than adding they were dealing with a host of issues concurrently.

Crowds were rioting in the major cities throughout the US. They were seeing spikes in crime not seen since the 1970s. The National Guard had been mobilized and curfews were in effect.

He needed to be with his family. Not here, running down some hunch of Enrique's. Enrique was right; this virus thing would be figured out and stopped. AngelGuard already had a patch, which meant they'd isolated the virus. Infected systems would just need to be quarantined and reset to their status prior to infection. It was a little more complicated than that, of course. But basically it boiled down to that when you took away the peripherals. When a system crashed or data was lost, it could all be brought back as long as an effective disaster recovery system was in place.

There was an upside to his and Sue's savings and checking account loss not being an isolated incident. He'd been thinking they were victims of identity theft. Had that been the case, it would have been an uphill climb to recover their losses. They might never fully recover what they'd lost.

But this...

This whole-scale collapse of banking networks was an entirely different scenario. It guaranteed banks would implement recovery systems; essentially reset customer accounts to their status 24 hours ago. Any transactions post infection would be retracted. It would be a tricky proposition. Some banks, the smaller ones that didn't have sophisticated disaster recovery systems in place might face losses. But his bank, which was a client of ComTek's, would be able to restore accounts to their amounts pre-infection, which would include his and Sue's.

At least in theory that's how it worked. But The Vault had never been tested on this scale. James looked around at the vast subterranean breadth of humming equipment. This place—a window into a post-apocalyptic underground world, if there ever was one—was about to earn its keep.

So much of what he did everyday was monotonous routine. To be in a situation where the worst-case scenario was happening was sobering. While he didn't have the impressive job title, or the fat paycheck, the value he brought to ComTek was about to be beyond monetary comprehension.

Trillions of dollars were safeguarded in this facility.

While he wanted to get home to be with his family, a part of him was struggling with a small, but critical omission. He was surprised that this place, which was about to become the most important facility on the globe, was unmanned, except for him and Enrique.

Security should be here.

The technicians, whose job it was to keep this place running smoothly, should be on site. *Where the heck were they?*

The place was a ghost town.

28

SUE looked frantically, but the jelly jar with the keys to the minivan wasn't anywhere to be seen. With dismay, she scanned the work area and adjacent shelves.

Over the years the place had become a storage depository for a thousand miscellaneous items. James had done a good job keeping things organized, but Sue knew it would take hours to scour the rest of the garage looking for the jar, and she didn't have that amount of time.

Her eyes darted to the garage door. She couldn't open that either. The clicker that opened it was locked inside the minivan. The button on the wall that used to open the garage's rolling door hadn't worked since they bought the place. It was on their long list of things to replace, but other things—like a new roof, furnace and air conditioning units, microwave, garbage disposal, the list was long—had taken precedence.

Sue pushed the button, but as suspected nothing happened.

Had the garage door started to open, the noise it made would have transmitted throughout the house. It would take the men a second, but once they heard it, she knew they'd come running. The men would have to unlock the deadbolt first. That would take them only a moment. She figured, at best, she and the girls would have less than a minute to get to one of their neighbor's houses.

That wasn't much time. Sue looked out the garage door's small windows. The driveway was long. They had a large yard. Across the street was Mr. Steven's house. To their left, over the dry creek bed that she couldn't see from her current vantage point, were the Wahl's.

Sue went to the quick-release cord for the garage door and pulled. The cord was supposed to disengage the electric motor and allow a person to manually be able to open the door. She went to the door and pulled, but it didn't budge. She pulled harder with no success.

She checked the cord again, but there was nothing else to pull. The electric motor was at least fifteen years old. It had been in the house when they purchased it. The rolling door, she knew, weighed several hundred pounds. She'd never budge it without the help of the pulley system.

Precious time was being wasted.

She gave up on the door.

They couldn't hide here. The men would soon figure—if they hadn't already—that she and the girls hadn't gone out the window, once they inspected the roof and drop-off that was involved. It would only be a matter of minutes before they searched the house.

If she broke the minivan's window to get the clicker, the noise was sure to draw the men. They wouldn't have enough time to run away. Sue bit her lip and made a decision. She told her girls to hide behind the minivan.

Hannah whimpered.

"Don't worry, Katie will be with you. Katie, watch over your little sister. I'll be right back."

Katie nodded. She was being so brave. Katie took her sister's hand and led her behind the minivan. Sue waited till they were hidden and then turned the deadbolt and cracked open the door that led into the house.

Taking a deep breath, she slipped inside with a lug wrench and headed towards the kitchen to get her purse, which had her car keys.

29

BY her best calculation only a few minutes had elapsed since she and the girls left the room upstairs. The men might still be up there, checking out the roof. She could only hope and pray that was the case. She paused in the hallway and listened, but didn't hear anything.

Her heart was beating so hard she was afraid it was going to leap from her chest. She moved forward, quickly and quietly. In her hand was the heavy wrench she'd taken from James's work bench. If anyone had asked her a day ago if she could ever hit someone with a lug wrench, she would have said never. The thought would have horrified her.

Motherhood, however, was a strange thing—it gave a person a unique perspective. Those men had bound and gagged her girls. She would do anything to protect her babies. *Anything.* She gripped the wrench.

Give me strength.

She reached the end of the hallway. She couldn't hear them upstairs. She peeked in the living room. There was no one there. She moved across the rug.

The TV was playing on mute. There was a black duffel bag on the couch. She saw plastic drop-cloths and rolls of duct tape. She shivered thinking what those were intended for. If she had any doubts, they were gone. These men had no intention of letting her and the girls live.

The kitchen had cupboards and drawers open. The place looked like it had been ransacked. Her heart dropped when she saw her purse wasn't where she'd left it. She quickly looked around and saw that it had merely been moved. It was next to the stove. She went over and was about to grab it, when she thought better.

She just took her cell phone and keys. She needed her hands; she couldn't be encumbered with a purse that might make noise.

The phone she slipped in her pocket. She held the keys firm so they wouldn't clink and give her away. With the wrench in her other hand, she headed back to her girls. As she entered the living room, she heard someone coming down the stairs. He was coming fast. *She'd never make it to the hallway without being seen!*

She backtracked to the kitchen and tucked behind the screen wall. She put her keys in her pocket so she could grip the wrench with both hands. The handle was warm and slick from her grip. She was sweating. She wiped the dampness from her hands and cocked the wrench back.

She could hear the man's movements. He was in the living room. It sounded like he was coming her way.

Lord, give me strength.

30

ENRIQUE pulled his hair. "I swear it was here."

James, resigned to hearing Enrique out, suggested they do a search. They set the parameters and focused on recent files. The search would only pull up files that had been modified in the last twenty-four hours. When that wasn't effective they expanded their search.

Still coming up empty, James suggested they cross-reference with internal memory files. Central IQ, where Enrique had first discovered the anomalies, utilized The Vault for redundancy backup purposes. Mirrored blocks of data were kept temporarily before being overwritten. Those blocks of data should align; if they didn't that might highlight the areas where they needed to focus.

Locating inconsistencies, differing bytes of data—the proverbial needle in a haystack—was one of those problem-solving tasks that James enjoyed. When glitches developed, it was usually old-fashioned sleuth work that resolved an issue. Some of it involved reverse engineering. He took apart the item in question and tried to recreate it.

James's methods were a little unorthodox, but typically they yielded results. Over the years, he'd written programs that were designed to root out anomalies. His tiger team was tasked to protect ComTek's network infrastructure. To do that, James had to put on different hats and sometimes think like a person with malicious intent.

While breaking rules was against his nature—operating in a theoretical realm was an entirely different story—he had no problems thinking like a hacker.

In fact, he more than enjoyed playing that role.

Being the hunter, instead of the hunted.

Hackers typically went for holes. Those forgotten back doors, which were intrinsic with most forms of software. Intuitively, James knew where to look, which in this business was ninety-nine percent of the challenge.

After running two sniffer programs concurrently, James came to a quick conclusion. Someone had taken elaborate measures to cover their tracks. They'd almost been successful.

Almost...

"Bingo."

"Shit boss—that was kick-ass."

It was only a small discrepancy, but it gave credence to Enrique's suspicions. Time logs had been altered, James's and Enrique's, as well as several others on their team. Neither James nor Enrique punched a time clock—they were both salaried employees—but time logs were automatically generated whenever a person logged on to the network. According to the redundant backup files, for the last several weeks James and Enrique each had shadows; meaning a third party was using their signatures to access the NAS Gateway.

Normally, it would be easy to bring up a snapshot that could effectively retrace keystrokes, but all that information had been wiped clean. Someone, who knew what they were doing, had surgically removed evidence, as well as key *crypt* files that would have allowed paths, key-ins and commands to be seen.

There were multiple security features that safeguarded ComTek's network infrastructure. The fact that someone had been operating under

James's and Enrique's signatures was cause for alarm. The NAS Gateway was central to all operations.

Granted, it was impossible for a lone operator to alter any data or programs without authorization. ComTek had safety measures similar to the military. Just like it took two officers to arm a warhead with their keys and passwords, it also took digital sign-off from two ComTek direct-line superiors to alter or access certain files.

Such checks and balances prevented confidential files from being improperly viewed, modified or misplaced. The NAS Gateway could only be accessed through Central IQ or The Vault. As James dug deeper, he realized the time log discrepancies were just the tip of it. Some of the search programs had turned up fringe material. On its face, it had nothing to do with breaches in security.

James explored the implications, clicking to several folders.

ComTek, like many companies, had strict rules on acceptable conduct. There were certain offenses that were grounds for automatic dismissal, such as inappropriately touching another employee, uttering a racial epithet, being intoxicated while working, or stealing company property. There were second-tier offenses that warranted a warning, or in some cases dismissal, if the infraction involved others. Viewing pornographic material online fit in that category.

ComTek was a zero-tolerance company. James and Enrique both knew the drill.

Don't do anything at work you don't want your employer to see.

HR gave that pitch to every new ComTek employee on day one. Personal emails were considered the property of ComTek and could be viewed at any time.

IT, in many ways, was Big Brother. While a person might be able to bypass filters to view inappropriate sites, masking such actions from IT was another story.

Enrique looked at James strangely. Which wasn't a surprise, considering what James had just pulled up. In the last three months, according to the log, he'd made multiple visits to chat rooms on his company-provided laptop. He'd also accessed sites, which judging by their names, TooYoung.com, Under18XXX.com, and others similarly named, were of the pornographic variety.

James viewed some of the chat room correspondence. According to the info on the screen, his handle was 'DaddyKnowsBest'. His *chats* appeared to be with underage girls. Briefly skimming the content yielded some disturbing exchanges.

James shook his head. It was becoming obvious that whoever had been using his signature hadn't covered all their tracks. This online record could easily have been expunged, at least on the surface, but there had been no effort to do so. It had been left to easily be discovered.

"Whoa," Enrique said.

James frowned and shifted uncomfortably in his chair. "This isn't me."

"That's what they all say."

James looked at Enrique.

"I'm kidding, boss. There's no way you'd be this stupid."

James took the ice pack off his ankle and shifted closer to the computer. "Why would someone do this? Cop my password to surf porn? It doesn't make sense."

The searches indicated other areas that weren't aligning. More red flags.

James's brow furrowed. "I'm going to check a few things. I want you to pull some things up."

James told Enrique where to begin. Then he started to dig.

31

BEING on a tiger team, as they were, gave James and Enrique special clearance, even more than their counterparts in IT. Every year they were required to submit to drug tests and have background tests run. The seven members of James's team were carefully vetted. For them, proprietary files off limits to other employees were just a few clicks away. Each of them had full administrator access, which enabled them to see almost any confidential file in the system.

On the screen were folders for each performance review James had had since he started employment at ComTek. For some reason, one of his sniffer programs indicated that several of these records had been changed in the last few weeks. He clicked open one of the files.

He'd never pulled these up before. The file he opened was over nine years old. It was one of his early performance reviews, just two years into his tenure at ComTek. He skimmed the form. It was the standard form that scored him in two areas: skills and behaviors. Those areas were broken down into various categories.

Skills and Behaviors

Integrity:

Customer focus:

Problem Solving:

Creativity:

Collaboration/Teamwork:

Taking responsibility:

Communication:

Technical knowledge:

// Leadership Assessment…

Next to each of the categories were columns with his supervisor's numerical scores and typed-in comments. Even though the review was quite a while ago, he recognized the high marks and remarks he'd gotten. There was praise for the 'deduplication' software he'd created.

That had been one of his biggest accomplishments. At the time it had been a big win for the company. Big being a gross understatement.

It had saved the company tens of millions of dollars.

Each year.

It also had opened up another revenue stream for ComTek. In fact, in some ways that software was partially responsible for The Vault being what it was today. But he never got credit for it. While it had been his baby, his supervisor had gotten the recognition, and been promoted because of what it brought to the bottom line. The software improved storage capacity by almost 1,400%.

That was huge.

Beyond huge.

That was back when James was certain he was on the fast track. *Make your bosses look good, and you're sure to follow suit. Big contributions get noticed. Pay your dues.*

Those adages still rung in his head. His supervisor and his supervisor's boss, who was head of the division, had said something to similar affect.

You're an ace.

You've got lots of runway son.

The sky's the limit for you.

He'd been given a copy of his review, which was standard procedure. He glanced at the bottom of the form. There was his signature. Both he and his supervisor had to sign the form agreeing to the scores and comments. The form would be put in his permanent record, which could be viewed by the senior team at any time.

The form was identical to the one he remembered, except for one thing. The last section. It was titled 'Leadership Assessment'. There was a small box where remarks could be placed. In that column were two words.

[Not promotable]

No explanation accompanied those two words. They stood there stark and cold. Two pairs of initials were next to those words. His supervisor's and his boss's boss.

James felt a lump form in his throat.

He closed the form and glanced at the change log for the file. *That had to have been recently added; that couldn't be right.* ComTek's proprietary technology kept a time-stamped log of the changes to every file. If it had been changed, he could find out. But this file's change log had only one entry—the one noting the file's creation. Those words were original.

[Not promotable]

James shook his head. He was getting distracted. This wasn't what he was here for.

With some effort, he shifted gears. He concentrated on the files that had been changed in the last few weeks. He pulled up the most recent one, which happened to be from last Friday when he had his annual review. Quickly skimming it, he recognized the part where his boss asked him to describe himself. Curiously, his response where he mentioned his "professionalism" was highlighted. James looked over at his boss's remarks.

James had a decent relationship with his boss and had reported to him for the last five years. They weren't what you'd consider fast friends, but their relationship was cordial and James knew his team's success made his boss look good. His boss had recently been promoted to VP in no small part due to the success of several major initiatives that James's team had spearheaded.

That seemed to be a theme with James's career.

Reading his boss's comments, however, did not reflect what James would have expected. It also did not match the form he had signed.

[James has an inability to provide an accurate personal critique. This response is disconnected from his performance. In the last few months, James has exhibited erratic behavior on multiple projects. I have concern for his mental state of mind. Let the record please note, that to date, James has been resistant to any form of counseling. This subject has been broached with him on two other occasions (see previous reports, #23-1 and #24-8). Recommendation to remove high-level clearance and initiate documentation process for immediate termination.]

James's face flushed. There was a 'yellow status' tag on the file, meaning the review was still in the queue for upper level sign-off.

This was a lie. *Erratic behavior? Counseling?*

He reread the last word in disbelief. *Termination?* James took a deep breath. He looked over at Enrique. "Found anything?"

"Not yet. You?"

"Check for dual-authentications. I think you're going to find that I accessed those key bundles you told me about earlier."

"What do you mean?"

"Just do it!"

Enrique looked over, surprised at his outburst.

James started typing quickly. If he was right about what he was thinking, what he'd uncovered was not the worst of it.

32

THE man was doing something in the other room. Sue heard what sounded like a zipper being zipped. *He was by the duffel bag.*

Sue listened; afraid to breathe. There was a pause where she heard nothing. Maybe he'd taken it and gone upstairs?

She stole a glance towards the kitchen's back door. She could unlock it and run for it. She could get help. Her girls were hidden; it would take some time for the men to find them. *But leaving her girls?* There was no way she could bring herself to do that, even if it might be their best chance of surviving this.

She gripped the wrench and listened.

She still didn't hear anything. Had he left the room? The silence was too much. It was as if she could hear her own heart thumping... so loud, if he was in there, she was almost afraid he'd hear it. She readied herself. It was time to look into the room.

"Da!"

He was still there!

"Understood, I'll make sure I get their blood on the man's clothes, but we have problem. No, no. We fix. Yes... Don't worry. It will be made clean." There was another pause. "What? Our fault? Enough! We did our side of deal. We downloaded marker. Now we clean up... leave. No more waiting for you with husband—you finish. Okay? Da!

"Vasily! Artem!"

Sue heard yelling and the man's voice receded. He seemed to be leaving the room? *Now was her chance!* She peered in and didn't see him. She moved quickly, going through the living room. She could hear shouting upstairs.

As she reached the hallway, she caught a glimpse of someone coming down the stairwell. He was coming fast! She hurried towards the garage door. Her flats smacked on the wooden floors.

She reached the door and fumbled with the key. Just as she got it in, she heard a shout. She turned. It was the man named Artem and he was coming towards her.

33

JAMES surveyed the screen and felt a sinking sensation. It was as if the floor beneath him had just opened. Data files had been altered on Enrique's computer, as well as the rest of the team's. The person responsible had erased their tracks. For the most part they'd been successful, but the one rule James knew, you could never fully erase anything in the virtual world. An imprint always remained—no matter how faint.

Scramble code and malware had originated from his own computer. His signature had been erased, but James was able to detect its ghost. By what he'd gathered, *he'd* commandeered his team's computers, as well as several hundred others within the network. *He'd* created slaves—a botnet—a zombie army of computers to fire off an assault.

Whoever had orchestrated this had made it look like he was responsible. They'd completed the charade by going to considerable lengths to erase the implicating evidence.

It showed a cunning mind at work, both in the sophistication of the operation and extent of the cover-up. Not dissimilar to perpetrating a crime using someone else's gun and tossing the gun in the river, but instead of tossing it into the deep current, it was tossed into the shallow area where it would indubitably get dredged up. After effort, of course, so the finders wouldn't suspect they were meant to find it all along.

Someone had set him up.

A cipher program masked the operation's true objective. James bypassed false authentication codes that were intended to throw off the scent. The attempts at media sanitization were sophisticated, but James was able to use back channels and determine what his doppelganger had been up to.

It wasn't pretty.

James retraced his signature's movements. At 23:03:45 yesterday, he'd sent a series of executable commands. Minutes later, at 23:09:10 a second wave of missives had been unleashed, followed by another at 23:09:12, 23:09:15, 23:09:18…

They continued every three seconds for three hours. Contained within each outgoing message was an attached file. The file name of the first was GreedKills.jwtLive. The name on the second was GreedKills.jwtRedux; on the third it was GreedKills.jwtRepeat. It was a new variant each time.

James realized what he was looking at was a blended attack, and judging by the evidence, he was the man responsible.

"Shit, hombre." Enrique had an ashen look on his face.

James took a deep breath. This explained things. Once unleashed this would impact every system it came in contact with. Not just the addressees, but also anything in their networks.

Everything going on, all the mess that was happening out there, the crisis in the banking community, credit cards not working… even the plane collision near his house might be attributed to this.

From the way this was done, some of the addressees he was seeing here… this could ripple everywhere. Infect entire networks. If it spread to networks, such as ATC, it conceivably could cause air traffic control towers to not be able to communicate with their planes. Anything linked to a grid, connected to the Web would be vulnerable. And it all originated with what was on the screen—these files, cheekily named 'GreedKills', had caused the chaos.

And James's fingerprints were all over it.

He stared at the screen.

"James?" His own name sounded strange. "James?"

"Yeah?"

"Someone's coming."

James snapped out of it and looked to his left. A light on the panel was blinking. It was the passive alarm system that blinked anytime a vehicle approached the front gates. He looked at the surveillance screens above them.

A white van with another one behind it had stopped at the barricade.

"Looks like Security. What do you want to do?"

James took another breath. What he'd uncovered was overwhelming. He fought off the paralysis that was taking over his body.

A dozen thoughts sprouted—variables and probabilities—each of them kept coming back to one thing.

Someone had set him up.

"I need time."

"Got it. I'll let Security know we're here; put them at ease."

James turned to Enrique. "You know this isn't me, right?"

Enrique nodded, earnestly. "Of course. Don't worry, I'll be back."

Enrique left and James closed his eyes. He took several deep breaths and rubbed his temples. He opened his eyes and looked at the glowing screen.

Alright.

James felt something tingling in his belly. He realized what it was.

It was anger.

34

SUE slammed the door behind her. Before she could lock the deadbolt, the handle twisted in her grip. The door was pushed in with such force that she was sent backwards reeling. She caught herself on James's workbench. Pain shot up her forearm and tools clattered to the floor.

She looked up and there in the doorway was Artem. His face had a look of wry amusement. He wasn't a large man, but there was a compactness to him that hinted of considerable strength.

His eyes surveyed the garage. "So this is where you are hiding."

The wrench had fallen from Sue's hand and lay on the ground. Artem glanced at it indifferently and stepped forward. Sue steadied herself on the table behind her.

"There now." He put his hands out, extending his palms. His heavily-accented voice was placating. It was a tone a person might use with a child.

"I hate we have to do this. Believe me, I get no pleasure. I ask you think of your girls. It doesn't have to hurt."

Sue's heart dropped with those words and her head followed suit. A snide smile formed on the man's thin lips. "There. I'm glad you understand."

Sue didn't make a move and he approached without concern.

"I promise…" He reached out calmly.

In a whirl, she jammed a screwdriver into the side of his neck. Artem screamed. She yanked it out and Artem stumbled back.

His hands groped for his neck as blood spurted.

He fell backwards.

Sue turned and looked frantically around the garage.

"Hannah! Katie!"

They both came from behind the minivan and looked at her with wide-open eyes. Sue ran to them and herded them to the side door. She opened the minivan and shoved them inside. She got in the driver's seat and automatically locked the doors. She clicked the garage door opener and fumbled with the keys.

Katie screamed.

There was a muffled sound of something hitting the minivan's side window. Sue turned to see Artem, blood smeared on his face and neck. His face was contorted into a maniacal snarl. He smashed a bloody palm against the window.

The window held. Sue turned the key in the ignition and the minivan started. The garage door, behind her, wasn't moving. She clicked the opener again.

Artem grabbed the door handle. Blood was oozing voluminously from his neck. His shirt was drenched. He banged the window again and looked around.

The garage door still wasn't moving. In horror and dismay she realized she'd disengaged the motor when she tried to manually open it.

Artem retrieved a shovel from the wall. He gripped the shovel with both hands. He began to wobble as if he was going to fall.

Something hit the other side window—the one on the passenger side. Sue turned and saw Vasily. The man rapped the glass. He was holding a gun in his other hand.

He leveled the gun towards her. "Out!"

Artem swung the shovel. It hit the windshield with a crash and the glass burst into a million spidery cracks. Somehow it held. Artem wobbled, then pulled back to swing again.

"Artem!" yelled Vasily.

Sue punched the accelerator and the back of the minivan smashed into the heavy garage door. The force of the impact threw her and the girls back into their seats.

"Mommy!"

Sue put her foot to the accelerator again.

Nothing happened.

The minivan had stalled. The garage door behind them was broken outwards and light was flooding in. Sue turned the key in the ignition and heard a tremendous noise. The passenger window blew out. Her girls screamed.

Glass was all over the dash. Sue turned and saw Vasily. He had the pistol leveled towards her. Its long silencer was smoking.

"Out! Now!"

Sue took her hands from the wheel.

Blaammm!!!!

The noise was deafening. Another shot rang out almost immediately.

Sue blinked, opened her eyes. Vasily was gone. So was Artem. She turned and saw someone coming through what was left of the garage door. Light was behind him and he was framed in silhouette.

The man approached. He was holding a shotgun. It took her second to realize who it was.

Dad?

35

ENRIQUE went through the airlocks and DECON chamber and headed towards the front entry. What he'd just seen James do on the computer was beyond amazing. He knew his boss was skilled, but he'd never seen anyone move with such speed when hunting down a security breach. The way he had taken apart such an intricate multi-layered infiltration was textbook, but it wasn't like any textbook he'd ever read at school.

Yeah, the man had skills.

Enrique moved quickly. He didn't know how much time they had. He paused briefly to look back at one of the security cameras and waved. He knew James would be watching.

The men were getting out of the first van. There were seven of them.

"We don't have much time," Enrique said. "He's picked apart what happened. I didn't like leaving him. We need to hurry."

The men nodded and followed Enrique inside.

36

SOMETHING wasn't right. James glanced at the surveillance screens. Enrique had spoken briefly to Security and now they were heading his way.

That wasn't exactly buying him time.

What was Enrique doing?

The men had gone through the DECON chamber without getting suited and had proceeded through the airlocks. They were walking with purpose, not pausing. No more friendly waves from Enrique.

This wasn't good.

James closed down the computer. He went to work quickly. They would be here in less than three minutes.

37

BOB Pulaski, who had used up his last shell, surveyed the rest of the damage. The men he'd shot were crumpled heaps on the garage's concrete floor. They weren't moving and by the look of it they appeared to be dead.

He could see Sue through the broken windshield. There was blood all over the minivan.

His heart dropped. Bob went to her. She moved when he reached in to open the door. "Suzy?"

"Dad?"

He touched her arm and she started to cry. "My girls."

"Where?"

"In back. Get them first."

Bob opened the sliding door and picked Katie and Hannah tenderly out. They weren't hurt, but look frightened.

"Are you going to hurt us?" Hannah said in a trembling voice.

Bob shook his head. "No, of course not."

Sue grabbed Bob's arm. "How many?"

He looked at her, puzzled.

"How many did you shoot?"

"Two."

Sue's eyes opened wide.

"What is it?" Bob said. As he uttered the question, he spied a man's reflection in the minivan's window.

38

"WHERE is he?"

"He's here," Enrique said. He looked up at the surveillance cameras. "He can't hide. We've got this entire place covered."

"I don't see him." The man that spoke was named Savic. His face had a feral quality to it: longish hair, hooked nose, and cords on his neck, as if ropes were buried just beneath his skin. Right now he wasn't happy.

"Hold on," Enrique said. "Let me pull up some other views." Enrique tried moving the mouse, but the monitor stayed dark. Puzzled, it took him a second until he realized the station was turned off.

He pushed the button to boot up the system. Nothing happened.

Enrique frowned and made sure the cords were still connected. There was nothing wrong there. He followed the wires, bending to look under the molded counter.

Enrique smirked, seeing what James had done. One of the main power cords was unplugged. *Nice try, James.* He knelt and plugged in the cord.

He sat back in the chair and pushed the button to fire up the box. The LED light blinked and the slim capsule-looking box *whirred* to life. A blue screen appeared on the monitor and stayed there unchanged.

"Shit."

"What is it?" Savic leaned in.

"Nothing. Give me a second," Enrique said. He rolled back his chair and looked under the counter again. As he did so, he noticed something on his pants and flicked it off. It was a piece of clear plastic. His foot crunched on another piece. *What the...?*

There were bits of clear plastic all over the floor. He then noticed, off to the side, some wires that weren't plugged into their data ports. He pulled one of the Ethernet cables out and saw its end was smashed.

"Fuck!" Enrique knew what had happened. James had pulled all the data cables out and stepped on their ends!

Enrique's jaw set. "This'll take me a few minutes. I need to restore connectivity."

Savic looked at his men. "Fan out and find him."

"Wait, hold on!" Enrique said. "I'll get it working."

Savic frowned and pulled out his gun.

Enrique looked at the gun in surprise. "What's that for?"

Savic glanced at his watch. "Did you send the video?"

"The second I got here. What's the gun for?"

"You're wasting time. Get the cameras fixed."

Not happy, Enrique went to get more cable.

39

JAMES moved deeper into The Vault. He was in one of the air shafts that distributed ductwork and miles of conduit throughout the facility. High voltage signs were on banks of equipment. He'd barely left the Fishbowl in time. He couldn't run with his ankle. The best he could do was move in a fast shuffle.

It felt like the earth was crumbling under his feet.

Enrique was in on it.

James was in a state of disbelief. What he'd uncovered, the breadth of the security breach; the fact that he was being set up to be the fall guy.

Enrique was in on it.

Of that he was certain. He'd taken those men right to him. As he got past the disbelief part, it began to make sense. His coming here was because of Enrique.

Enrique had wrapped things up neatly. He'd brought him to the scene of the crime. Instead of being home with his family as rioting was done in the streets, which any sane family man would be doing, James had come to a closed, locked facility. It only looked incriminating. If Security found him, they'd take him in and the way the evidence was stacked against him, he wouldn't stand a chance of defending himself.

Enrique and whoever he was working with (his boss?) had done their worst. By all accounts, James had orchestrated the attacks and commandeered his team's computers. They'd spliced in just the right details: the performance reviews, his surfing of pornographic sites at work, his web chatting of underage girls. It was character assassination.

Sublime in its smart-bomb precision.

It destroyed his credibility and called into question everything about him. Forget about being seen as a wholesome family man—what else was a lie, people would wonder?

He'd never have a chance to counter the charges that would be leveled against him. They'd effectively buried him. And now they wanted to take him in. At this very moment Security was searching for him. To buy himself time, he'd disabled *Phalanx*, the 360 security shield that controlled the surveillance cameras. Enrique might figure out how to get the system back online. However, he was in for a surprise or two once he got the computers working.

Without the cameras they would have to systematically comb each floor. That would take a while. There were multiple places to hide. He thought quickly; knowing decisions now—left or right, up or down—were like the last death throes of a chess match. Depending on which way he went now would dictate how quickly this game ended.

As he moved past a vertical wall of high voltage wires and mechanical equipment, his mind felt as if it were free falling. He hadn't seen any of this coming. It didn't make any sense. James struggled to think. He needed to come up with a plan.

He went through a cased opening and entered a cavernous space. He looked over the guardrail and headed down. His ankle was holding up, but he didn't know for how long.

He reached the bottom landing. Off to the side, there were rows of lockers. Some of the engineers stored their tools down here. James paused. An idea, or the beginning of one, formed in his head.

He found a duffel bag in one of the lockers and began to load up with tools. Using a screwdriver, he popped a cabinet's lock and retrieved two utility laptops, several spools of cable and some duct tape.

Outfitted with what he needed, he went deeper into the bowels of the facility.

40

BOB had seen it in Saigon, Quang Tri, and more areas in Vietnam than he'd care to remember. He'd seen it again one night off the Ivory Coast while working on one of BP's rigs. Seven of his men had died when Nigerian gunmen had come in their boats.

Seeing death was always a surprise, none more so than when it was your hands that caused a human being's demise. There was a rush of adrenaline that flooded one's consciousness like a river washing away thought. Later, upon reflection, came the horror of what had been done, as faces, emotions, guilt and demons clawed for attention. But right now those struggles and voices were pushed aside.

"What is it?"

His own words...

Answered by the reflection in the glass... the fear in Sue's eyes.

IF time could stop...

Be seen from a different perspective.

Bob wasn't an intimidating presence; he wasn't tall and he didn't have a broad frame. But working on a rig for thirty-five years, drilling miles of pipe, moving equipment around that could make his hands bleed—gave him a strength that a person wouldn't see just by judging his outward appearance. Only an observant eye might notice the cords on his wrists and thick calluses on his hands.

He was sixty-two years old. Almost twice the age of the man behind him.

THAT man, reflected in the glass—who had survived firefights with rival Chechen gangs, was a soldier in the Solntsevskaya brotherhood and had just seen two of his comrades, Vasily and Artem, killed by Bob's gun— was, if anything, supremely overconfident. He was a killing machine, and his arm outstretched, a pistol in his cold, firm grip, pointed at Bob's head, was all in a day's work for him. Tomorrow he'd mourn his lost brethren; today he'd brain an old man.

He couldn't have been more mistaken.

BOB instinctively reacted with a speed that belied his age by several decades. The stock of his shotgun smashed into the Muscovite's jaw. It shattered the man's jaw on impact. The man's pistol discharged as the man went down. The errant bullet missed the girls and lodged in the wooden joists above their heads.

Bob moved quickly, almost a blur. The man was down, but not out. He disarmed him, snapping one of the man's fingers in the process. As the man tried to rise, Bob took him down for good with a forearm blow to the temple.

The man crumpled. It was over.

"IS he dead?" His daughter with her hand to her mouth.

Bob knelt and checked for a pulse. "He's alive."

There was a delayed reaction, and then Sue began to sob. Bob rose and stood there awkwardly. He wanted to reach out, comfort her, but it was as if he was suddenly frozen. All his energy expended, unable to even reach out and touch his daughter.

He stood there as Sue brought her girls to her and hugged them.

Tears flowed.

A tightness squeezed Bob's chest. He knew their innocence would never be the same. He felt sorrow for that reality, particularly for Katie and Hannah. He'd seen death at an early age too, and knew the loss it brought. It was as if color drained from the sky and grayness seeped into the days of youth.

Eventually the tears ebbed and Sue stood and led her girls back into the house. Bob didn't follow, but tended to the man he'd taken out. He found some duct tape and bound the man's arms and legs. As he wrapped him, he saw the tattoos.

The tattoos made him pause. He'd seen tattoos like that before. It had been in the Ukraine, and the man that had those tattoos had been in the employ of an oil czar.

A bad sense of foreboding followed Bob as he went inside.

He found Sue in the living room. She was wiping something from her daughter's arm. "They cut the phone lines," Sue said. "I've tried calling with my cell phone, but I only get a busy signal."

Bob nodded and set down his shotgun and the guns he'd collected. "Who were those men?"

Sue shook her head. "I don't know." She looked at him. "If you hadn't come when you did…" She trailed off. "How did you know?"

"Your cat."

She looked at him, puzzled, and Bob explained. He told her he'd rung the doorbell and thought they weren't home. He'd left and had seen their cat crying on the stoop. "I came back. I didn't think you'd leave your cat. Not with what was going on."

"So that was you… ringing the doorbell?"

Bob nodded.

"Tigerlily?" Hannah cried.

"Mommy, unlock the door."

"Okay…"

Sue opened the front door and the girls called for their cat. Seconds later, a large calico came running up the steps, crying loudly.

"Hey, *Bawler*," Bob said, as the cat preened.

"It's Tigerlily," Hannah said, scolding.

Sue glanced at Bob. "Do you think they'll be okay?" she said softly.

Bob nodded. "They'll be fine… they're young." He knew that was what she needed to hear.

There was pain and hurt in her eyes, and Bob wished he could make it go away. Emotion welled up inside him, and he turned away. He walked around the room. There were sheets of plastic on the floor. A duffel bag had been emptied on the couch. None of this looked like your typical robbery. This was something else.

That bad feeling came over him again.

"Do you mind if I look around?"

41

IT was past midnight in snow-laden Moscow and the smoky clip joint was filled with regulars. Semion Mihajlovic stubbed out his Davidoff cigarette and lit another.

He was a squat man with fleshy jowls. Deep brows gave his face a primordial profile. His suit was tailored and expensive; his pinky ring and gold watch were encrusted with diamonds. As head of the *Solntsevskaya bratva*, or Solntsevskaya brotherhood, the most powerful organized crime family in Moscow, Mihajlovic was far removed from the common ilk that bottom fed in the backstreets and alleyways of his city.

He and his men operated differently from the other crime families in Russia who adhered to an arcane and antiquated value system, where being *vory v zakone*, or 'thieves in law' was considered a badge of honor. For those men, strict codes of lawlessness fettered their lives. The Solntsevskaya bratva had expanded beyond such narrow-minded thinking. They lived by their own set of rules and their operations spanned the globe.

Fortune 500 companies had nothing on the Solntsevskaya bratva. They were a multi-billion dollar organization in many ways more powerful than the Cosa Nostra or South American drug cartels. Over twenty-thousand strong with a presence in Asia, Europe and America, they operated without impunity or fear of the law. They had their hands in everything, everywhere.

While their roots were in prostitution, human trafficking, arms dealings, and illegal drugs, they'd expanded significantly in the last decade into pseudo-legitimate businesses and considered themselves at their core reborn as true businessmen.

It was an attitude that was promoted, even flouted by Mihajlovic. For all respective appearances—the bodyguards, armor-plated Rolls, lavish lifestyle with flats in Moscow, Venice and Nice—he maintained he was a simple businessman that dabbled in wheat commodities, real estate and oil futures.

His designer phone pressed to his ear was standard for him. When he wasn't talking on it, his stub fingers held on to it, expecting his next call. Most, if not all his business was transacted on the phone. Even when one of his girls attended to his needs he held onto it. It was his thing.

Right now he wasn't pleased.

"What do you mean you haven't had contact?"

The voice on the other end was filled with static; it was an overseas call. Mihajlovic snorted; a sign that sometimes preceded violent explosions he was prone to have on occasion.

The two men near Mihajlovic's booth glanced at their boss. They were standing several paces away. Each was built like a tank, and topped out at over three-hundred pounds.

Mihajlovic snorted again. "What about *Angelguard?* Where are we right now?"

He nodded. "And the accounts? The money? Hmn. Da!"

Mihajlovic clicked off. He took another drag and leaned back. His enormous potbelly threatened to launch the pearl buttons off his shirt. His eyes trolled the room. Near the Lucite bar, which glowed with a purplish cast, he saw a *Krasivaya* he hadn't seen before. She looked Czech: round face, body long and lissome. He nodded at one of his men, and the man came and stooped over.

Mihajlovic said a few words and the man nodded and walked towards the bar.

Mihajlovic rolled his lower lip inwards and fiddled with his pinky ring. Waiting was tiresome. He needed something to relax, take his mind off things. His eyes took in the girl as she walked over. Her legs had a slight wobble as she walked, indicating she hadn't yet mastered the art of walking gracefully in six-inch stiletto heels.

Mihajlovic made a call on his phone.

"Get in touch again. If no contact, have them send more men." He clicked off as the girl—barely more than a teen—slid her shapely tush into the seat across from him.

"What's your name?"

She told him.

"Do you know who I am?"

The girl nodded.

"Good. Champagne?"

The girl smiled and showed off snaggly, uneven teeth. Mihajlovic snorted, displeased.

"You're an ugly one aren't you." He laughed a throaty belly laugh. "Don't worry, I won't throw you away. Just keep that trap closed." He signaled with a finger. "Victor, champagne! *Shevelis!*"

42

VISITORS from corporate sometimes commented on it. The Vault was that kind of place. It evoked unique first impressions. *Unworldly* was a term bandied about. There were other terms used to describe the place. *Muscular. Twenty-second century. Hard.*

They all fit. For James, he usually thought of that movie *Aliens*. Particularly the first few times he'd gone down to the lower levels. He'd seen that movie as a kid and it had scared the bejesus out of him.

There wasn't the moisture component, dripping water everywhere, nor was there the slime. And definitely not the rust. But there were the catwalks, the metal grate floors, the open elevator lifts, the huge utility lines running overhead and along the walls.

There was also the noise. The constant whoosh of air handlers and humming of equipment. That was down here. All of it industrial and brutish.

The Vault hit all the cues. Big time surround sound too.

WHOOOSH...

The cooling this place required was unreal. It was like a wind tunnel in spots.

Constant.

Overpowering.

If you weren't in the Fishbowl you were assaulted with it. Many of the technicians wore earplugs; some even wore the heavy duty kind used on firing ranges. The decibel levels varied, depending how close you were to the air handlers or the other banks of equipment. In some areas of The Vault the noise was as high as 81 decibels. You almost had to shout to make yourself heard above the din.

A technician had once regaled him with details. Apparently 85 decibels was the cut-off point the federal government cared about. After that point employers were required to protect their workers. OSHA standards is what the man said. The technician mentioned he'd even brought in a decibel reader.

It hadn't proven his case. 4 decibels too few. ComTek had listened to the man's complaints and promptly ignored them.

They'd spent over two billion dollars on this facility, but the cost for a little ear protective gear to improve the work environment for their employees was just too much. *Gotta draw the line somewhere,* the technician had been told. Just deal with it.

James wasn't surprised. That was standard M.O. The number crunchers always said no.

The technician had his own theory. In his mind, he understood their logic. It made sense to save twenty bucks on ear protective devices. But as for other capital expenditures, they were always inversely in proportion to what level they were connected to wants of upper management.

For instance... Corporate retreats for VPs and above—there was a special $289,000 slush fund for that allotted each year. And one corporate jet wasn't enough for the CEO. He had to have two. That cost $333,000. A month!

You don't even want to know what it cost to remodel the CEO's office. See, we're in a turnaround...

The man had a knack for impressions. Could do a mean CEO. *That's right, a turnaround. Need to get that stock back up. Can't do it from this crummy office. Goddamnit. Twenty thousand for a rug? Just do it!*

141

Twelve thousand for a new hutch? Goddamnit, yes! It's a bargain. Dennis Kozlowski owned the damn thing and he paid a heck of a lot more than twelve thousand.

No lie. Serious. It actually belonged to Dennis Kozlowski. *Kolinsky? Wait a second, you're not related are you?*

The technician had a sense of humor.

Different departments, same challenges. James had trouble requisitioning funds for his own team. New software to replace his team's outmoded, three-year old, almost obsolete IT Security? Forget it. Make do with what you got.

Figure it out.

Be creative.

Buzz phrases; he'd heard the same pithy platitudes.

WHOOSH...

It had been near here that the technician had bent his ear. *Can you believe that? Told me to go to Home Depot. Buy it on my own dime.*

James had nodded, smiling. He'd liked Jerry.

Wasn't much longer after that he'd heard the man had moved on 'to seek other opportunities'.

Thing was—Jerry had had a point.

The whoosh sound was more than just an annoyance. It created a pressure that built up in the head. Made it hard to think.

Drowned out other thoughts.

Not good. Particularly not now, considering that James needed to be able to think.

He looked over his shoulder again.

A long row of cabinets, all painted a bright orange, tracked down a wall. The ceiling, ten-foot overhead, was filled with power lines encased in braided stainless steel conduit. Vertical ductwork bisected the floors.

Down a ways there was a metal railing. He could still see the blue-painted metal beams supporting the monolithic slabs of concrete and steel deck. Cavernous spaces beyond.

Could have been the belly of a futuristic ship.

He kept moving. Somewhere near here he remembered seeing one. One of the hubs.

They were throughout the facility for technicians to use. Any of them might work. The difficulty was going to be in finding one out of sight. Most the hubs were in plain view.

He couldn't use those. Security was looking for him right now. He needed to pick a discrete spot. Someplace that was tucked away, close enough to ductwork.

That was key.

Be creative.

He could do that.

He slowed down. This was looking familiar. He'd been here with Jerry.

There, ten paces ahead, just as he remembered. Couldn't see it till you were right upon it. It was along the wall, fully hidden by the orange cabinets. One of the diagnostic hubs.

James set down the duffel bag and pulled out some of the items that he'd taken from the locker area.

Screwdriver in hand, he went to work.

43

IT didn't take long. James stepped back to take a look.

The utility laptop, which he'd inserted in the duct, was fully out of sight. The grill was repositioned back as it was. A cord, discretely hidden, came from inside the duct. It was taped so that it tracked behind some equipment and disappeared.

He checked the other laptop to make sure it was picking up the signal. Seemed to be working fine. Plenty of battery power.

That was good, he was going to need that. He put the laptop in sleep mode and loaded the tools back into the duffel bag. The duct tape had come in handy.

Duct tape. Over a million uses for the stuff.

He sat down. Make that one million and one. He doffed his shoe and wrapped his ankle. Gingerly, he tested the result. There was still a sharp pain, but it helped some. What he needed was to stay off it, and to elevate and ice it. Wishful thinking, of course.

He laced back up, got rid of the booties, and picked up the duffel bag and moved on. His head ached from where he'd hit it earlier. His cut had scabbed and his hair was matted with dried blood. His back was sending warning signs it was about to flare up. Aside from those minor particulars, he was doing fine.

He had a moment where he saw the irony. A simple cold could make him crabby and irritable. Sue always said that he—and sometimes upped the ante to include all men with her comment—were such babies. The girls would get a cold and soldier on, but if James got just the hint of one he'd inevitably complain and go to bed.

In most other things, however, he wasn't a whiner. He'd grown up in Philly; a blue-collar neighborhood. It wasn't a place for whiners. He used to make money cleaning up his uncle's place after school. His uncle owned a sparring club and gym. James had done his fair share of getting on the mat. Pain, his uncle would say, was all in the head.

There was truth to that statement. He'd spared with some talented fighters; a few that had gone to the next level. James was a skinny kid back then, and quick on his feet. He'd liked boxing, but it was wrestling he'd excelled at. He was a natural and had that unique combination of leanness, speed and brawn.

It was hard to believe—he was forty pounds heavier than the kid he used to be. His reflexes weren't the same—not even close. Just a few hours ago, he'd allowed a man to pull him from his car without even resisting.

That wouldn't have happened twenty years ago.

He'd changed.

Still, even that considered, muscle memory was a strange thing. It never really went away. The body remembered. It might wheeze and resist when pushed, but it went along, forgetting its current atrophy.

He hadn't eaten today, but he wasn't hungry. It was like reserves were being tapped into. He was remembering the person he used to be. The person who didn't quit. The fighter.

It used to be a mantra for his life.

He'd gotten a scholarship for wrestling at Penn State and had pursued a mathematics degree. It was an odd choice for a jock, but it was something he was passionate about. He'd gone on to get his masters in computer science.

When he graduated, he'd had some attractive offers from some big names, but instead of going the traditional route he'd gone with a startup out in California. It never got off the ground, but James didn't let that deter him. He'd taken an equity stake in another startup, till eventually he tried his own thing. Sue, his sweetheart in college, stayed with him throughout.

They'd lived in a rental; a tiny three-hundred square foot apartment. They'd married—a small affair with just a few friends and select family—and put off having kids as James took a fledgling concept and tried to hit it big. He'd swung for the fences.

Years went by. Sue's job paid the bills. James's didn't.

At thirty-two, after eight years of failed starts and false hopes, James had a crisis moment. They couldn't afford the airfare to go to his dad's funeral. Their credit cards were maxed out. Their car was a junker and wouldn't make a cross-country trip. His mother, who was on a fixed income herself, had to lend them the money, much to his shame.

It wasn't long after that that James took a job out East at ComTek. The company was located in Raleigh, North Carolina. It was a stable job with a real salary, instead of a promised big payout, which was always another year away.

They'd tried to start a family, but after a few years they realized something was wrong. Sue was eventually told by the doctor she would never have kids. James had blamed himself. He'd been the one putting off having a family. He thought they'd missed their window. *Sometimes nature shuts the door quickly,* the doctor had said.

Sue never once blamed him. Even after all the doctor visits, Sue refused to believe she couldn't get pregnant. *I'm going to have your child,* she'd said. James had thought he could never love his wife more than when she said those words, even as much as they pained him.

Two years later, on a cold rainy day in December, Sue told James the news. She was crying.

They each were thirty-seven and they were going to have a child.

There weren't words to describe what they felt. But it only got better. When Katie entered the world and James looked down on her beautiful scrunched-up face, he'd had an epiphany moment. He told himself he would never put his family's security in jeopardy.

He'd stopped putting energies into the stuff on the side. The programs he was writing after work; the new operating software he was creating; the website he was working on, which he was trying to get angel funded. He'd been trying for close to fourteen years. It was time he faced the facts.

It wasn't going to happen.

But he refused to let that get him down. He made a decision then. He redoubled his efforts at work, really applied himself. There were other avenues to success.

He had to play catch-up, of course. He wasn't a Young Turk, but the corporate world could provide a decent life for his family. A secure life with a stable paycheck.

They socked away money diligently for retirement and the girls' college funds. They incrementally paid off their debts. They made do with little. They didn't take extravagant vacations. They enjoyed the simple things.

Two years later they had another miracle when Sue gave birth to Hannah.

James was committed to the role of supporting his family. It was different than his dream, but it was perfect in a different way. While he had some regrets, he didn't regret for one day the choices he'd made. Lofty dreams were for people with no dependents. There was no way he would put his family at risk, chasing after stuff that might never materialize.

He wasn't going to be that guy who wasn't there for his family. He worked hard and his hours during the week were long, but the weekends were all family time. He spent time with his wife and kids.

He thought he'd done the right things. Made the right choices. Now here he was, forty-two years old. Playing by those rules—doing what he thought was safe—hadn't quite worked out as he planned. Someone had taken that security from him. Whisked it right from under his feet.

They'd put his family at risk. They had set him up for something he didn't do, and the way it was looking he was going to go to jail for a long time. He was going to be taken from his wife and girls.

But the people who had set him up had overlooked one small detail.

The man he was.

James Kolinsky wasn't someone's whipping boy. He may have failed in his life's ambition, but there was no way he was going to fail his family. They were the most important thing to him. Even more important than his dreams. He realized that when he tucked his girls in every Saturday and Sunday night. They and his wife were his rock, his life, and there was no way he was being taken from them.

No way.

James found a spot by some switchgear. The noise wasn't as bad here.

He took out the laptop from the duffel bag. The other laptop, the one he'd hidden in the duct, was patched into the system. He'd preconfigured its interface to handle the embedded security. His laptop's wireless connection should be able to connect to the hidden laptop, which in effect would work like an improvised router. At least in theory.

He waited as his laptop searched for the connection. It took several seconds...

He was on.

So far so good. He had access to the main matrix. He could connect remotely from anywhere within the complex. Not just the hubs.

One challenge figured out. He was mobile.

He assessed his options. The Vault had emergency exits situated throughout the facility. Each of those would trigger alarms if they were opened. He knew Security was searching the floors above him. Where though, was the question? He needed more info if he was going to stay ahead of them.

He went as fast as he could. In the back of his mind, independently of his focus, he chewed on the fact he hadn't recognized the men. The Vault had three Security teams that rotated around the clock. James thought he knew all of them. The men he'd seen in the surveillance video were new.

That introduced another variable. Whatever was going on wasn't isolated to Enrique and one or two others. There were more involved. They weren't working in a silo. Too many factors came into play. To do what they'd done would take a coordinated effort. Others—more insiders—working with the same aim.

For what purpose, though?

Another question that needed an answer.

He was starting to see what lay ahead of him. These people, whoever they were, thought they'd found the perfect stooge for their plans.

Well...

Not if he had any say about it.

44

FIRST thing on the list, he needed to know where they were. He'd disabled *Phalanx*, but there were other ways he could keep tabs in The Vault.

On his laptop, he pulled up several views. He clicked from one to the next. Each were montages of color; streaming sensor readings. The thermographic images showed gradients of temperature: white being the warmest, red and orange being warm, and blue being cold. Throughout the facility were FLIR; 'forward-looking Infrared' sensors that were connected to the environmental systems.

The equipment in this facility put off massive amounts of heat and the cooling systems had to be monitored at all times. The FLIR helped regulate those systems. It was a back office, intuitive system; the PdM components operated autonomously and never needed maintenance.

He knew Enrique hadn't been trained on it. If he had, he'd be able to use the FLIR sensors like James was using now—albeit somewhat unconventionally. The FLIR sensors, in addition to monitoring temperature, in a rudimentary way could detect movement. James was able to see where his hunters were. It wasn't pinpoint accurate, but it was better than being blind.

He spotted a group of them. He could see them moving. They were two floors above, systematically combing the floor, looking for him. There were five. No, make that six.

The others were in different spots. Two were in the Fishbowl. One was near a larger heat mass that appeared to be a vehicle, which was in the loading dock area. There was a tenth on the first level.

He flipped to other views. Screen after screen.

There were tens of thousands of servers in this facility; all of them were arranged in stacks, like library shelves. On the screen they looked like lava flows, red and orange in running rows. The Stacks were the lifeblood of this place. They stored the data.

Other equipment was putting off heat, as well. The switchgear, PDU transformers, UPS modules, APC Megawatt backups, and all the other equipment that comprised the power grid. Multiple 480 Volt AC feeds supplied the grid. This facility was a power hog on almost unfathomable levels. 80 megawatts. An entire power plant, two miles away, was needed to run this facility.

All that power and data storage meant heat. Lots of it.

James flipped through the views.

In other quadrants, masses of blue showed the cooling systems. The thermal storage tanks with their *Cryogel ice balls.* The chillers ran on solutions of water and 28 percent glycol. Those Cryogel ice balls, which were 4-inch polyethylene spheres, were frozen at night. They cooled the water/glycol solution during the day.

Huge tanks, air exchangers, mechanical equipment, ductwork... all of it... was visible on the screen. Colors of blue and orange.

James kept scanning. He found the last two men. White and red traces. Both moving. They were near the generators. Pieces of equipment the size of boxcars. Level two.

That made twelve.

Enrique was most likely one of the men in the Fishbowl. The other eleven heat signatures were Security. Security, which had gone through

DECON ignoring protocol. James had gotten a brief look at them on the cameras before he disabled Phalanx. They were a mixed crew; some of them had visible tattoos. None of them looked familiar. They were wearing the gray shirts that Security wore, but that's where resemblances stopped.

He didn't recognize one of them. Not one.

Security typically was comprised of six men. Six was the standard crew size. Six. Not eleven. And they hadn't suited up.

Eleven men recently hired? What were the chances of that?

James watched them. Blobs of white and red moving. Two floors above.

He had some time.

He focused his attentions on following the cyber trail. The blended attack, which he'd purportedly orchestrated, had come from hundreds of email accounts. Each from different computers. It had been coordinated from a central source.

The bot-infected computers had carried out instructions, unleashing their missives every three seconds with malicious code. He looked at the attached files.

GreedKills.jwtLive   GreedKills.jwtRedux   GreedKills.jwtRepeat

New variants each time.

They were being sent to host addresses of different ComTek clients. He looked at the CIDR notations.

192.168.100.1/24

192.168.100.1/25

192.168.100.1/26

They were routing prefixes; IP addresses of networks. He pulled up ComTek's database and checked against the list. The routing prefixes matched clients of ComTek's.

Some were banks. Wells Fargo. Bank of America. J.P. Morgan. Citigroup. SunTrust.

Every bank that had a service contract with ComTek was receiving the emails. They were being sent to back-office servers. ComTek frequently sent security updates. It was all automated. It protected the systems and kept them working correctly. ComTek seamlessly backed up their clients' data 365/24/7.

These emails were not normal updates.

They contained a worm.

A worm that was infiltrating each bank's security network, bypassing their triple-tiered firewalls. It was replicating with each breach. Piggy-backing behind it were a series of programs that were doing their worst.

Confidential files were being compromised. Account information was being overwritten. Numbered accounts were directed to renumber themselves every few seconds.

The result was crippling. It was crashing their networks. James realized what he'd seen with his own bank account was happening on a grand scale. Transactions, millions of them, were cross-pollinating other accounts. It was essentially taking every account out there and intermixing them.

In his case, the transactions had yielded a negative result. The inverse would be true, as well. Other accounts were probably seeing the exact opposite. Accounts growing obscenely, fed by hundreds of random transactions from other accounts. Cash infusions, deposits, wire transfers.

It was taking all the funds out there and distributing them randomly. Some winners. Some losers. A big time crap shoot. *Hello Las Vegas.*

James took a deep breath. The scale of this cybercrime was enormous. This made past viruses look puny in comparison. *Nimbda, Code Red, MyDoom, Sasser.* All of those had snarled or stopped Web traffic and caused problems. But none of them had meted this sort of destruction.

And he had done it. His digital fingerprints were all over this nightmare.

He had an astral body moment.

He looked around. The mechanical equipment was humming softly. *The eye of the storm*, he realized. This area of The Vault was partially insulated from the regular noises. He couldn't even hear the air handlers from where he was sitting.

But out there was something else. Out there, not in The Vault, but the real world. A financial chimera that he'd caused. A virus plague spreading like locusts. The breakdown of the entire banking infrastructure. A cyclonic trail of damage, vortexing out of control, hitting other systems…anything that was remotely linked to banks. Payment servers, credit cards, online banking institutions, retail centers' back-office systems…

In short, commerce itself.

The repercussions were almost too much to think about. He was getting distracted. His mind going off on unhealthy tangents.

He stretched his neck. He'd gotten stiff from looking at his screen for so long. He'd been absorbed.

Too absorbed.

He flipped to the FLIR and toggled through the views. The six men were no longer two floors above. It took him a moment to find them. He could see their heat traces, white and red, moving.

They were one floor above. Based on the direction they were going they had just started searching that floor. *Good, he was okay.* That would take them some time.

With a few clicks, he went back to his previous screen.

He needed to learn more.

45

SNOWFLAKES. It was a good analogy. All the same, until you looked at them closely.

James realized that everything was not what it seemed. He discovered that when he compared the different variants of the worm. One of them had a back-door component.

Hello.

That changed things. This wasn't just a rogue operation meant to slice and dice. There was order within the chaos. A back-door feature meant things could be controlled.

Control. The hacker's oeuvre.

Parse it down and that was what it was all about. Control, or finding a way to control. Manipulate, take over, make your server mine, your computer mine.

I own you.

James examined the code. It was definitely different than the others. Not just a carbon copy with a few tweaks. The code contained an implanted series of directives.

James isolated it. It was a matter of taking it apart, looking at its constructs. This variant of the worm was exploiting a vulnerability within the banking networks. It almost looked like something copped straight from a Zeus crimeware kit.

No, that'd be too easy, but there it was. It was so basic. Elemental.

A zero-day vulnerability. The banks were using old servers.

Are you kidding me?

He shook his head. It just didn't seem possible. Any routine Security Audit would spot these types of vulnerabilities in a second. Every server—didn't matter, which one—had vulnerabilities. They all had them. Even the most expensive, high-tech ones money could buy. Nothing was ever fully secure. There were always vulnerabilities some *cracker* could find. The key was to address them. Make those servers secure before they were put online.

These were old servers. Granted, they were back-office ones, but it didn't matter. It was a no no, and three of the seven major banks were using them.

That explained them going down. This little worm had found the holes.

And this little piggy went all the way home.

James double-checked. It seemed crazy, but there it was. He checked all of the worms. There were hundreds of variants. He focused on two more that shouted out at him. Two more with back-door components. Again using something straight from a crimeware kit.

Whomever had created these little nasties had had some help. They'd gone to the *Home Depot for hackers* to get some extra tools.

He looked at the binary code. It was definitely from a kit. At least this section was. Most likely it had come from a Zeus crimeware kit. Anyone could purchase them online. They were available to any wannabe hacker. The underground economy was flourishing with the things, selling them for profit.

There were other makers of crimeware kits. *Fragus. SpyEye.* They all served the same purpose. The kits gave instructions for how to customize malicious code. Basically taught beginners, rank amateurs, how they could steal data, confidential information. It lowered the bar. Made anyone an instant player in the cybercrime realm.

In the last few years the kits had gained in popularity. They were all over the Web. Thanks to them there were now tens of thousands of new malicious code variants out there.

And James was looking at three of them right now.

Interesting.

Maybe the sophistication of this thing *wasn't all that.* To cop a phrase from Enrique. *Was this your work, Enrique?*

It certainly looked like it.

Enrique was skilled, but he had a proclivity for plagiarism. Most of his best ideas came from others. James knew how Enrique worked. The kid took shortcuts. Didn't like to do things the hard way, if there was a faster, more expedient method.

There was a laziness to that attitude. He used to scold him for it. Because sometimes it meant he got sloppy.

RAS, eh Brutus. Reticular Activating System.

James put a lot of weight in RAS. Once his mind was made aware of something, it was like his mind expanded. Was able to see more of the big picture.

RAS was a natural phenomenon. Medically it was described as the ability of the mind to have a heightened sense of bodily and behavioral alertness. Everyone had it.

You buy a car. One that you think is slightly unique, maybe because of its model or color. The second you get on the road, though, you start seeing identical cars to yours everywhere. Seems like everyone owns a champagne-colored Jetta.

Thing was—they were always there. You just never noticed them. They weren't on your radar. To you they were invisible. Invisible until you bought one.

RAS.

It just took a little prodding. Once you tapped into it. Allowed yourself to stop focusing on the details, it was like seeing with 3-D vision. Seeing what was also there—just invisible because it was flattened temporarily so as to exist in two dimensions. Accordion those dimensions out to three, and suddenly you could see what you were looking for.

It didn't take long. There it was. James smiled.

A tertiary program, layered in the code.

He knew what the back-door component was doing. Not only that, he had the key. A vulnerability to exploit.

There was an often-repeated list of cardinal rules in the information security business. Anything can be broken into. Nothing was fully secure. No firewall exists that can't be breached. No crypto is unbreakable.

Those same themes held true for worms with back-door components. Creators were always mistaken into thinking they controlled them. Which for the most part they did. Unless someone else took that control from them.

Flipped the tables.

You own me.

Right back at you.

Control was all in the eye of who did it best.

James paused.

The smell of chum in the water had made him get carried away. He'd let time slip. Not good.

He toggled back to the FLIR.

Shit.

His forehead creased. The men weren't on the floor above him. With a few rapid clicks he brought up other views.

Shit.

Where are you guys?

158

It took him a moment. Then he found them. Six heat traces combing another floor, moving methodically. There was a seventh heat trace close to where they were. That heat trace wasn't moving.

It took him a second to realize why.

That seventh heat trace was him.

46

IT was a ghoulish inventory: duct tape, bleach, cleaning solution, Saran Wrap, plastic sheeting, contractor-strength plastic bags, two hacksaws, some technical gear of unknown purpose, several 10-gig memory sticks, an assortment of weaponry, several clips of ammunition, a knife with Saran Wrap wrapped around its handle, and lastly a folded letter.

Sue handed it to him. Bob read the first few lines again. It was a journal entry, printed on ordinary copier paper.

Forgive me Sue for what I am about to do. I know you and the girls will soon be in a better place. This is no place for us...

The passage, dated yesterday, went on to say that this would be his last entry. There was something printed on the other side. It was a recipe for spicy salmon.

"There was some paper in the tray."

It had been printed on the printer upstairs. James frequently saved paper by printing on the backs.

Sue told him she'd uncovered the journal entry on the screen, by clicking the computer out of hibernation. She'd tried to scroll back to previous entries, but a password box appeared and had closed down the file. It appeared to be encrypted.

"James didn't keep a journal," Sue said.

"As far as you know."

"I know my husband. They did this. They intended to make this look like James typed it. But this isn't him."

160

Bob frowned. He glanced out the window and surveyed the yard. His truck was in the driveway. To the left and right were woods. There was a house across the street, and a curving driveway to the left, but otherwise this house was tucked back and out of sight.

The house, Bob realized, even for being in a neighborhood, was very secluded. The gunshots should have drawn some attention, but no one had come to check on the family. No police or concerned neighbors had rolled up or walked into the yard. A bunker mentality had taken hold of the city, and it seemed to have taken hold of this neighborhood, as well.

Sue tried calling the police again with no luck. She called the fire department again.

"It's still busy."

Bob's eyes strayed to the keys and cell phones he'd taken from the men in the garage. The keys were to a Mercedes, but there was no car anywhere near the house. The men hadn't had any form of identification on them.

"We need to go," Bob said.

"I know," Sue said.

47

PETER was not happy. He had just seen ten large slip through his fingers.

"They've taken us off?"

Denis nodded.

An hour ago they had left the mark's Jap car. It had been in some sort of wreck and abandoned on the road. From there, the trail seemed to have gone cold.

Peter looked at his partner. "I don't like being teased."

Denis shrugged. "Five thousand is five thousand."

"But it's not fifteen."

"Nope."

Peter took a drag on his cigarette and flicked his butt out the window. He didn't want to let this one go. "That file have his address?"

Denis grunted an affirmative.

"Plug it into the GPS."

48

JAMES wasn't thinking this, but it was there in his head. He'd had discussions with colleagues before. There was a certain body of thought regarding hackers.

Hackers were notorious for having multi-personalities. They were the ultimate ciphers, nonentities, blank slates. Individually, they belied labels. They were who they wanted to be. Morphing at will.

As a group, however, they began to coalesce into definable terms. As one voice, they romanticized their profession. They even viewed their *profession*—if it could be called that—as a legitimate occupation. They saw themselves as having a unique role in the world. As liberators. Freedom makers. Heroes for the masses.

Hackers were leaders. Multiplied one thousand times one thousand. They were one, and they were a million.

There was a communistic cant to their credo. Knowledge for them was meant to be shared. Any knowledge that was hidden, kept from the general collective, had to be outed, by any means necessary.

The light must shine on every dark corner.

Hackers were paradoxes.

They lived by their own rules. The irony was that while they broke rules, they believed in the absolute power of rules. Knowing how things worked, the rules that governed what made $2 + 2 = 4$ or $x * y = z$ enabled them to manipulate the rules as they saw fit.

Hackers were artists.

Masters of a timeless art form. An art form that wasn't *new*. Its birth actually preceded computers. Not by decades, but by millennia. The romanticists in the hacker realm drew lines to the ancient Greeks. Pythagoras with his *Pythagorean Theorem*, pulling away the curtain on Euclidean geometry. Showing how it worked. Revealing its secrets.

Revealing the truth.

Hackers sought the same truth. As a collective, they lived by a "Hacker Ethic" that touted the appreciation of logic as an art form. Their end game was the free flow of information. Making all information available to the masses. Because with knowledge was gained a better understanding of the world.

Pythagoras, in his day, sought the same objective.

Knowledge for one. Knowledge for all.

Hackers were purists.

Poetry. Haiku. They felt a familial connection to those arts, however tenuous—rooted in how they saw *elegance* in code.

Brevity. Using the minimum number of binary bytes to paint a picture. Just like haiku, or poetry did with words.

Leaders, paradoxes, artists, purists. Hackers were all of these things.

James was a hacker.

He just didn't know it.

While his job as an information security engineer was to police and secure, he was a hacker that hadn't been liberated, yet. One thing, though, his mind had the gift that all hackers had. Because there was one other absolute truth.

Hackers were hacks. They espoused all sorts of bad analogies.

The rabbit who thinks he's a wolf always faces a grim end.

James was glued to his laptop's screen, like a moth on a flame, his wings glowing pyrotechnic. He saw the heat trace that was him, which wasn't moving. That was him.

A truth.

There were six other heat traces. All moving. All moving towards him.

Another truth.

He snapped out it.

Stupid.

James slipped his laptop in the duffel bag. He moved down the aisle, past the switchgear.

He had eyes but he wasn't using them.

Those men had cut him off. He'd seen it on his screen. Computed it instantly. Visualized the chess moves before they happened. There were lifts and stairwells throughout this place, and somehow James was obtuse enough to let them get too close.

They had him boxed in. They'd cut off his moves. He would never make it to the closest stairwell. He couldn't head towards the central core, either.

His options were limited. Head north, stupid, and go to the end. Stop at the Cryogel tanks and wait till they find you. James figured that would be in about five minutes, at best. If he put on his invisible suit and clicked his heels three times.

Shit.

He'd gotten sloppy. And he knew better.

Cardinal rules. Another often-quoted one: always prioritize your threats. Anytime he performed a security analysis on a piece of equipment—such as a new server or router—that was always forefront in his mind. What is the first thing he needed to worry about? Second? Third?

It was critical to make a list. Make it to ad infinitum, if necessary, but never lose sight of what things mattered most.

First major threat, second major threat…

Okay…

Threat number one: you have Security looking for you. They get you. Game over. You're done.

Jail time. Say goodbye to your wife and kids. Spend the rest of your life in an eight by ten cell. Get cozy with Bubba, your three-hundred-pound bunkmate who insists on being on top.

Got it?

He was so angry with himself, he wanted to hit himself. Bodily make himself suffer.

Calm down. This was not productive.

They didn't have him, yet. Until they did, he had options. Just figure them out. Option number one: hide. Option number two…

Think James. He visualized the floor plan in his head. The Cryogel tanks were the best place to go.

He gripped his duffel bag. He took a left at the end of the aisle. A quick right past some utility cabinets. Twenty feet ahead was open space. A great big cavernous room that housed the tanks.

No choice. Where he was, was no place to hide. He entered the room.

The rabbit was coming out of its hole.

Hello, big bad wolves, come and get me.

His mind was a gelatinous mold of free-flowing garbage.

The room was filled with vibrations.

WMMMMM…

A reverberating, eternal echo. James seemed to recall that Jerry had said this was the loudest space in the entire Vault. 81 decibels.

It sounded louder than that. Not that James was an expert. The one bright side: James didn't need to worry that the tools in his duffel bag would clink and give him away. He could clap his hands and stomp his feet and no one was going to hear him.

What he wanted to do was scream.

No time for that, stupid.

James moved quickly across the open floor. He felt so exposed. Those men had been close. If they reached this room, he was a sitting duck.

He didn't want to go out like this. Not when he'd gotten close. He'd just started to see the light.

The door was cracked. The back door that would reveal the truth. Reveal why he'd been set up.

The truth.

Answer what he needed to know.

49

THE open space felt interminable. James moved as fast as he could. It was only thirty yards, but it felt like forever he was out in the open.

Breathing heavily, he made it to the Cryogel tanks and went behind the nearest one. Up close, the tanks were enormous.

Made of ASME Code steel, they looked like grain silos. Fed by insulated lines, they were the key component of the Cryogel Ice Ball™ thermal storage media. The insulated lines led to a field of chillers that were all housed topside. The chillers ran during the night to save on energy costs. Energy was expensive. Running during non-peak hours more than halved the electrical bill for this facility. An electrical bill that was in the tens of millions of dollars per year.

Electricity didn't have a shelf life. You either used it, or lost it.

That's where the thermal storage kicked in. The solution in the tanks, infused with Cryogel Ice Balls, circulated and stored the energy. Energy, which was released 365/24/7 as air conditioning.

The tanks had steel ladders on their sides. James gave them one look and felt a wave of nausea come over him. He looked around. There was little cover where he was. Security would spot him the second they walked around the tanks.

He took a deep breath. *You can do this.*

He stepped to one of the ladders and took hold of the lower rung. He started to climb. Above him, the top of the tanks seemed to kiss the steel deck. He climbed with the duffel bag slung over his shoulder.

He hated heights. It was a fear he'd had ever since he was a kid. As he'd gotten older, it'd just gotten worse. Cleaning the gutters of his own house, perched on his twenty-four-foot ladder, always gave him the cold sweats. And that was only two stories. These tanks were over four stories tall.

Vertigo was a strange phenomenon. Take a six-inch-wide plank and ask a person to walk across it, and a person could do so easily. Now take that same plank, place it thirty feet in the air and ask that person to walk it again. That was another ballgame altogether.

James didn't like heights. Period.

He flew in airplanes, begrudgingly. He had to shut the port window every time. He hated seeing outside. His hands went clammy during takeoffs and landings. It never failed. He always felt ill hours after a flight. All those gastric juices still churning in his stomach.

He went up one rung at a time. He didn't look down. It was painstaking.

The steel rungs dug into his sweating palms. His ankle was hurting. He kept going. Shutting out everything. No noise. No fear.

Just rungs. Concentrate on the rungs.

He was almost there. Just a few more rungs to go. The duffel bag started to slip. *Shit.* He gripped with one hand and used his other hand to push the strap back on his shoulder.

He happened to look down. That wasn't a good idea. It broke his focus. No longer was he looking at the white enamel paint in front of him. His vanishing point accelerated, stretching like a bungee cord running away from him, making his eyesight undulate.

It was a long drop. The rungs of the ladder receded smaller and smaller. He felt queasy, dizzy, but that wasn't the worst of it.

Down at the bottom he saw something moving.

Shit.

It was a man. Security.

50

THREE and a half stories in the air, James froze, doing his best imitation of a Cryogel Ice Ball. The man below hadn't looked up, yet. If he did, James would be spotted instantly.

James snapped out of it. *Move.* He took hold of the next rung and stepped up another rung. The noise...

WMMMMM...

...cancelled out all other sounds. James continued up. The top was close.

He looked down. The man was moving to the left and still hadn't glanced up. James monkeyed up the last two rungs and drew himself up. He reached for the guardrails and stepped onto the top of the tank.

He was almost close enough to the ceiling that he could touch it. When he'd looked up from the bottom, it had appeared the tanks were flush against the steel deck. Once on top, though, he realized there was actually about eight feet of clearance. If he stood and hopped a few inches he'd be able to touch the ceiling.

Just that thought made him dizzy again. He crouched down on top of the tank and caught his breath.

Okay... he needed to look. He edged to the lip and looked down. The man had moved over to the next tank.

James watched, transfixed.

Security. Or someone posing as Security. The man stopped. Glanced around. He touched his ear and seemed to be speaking to someone.

The man suddenly looked up.

Shit. Slow to react, James pulled his head back.

Had he been seen? The man had definitely looked up. Even if he'd been looking elsewhere, his peripheral vision might have caught the movement. *Darn it.*

Why did he have to look? Because he was an idiot. Once again he was his own worst enemy. He needed to be smarter. There were other ways to look.

James opened the duffel bag and drew out the laptop. He tapped a key to take it out of sleep mode. He brought up the FLIR. The screen was already showing this space.

It didn't seem so large on the screen. It was a bird's-eye view. The tanks just small masses of blue.

He zoomed in. The tanks grew larger. He adjusted the settings, tweaking three sets of coordinates. The software was pretty amazing. It was almost like seeing things in three dimensions.

Massive amounts of blue. The tanks were heavily insulated. Their outer casings were made of double-walled steel. Sprayed-in insulation gave them a high R-value. But still, as a collective, they registered as an end sum of blue.

Blue. Cold.

James became conscious of it. The tank *was* cold. His disposable scrubs, made of paper-thin Tyvek®, gave little to no protection at all. The steel on top of the tank seemed to radiate a chill.

He placed his hand against the steel surface, and just as quickly drew it away. It was more than cold. It was freezing.

James started to feel the chill coming through the bottom of his soles. He ignored it and fiddled with the view on his screen. He saw heat signatures. There *he* was on top of the tank. And there was Security just one tank away, forty feet below. The man was in the same spot. He hadn't moved.

James toggled, looking for the others. He spotted them. Five of them. They were in other areas, spread out, combing the remains of the floor.

James looked back at the man at the base of the tank. Maybe the man hadn't seen him. If he had, he'd be moving. Heading up the ladder James just went up.

With baited breath, James watched the man. What was he doing? He was still in the same spot.

He brought up several views simultaneously. They were just vignettes. Too small to see details, but enough to see the movements of the others.

The other five were all moving. The man James had glimpsed still wasn't. It was like watching a video game. White/red dots moving in random ways. Two of those dots not moving. One of those dots was James. The other was Security, who might have seen him.

James started to get a bad feeling. The dots seemed to be moving in concert. It took him a second, and then he realized it. They were all heading to the man who wasn't moving.

Not good.

That meant the man had seen him. He'd called the others. Probably after James pulled his head back. He'd seen the man touch his ear. The man had a communicating device. One of those earplug things, Bluetooth, or something similar.

Shit.

They were definitely all heading to the man not moving. Several of them jumped views, moving to the next frame. James closed the other views— one by one. He just needed one view now. All six were near the tanks.

Near his tank.

Their heat signatures were amorphous blobs, but zoomed in close, James could see vague body outlines. Make out arms, legs. They were standing together.

The man who hadn't moved was in the middle. He suddenly raised his arm.

WMMMMM...

The noise. The coldness of his soles. James was suddenly attuned to it all.

He watched as the man put down his arm. He stayed there while the others—all five—split up. What were they doing?

He soon had his answer.

There were five Cryogel tanks. Five men. They each were going to a ladder.

51

THE mind is a resourceful creature. It can surprise you when least expected. Even as Security was walking towards the ladders, James's mind leapt ahead, flipping through his options.

One.

The duffel bag next to him held various tools. Tools that could be thrown to create a distraction. The reverberant din of the space, however, eliminated that option from being successful. Any noise it would have made landing would have been cancelled out. No clanging sound would register loud enough, and even if it was heard it would only make the men more determined to thoroughly search this area.

Two.

The top of the tank was a small contained space. Its diameter was about twelve feet. No cover at all. Once one man reached the top of his tank, he'd have a clear view across the tops of the other tanks. No hiding place there.

Three.

Above James was the ceiling. A steel girder was just within reach. He could jump and grab it; pull himself up. What then, though? He'd still fully be in view—dangling, exposed. His eyes tracked where the girder led. Even if he fought off his fear of heights and was able to monkey bar it (a physical act, he wasn't even sure he could do), that girder led nowhere. He'd have to go over two of the Cryogel tanks to get to its end. No option there…

On his laptop the FLIR was showing the men at the ladders. They were starting to climb up.

Four.

James could crawl to the lip of his tank and hang off. He would have to hang from the opposite side of the men. The coldness of the tank would freeze his hands in moments. He might be able to hold on for thirty seconds at best, before his hands just became numb. And there wasn't any side of the tank where he'd be completely hidden. Once one of the men reached the top of his tank they'd be able to see him hanging off. That wouldn't work. Good too… because that option sucked.

Five.

James's eyes rapidly flicked to his laptop. His mind was ahead of him, already synapsing another option. He started typing quickly and pulled up the back-of-house software that was tied into the IMDS systems, which monitored all emergency exits.

With a few clicks he accessed the 'controller interface'. He flipped through the modules and found the zones that regulated this floor. All emergency exits were tied into the grid. There was an override function that enabled diagnostics to be run. That feature was used to verify systems were working correctly.

James triggered two faults. That would send an instant relay back to the grid. According to the monitors one of the emergency exits on this floor had just opened. There was no noise and no flashing lights that would result in that act. But there was a small audible alarm that would register two floors away in the Fishbowl.

The Fishbowl.

Enrique was in the Fishbowl.

James pulled up the FLIR. He could only wait now. He figured he had about twenty seconds before the first man reached the top of his tank.

52

SUE read the journal entry again. The last lines were as strange and disturbing as the rest of the letter:

...this will be my last entry. Tomorrow the world will see. The son of an immigrant's son, a man given scraps and told to like it, says "No more!" Tomorrow I make you greedy bilious bastards bleed green!

JK

She knew this wasn't James. While its full meaning eluded her, she had no doubt that the journal entry was meant to be seen as a confession of sorts. Those men had intended to kill them and make it look like James was responsible.

She recalled what she'd overheard one of their captors say:

We did our side of deal. We downloaded marker. Now we clean up...

They had planted that evidence on the computer.

Now we clean up...

Not much fuzziness with what that meant.

The propane tank that those men had taken from the grill outside, which was now halfway up the steps. The plastic sheeting that the men had begun to tape on the door. The other grisly items Sue and Bob had discovered, the hacksaws, the knife...

The man had said, *I'll make sure I get their blood on the man's clothes...*

Their blood. Which probably meant hers and the girls'. It would have been on James's clothes. One more piece of evidence, making this horror show look like something else. The men hadn't had time to finish. Sue had gotten the girls away just in time.

A chill went up her spine thinking what almost happened. But why? Why would they do this to them? What possibly could be their motive? Such a heinous act... to kill a mommy and her girls?

"Are you ready?" Bob said.

Sue picked up the bags she'd packed. She'd thrown in clothes, toiletries and other essential items. She didn't know when they'd be back. A few moments ago she'd called James, but hadn't been able to reach him or even leave a message. She didn't like leaving like this, but she knew it wasn't safe here. Those men hadn't finished their job and they didn't seem to be working alone.

"C'mon girls."

They went towards the door.

"Hold on," Bob said.

"What is it?"

Outside, a black Suburban was pulling into the driveway.

Sue looked at her father, fearfully. They'd waited too long.

"The back door," Sue said. "Hurry!"

53

DIRECTING things from the Fishbowl, Enrique cursed under his breath. The passive alarm had gone off. Two floors away, the men had triangulated the area and searched, but hadn't found any trace of James.

Enrique looked at the monitor and the alarm matrix clearly indicated a door on one of the lower levels had opened just two minutes ago. "That can't be right," he said adjusting his Bluetooth headset. "He should be right there."

"You said you'd have the cameras working!" Savic said.

Above them the surveillance cameras were showing only blue screen. They couldn't use the cameras to locate James.

"I need more time," Enrique said. He couldn't figure out what the hell James had done. He'd tried everything he could think of to get Phalanx back online. It had been working when he left. James would have had only seconds to sabotage it—it had to be something simple.

Another small audible alarm sounded. Enrique's concentration was interrupted. The alarm matrix was indicating that a door on one of the upper levels had just opened.

"He's up a level from you, near the stacks, quadrant three!" As soon as he said it, he realized that couldn't be right. That was clear on the other side of the building. James couldn't have opened both those doors within two minutes apart?

Enrique put his hands to his temples. His head was throbbing from a massive headache. This was not how this was supposed to be going down.

He'd been tasked with getting James here. He'd done his job and now it was time to wrap this up and…

Enrique froze. The monitor in front of him had gone dark. *What?*

"Fuck!" he screamed.

54

THE four of them ran to the kitchen. Sue opened the door. The backyard led to woods. There was a stretch of grass that now looked endless. They'd never make it to the tree cover in time.

"We can hide under the house," Sue said.

They went down the steps and into the flower bed area. The house was slightly raised and wood lattice skirted the perimeter. A spot behind the bushes was accessible. Sue peeled back the lattice, which was not fully connected to its post. "Girls."

The girls didn't balk, but crawled through the opening.

"I'll head to the woods, draw them off," Bob said.

Sue shook her head. "No, get in, you can fit." Her voice was firm. Her dad looked at her and a grim smile creased his face. He nodded. He got on the ground and squeezed through the opening. He barely made it; the crawlspace was tight. He moved to where the girls where, crawling on his belly. Sue followed, briefly stopping to arrange the lattice back as it was.

"Mommy, I see a spider," Katie said.

"It's okay, it's not going to hurt you. We have to be quiet," Sue whispered.

There was about two feet of clearance to the bottom of the joists that supported the house. In some areas the dirt wasn't level and it got tighter. They were all on their bellies. The place had a smell like that of a dead animal that had been decomposing for a long time.

"We need to move in," Sue whispered.

"Mommy I don't like this," Hannah whimpered. "There are bugs here. It smells."

They could see through the latticework in some areas. In other areas there was stacked cinderblock and concrete piers. Sue caught a glimpse of movement near the perimeter. Bob motioned to her and pointed.

The men who'd been in the Suburban were walking around the house!

55

JAMES tucked himself behind two structural columns. His adrenaline was just coming down. That had been way too close, on so many levels.

The fact he'd made it down from the Cryogel tank in one piece was accomplishment enough. Add in all the other stuff, and he was surprised his ticker had held up. His heart had been beating so fast when those men were climbing the ladders. Any second he expected one of the men to reach the top.

When they didn't, when it became obvious they were going down, James's heart had skipped two beats, at least. James sucked in some much needed breaths. He'd made it.

Good.

Now back to work.

He was in a good spot. The men had already searched this section. They wouldn't be coming back to this area anytime soon. The closest heat signature to his was one level away, and completely on the other side of The Vault.

He was good for now. *Seemed like he'd said that before.*

He went back to the cyber trail. Jimmied open the back door. *Now let's see what you little beasties are up to…*

It didn't take long to get back on track. Like flipping a light switch in his head. Going back to where he was, laying plain the tertiary code, figuring out what it was doing.

Some people were all thumbs when it came to using their hands. James always said he was all tongue when it came to languages. Partly true.

He'd taken six years of Spanish, four in high school and two in college. He could barely speak it, even in his sixth year, when he was supposed to be at the fluency stage. All tongue. No ear for language.

Seeing was something else, though. James could read Spanish, well enough. Write it passably too. Still could, twenty years later, if he was hard pressed.

He had an *eye* for language. It was just something he was good at. Hard to explain. The best analogy might be the same mystifying condition that made an idiot savant brilliant in math.

Numbers, words, symbols…

On screen or on paper, all of those characters just sort of gelled for James. The languages he knew, however, weren't your run of the mill ones.

Pascal, BASIC, Psuedocode, HyperTalk, JavaFX Script…

He knew over thirty of them. Programming languages. Down cold.

If robots ever invaded the earth, he'd make a crack interpreter. Just set him up with a keyboard interface and let him go.

He let his fingers do the talking. He used an <s:token> UI component. First he needed to secure his JSF forms against (XSRF)—cross-site request forgery. It was a serialized view. Passed in the javax.faces. ViewState parameters set.

All gobbledygook. But it held meaning for James. He continued to type.

sha1(signature = viewld + "," + formClientld, salt = clientUid)

He was using unique identifiers…

Making sure that what he did couldn't be traced back to him. That was one of the secrets. When you messed with back doors you needed to make sure you were quiet. Didn't want your footsteps giving you away. Not when you planned to take the keys away. Lock that door up.

Make it yours.

I own you.

James paused. He knew what the tertiary code was doing.

Whoa.

James ran an algorithm to confirm it.

Yep.

Wow.

Holy fucking shit.

56

THE estate, nestled in an enclave of five and ten million dollar homes, was ringed by a high brick wall. Large wrought-iron gates opened for a black sedan and it drove up the curving drive.

"They're here," Nick Paulson said.

Rex Portino nodded. He was a fit man with dark olive skin and aquiline features. His hair, preternaturally white, gave him a distinctive flair. When his eyes narrowed, his crow's feet were like dark crevices.

"Alanna, make them comfortable."

The girl, an attractive brunette, nodded and left the room.

Portino finished up his call. "—two hours from now. Yes. We'll do it then. I'll keep you posted." He set down the phone.

Paulson looked over, smugly. "How are our New York friends?"

Portino gave him a dismissive glance. "Aren't you supposed to be taking care of something?"

Paulson shrugged. "It's done... nothing more to do."

Portino raised an eyebrow.

"Not to worry," Paulson said. "When this gets investigated, they're going to see his face front and center. The van rental is in his name. Enrique did his part, just as we wanted."

"I don't like when things get off track."

Paulson shrugged again. "Well, he didn't exactly do what we thought he'd do. Guy was a creature of habit. He was supposed to just go home."

"He seems to have done several things we didn't anticipate."

186

Paulson shook his head. "We're good."

"See to it that we are. My associates have expectations and we don't want to disappoint them."

"No, we wouldn't want to do that," Paulson said with a smirk.

Portino's eyes narrowed.

"I said we're good." Paulson flashed his pearly whites. "They're waiting. You ready?"

57

THE men who emptied from the black Suburban were armed with Uzis, slung around their necks. Two entered through the garage. The other three circled the house to secure the perimeter.

They moved as one unit and kept a close look on their watches as they made their way through the house and scoured the yard. The two that entered the house came out with the wounded Russian. They placed him in the Suburban and went back to retrieve the two dead bodies. The men were short in stature, but had no problem hoisting the vinyl body bags which weighed close to two hundred pounds each.

They stacked the two bodies in the rear of the Suburban. Their other three associates joined them. Rapid-fire Mandarin was exchanged and duffel bags were grabbed from the cargo hold.

Back inside the house, they systematically cleaned each room. Bleach and other chemicals were used liberally. Blood that had been spilled was effectively erased—DNA checks, if they were ever done by an investigating agency, would yield nothing.

Vacuums were used in the garage to quickly suck up spent cartridges, buckshot, and other telling debris that littered the floor. Incriminating items inside the house were quickly packed in bags, removed and placed in the Suburban.

A match was lit and the men quickly filed back into the Suburban. The fire was just beginning as they pulled into the street. By the time they drove away the garage was in full blaze.

The entire job had taken less than twelve minutes.

58

THIS was bigger and nastier than he thought. And he already thought it was pretty big and nasty. James swallowed. He was beginning to see more of the big picture.

Big.

Now that was a major understatement.

He didn't have a monitor big enough to capture its breadth. Even before this went down James was the paranoid type. It went hand in hand with his obsessive compulsive tendencies. Like it or not, paranoia was hardwired in his DNA. He always blamed it on his job, but that was only a half-truth.

Half true in the sense that he was paranoid long before he became an information security engineer. Granted, his job did nothing to help his situation. It was like an alcoholic running a liquor store. He saw way too much for his own good. His worldview was filled with keeping abreast of the latest phishing scams and hacking techniques out there. He'd seen firsthand some pretty sophisticated *black hat* operations.

And with each there was usually one characteristic that was a common thread: the threats were cloaked in anonymity. Spawned by unknowns. That was the baneful reality of the information security business.

Threats he saw could have originated from kids, college students or eighty-year-old grandmothers. He never knew. Hackers were nameless. Faceless. Operating not from a static point, but from dynamic ever-shifting portals that were next to impossible to pin down. The Web was a playground for those who wished to remain anonymous. Identities were too easily hidden.

What with all *the onion routers* out there. TOR, for short. TOR was a second generation low-latency anonymity network of onion routers, which enabled users to communicate anonymously on the Internet.

Bunch of bullshit, is what it was.

It worked at the TCP Stream Level. Instant messaging, Internet Relay Chats (IRC) and Web browsing could all take advantage of it. It gave one a license to do bad things. View bad things. Be a bad thing.

It hid who you were.

Like Russian nested dolls—those painted Matryoshka dolls that decreased in size and were placed one inside the other—with very little effort a person could essentially do that—pose as someone else, whom subsequently could pose as another... With onion routers that's what happened. The sequence kept going, till the person's true identity was erased and impossible to trace with any degree of certainty.

The public frequently had preconceived notions that hackers were fringe threats: disgruntled techies that operated out of their parent's basement; lone individuals usually more interested in causing mischief than real harm. James suspected that wasn't the case for a lot of what he saw. Crimeware kits aside, some of the malicious traffic out there was just too coordinated, too sophisticated to be done by amateurs. He knew there were groups out there. Well organized... highly tech-savvy... that targeted companies and governments.

That was his paranoid side taking flight. But that bird had some wings.

Pterodactyl-sized wings.

And he was seeing sightings all the time. Not that long ago, one of ComTek's competitors had had a serious security breach. Two million customers of a national bank had their data stolen. That one had really hit home, as it wasn't so dissimilar to the data tapes that ComTek lost (or had thrown away by the cleaning service).

But in the case of their competitor, the data stolen didn't languish in the trash, or find its way to some dump. It was taken, deliberately, by an outside entity. The information contained social security numbers, account information and other particulars. The security breach was never disclosed, least not until recently.

James had read about it in an IT trade journal. It barely made the news. And when it did get disseminated nationally, it was just a blip of an article on page 7 of the Wall Street Journal.

To James the news further validated all of his suspicions and paranoia he'd had over the years. It was the tip of the iceberg and lurking beneath was the monster that no one saw. Hidden from sight, but in plain view, at least to James, if no one else.

His eyes were wide open.

Paranoia, paranoia, self-destroyer...

He knew what was out there.

Page 7 of the WSJ summarized one example. In thirty minutes, thirty million dollars had been taken from ATMs in twenty-seven different countries. The theft was all the more amazing, considering that each ATM withdrawal was only three hundred dollars. To put that in context: 100,000 fake credit cards would have had to been manufactured, distributed, and then used simultaneously in twenty-seven different countries to take that amount of cash.

Some criminal outfit had coordinated that operation. It couldn't have been done by a few people. Just from a logistical standpoint, it would have taken hundreds of people—mules and soldiers—to hit the ATMs, each making dozens of withdrawals. That fact, when James read about it, had chilled him to the bone. Major multi-million dollar corporations would have difficulty pulling off that type of seamless operation. There were criminal outfits out there that were pulling off capers more sophisticated and audacious than one could imagine.

And right now that theft looked minor—like some five-year-old kid stealing chewing gum from a convenience store—in comparison to this.

On the surface, those viruses *he'd unleashed* had done some major damage. "Created complete chaos" would be another way to describe it. But underneath it was far more insidious.

Criminally insidious.

That tertiary program, buried deep in the code, was siphoning off minute amounts from banking accounts each time. Singularly the amounts were negligible, just pennies, but it was happening to millions of accounts every few seconds. At that rate, every minute roughly equated to hundreds of thousands of dollars. The runtime factor was set for twenty-four hours, of which twenty-two hours had already elapsed. By its end, if this continued to play out, over three hundred billion dollars would be siphoned.

James had just run an algorithm to confirm it.

300,000,000,000 dollars.

Just the amount of zeros was staggering. It was a mind-bending sum.

Three hundred billion dollars.

That was one big number. Enough to shock anyone, himself included. Shame on him, though, he shouldn't really be surprised. He should have known this was all about money. Taking money to be exact. That was always a concurrent theme with cybercrime—money.

Three hundred billion of it. A god-awful lot of dough. But truth was, even that gargantuan number could be humbled. Put in perspective. That amount roughly equated to less than six percent of the entire pool. Over five trillion dollars were warehoused in the banks and financial funds that utilized ComTek's data recovery systems (i.e.: The Vault).

That money was parceled into almost infinite arrays of blocks of data. Those blocks, measured in bytes, bits and factors thereof, represented the monies of individual accounts. There was no vault that contained that amount of hard currency.

Collectively, looking at the entire money supply in the US, which was sometimes referred to as 'M0' or the 'monetary base', there was less than one trillion dollars of hard currency in total circulation. The majority of monies was in electronic form, in checkable deposits, saving deposits, institutional money-market funds, short term repurchase agreements...

Everything today was electronic. When employers paid their employees, they didn't hand them cash, they issued them checks, which were deposited into their accounts.

Like modern-day markers those checks were essentially 'virtual money'. That was how the banking system worked. Everything was electronic. Monies were just bytes of data. And those blocks of data were being diced-up and filleted thousands of times, while simultaneously minute amounts were being siphoned and stashed in what appeared to be temporary holding accounts.

Temporary...

Bytes in the void.

James looked at what was on his screen. It was an inscrutable morass of numbers, letters and symbols. Streaming data he'd culled from one of the back doors.

Not quite *Western Union* here, but something else. *Fed Wire* was how many banks made wire transfers, particularly large sums of cash. The Vault backed-up all that type of data. But this wasn't that.

What was this?

It was a black hole is what it was. And all that cash was going down it. *Slurp.*

Three hundred billion dollars.

Well… it might have been too late to stop the malicious code from doing its worst, but there was one thing James could do. Follow it. See where that money was going. From what he could tell, the cyber trail had several wormholes. Not just one, but five. And that money was slipping down them into these transitory black holes. Escrow accounts without any visible bottoms.

Intersante.

James paused. He was on the cusp, he felt. Those black holes were about to close up. In about two hours the runtime for this operation was set to end. At that point this was all over. That money would be gone. *If it wasn't already.*

Time to find out. There was a trail, however faint. Just a tendril… but it might be enough.

Of course…

He flicked to the FLIR and gnashed his teeth. Right on cue. Just when he was sinking his teeth into this too.

Time to move again.

James stashed his laptop in the duffel bag. Several ideas were streaming in his head on parallel paths. He needed to do several things, and do them fast.

Prioritize. Threat number one, threat number two…

Full of purpose, he headed towards The Stacks.

59

HE took a slight detour on the way. Two hours, and then three hundred billion dollars was gone. Not if he had his druthers. Tag this on him. Make him the fall guy.

James was beginning to piece some things together. There was a term used in information security… *Chained Exploit.*

The easiest means to an end was never the direct path. You didn't go through the front door to get the goodies. You arranged a sequence of events, strung together a *chain* of *exploits.*

James was one of those links on that chain. Whoever had orchestrated this operation—Enrique and company—had compromised James. They'd exploited him. Put him in the cat seat calling the shots. Or made it appear that was the case.

When this got investigated in the next few days—*hell, next few hours*—James would be where the blame went. Simple. He'd gone postal. Messed a lot of stuff up. He was *mentally unstable*. Said so in his file.

All those worms wrecking their havoc. That was a lot of noise. A diversion. It took attention from what was really happening.

Two can play that game.

James reached the APC Megawatt backups. The Vault was a power suck. Power, electricity to be exact, is what made this place run.

80 megawatts was nothing to fool around with. You could run a small city with that type of power. One thing about data centers, they weren't green. Their carbon footprint was scary. Industrial factories spewing

black smog had nothing on large data centers. Particularly one this size.

This was the mother ship of all data centers. Sucking power like there was no tomorrow. *The way things were going, who could blame it.* Tomorrow wasn't looking so good.

Particularly not for James.

James looked around. The power grid was one monstrous beast. The APC Megawatt backups were just one component. Those battery cabinets each weighed over four tons. And there were dozens of them.

You also had the generators—they were located in another area. Each of those babies were the size of box cars. Add in the other UPS (Uninterrupted Power Supply) units, the PDU (Power Distribution Units), switchgear, distribution wiring, and all the other related components and you had one big, gigantic, mack daddy bunch of badass electrical shit.

All run by 480V power lines. Each one with enough power coursing through them to fry an elephant. Make him into one burnt crispy.

James knew what he needed to do. He found the manual. It was called "the book", and it was off limits to anyone and everyone. He had to pop the lock on the cabinet to get it out.

It was a heavy tome. Full of forty pages of cautions and warnings. The other hundred and ten pages detailed the shutdown sequence.

So much for having just a simple kill switch. Murphy's Law. Nothing was ever easy.

He got started.

60

DATA Centers have a love/hate relationship with electricity. James was more than up to speed in that arena. His job was completely intertwined with understanding power. What it could do, what you needed to avoid, and what you should never do.

He was about to open door number three. *What you should never do.*

Cut the juice. Initiate the shutdown sequence. Flip the switch.

Technically, according to *the book*, it wasn't one switch, but a whole freaking lot of them. Semantics aside, flipping the switch was a no no. There was a reason there were three sets of redundant backup systems. You never wanted to shut a data center down.

Never.

Power kept the equipment running. Kept things like *loss, corruption of data* from happening. When a data center goes down, bad stuff could happen.

Words like "bump", "brownout", "blink", "surge", "spike", "wink", all innocuous sounding terms. All not. They meant bad things when used to describe electricity.

Power disturbances were not good. *Transients, sags, swells, waveform distortions, voltage fluctuations.* More power terms. All not good.

When power was shut off, it had to be done so very carefully. If not, things like explosions could happen.

Technically, a place like this, should never cut the power.

Power. Uninterrupted continuous power. That was the deal. Keep it going.

Data centers shouldn't lose power.

Of course, it happened all the time. Usually in Tier 1, 2 and 3 facilities. Occasionally—no, make that rarely—it happened in Tier 4 facilities. But a Tier 5 facility like The Vault?

Never supposed to happen.

Never.

Ever.

Well, as they say, there was always a first time. James just hoped he knew what he was doing.

Time to make things right.

He took a deep breath. Took another one. *Oh baby...*

Why did he talk himself into doing these things?

Because according to his latest performance review he "exhibited erratic behavior" and needed "counseling".

61

THERE was a method to his madness. There really was. *Keep telling yourself that, boss.*

James was by the main switchgear. It was a long bank that could best be described as looking like a bunch of grey-painted lockers. Except instead of plain metal doors, they had blinking LEDs, voltage meters and other things on them that made an audiophile's high-fidelity sound system look like a joke. This was for serious badasses. Electrical engineers certified and trained on this type of equipment. Not for information security engineers. Not trained and not certified on this equipment. *Who was he kidding?*

Did he actually think he could do this?

He better be able to was the correct answer. He'd just turned off the first series of breakers. No going back now.

He stepped over to the next panel. The book—he had to give it credit—was laid out so that even a complete neophyte could follow it. Complete with color graphics showing what to look for, what to do. The steps were clearly enumerated.

The 'skull and crossbones' and 'lightning bolt' icons sprinkled throughout the book were a nice touch. Guess those meant death. Surge. Explosion. Don't do that.

The boldface text provided some subtle emphasis in spots. [Once initiated, steps 1-5 must be done in sequence and to completion. There should be no delay or interupption as this may cause a bump in current.]

James paused, wasn't *interruption* spelled with two r's, not two p's?

He was pretty sure.

Concentrate. He was getting distracted. Not what he should be doing. That innocent-sounding word "bump" wasn't something to gloss over. *Bump* was bad news. He knew enough to be dangerous. It could happen with improper switching of inductive loads. He needed to fully complete the sequence, otherwise he could be looking at a loss. Corruption of data.

All those small talks with Jerry had drilled one thing in his head. This was a serious place. For serious a-holes.

Kaboom!

That was Jerry's sense of humor coming to haunt him. Guy had yelled that when he'd opened one of these panels.

James buckled down and reminded himself of his end goal. This needed to be done. No fuckups. No explosions.

Five minutes later he was done with steps 1-12. Only 82 more steps to go.

He checked the FLIR. *Shit.*

He better start moving fast. There were three heat signatures in Zone 13. That was one floor below him. *Directly below him.* All they needed to do was get on the closest lift and he was in trouble.

Trouble.

He looked around at the humming equipment—coursing with crackling, death-ray voltage enough to raise Frankenstein from the dead. Strangely enough, he didn't see the humor. That's because in the back of his mind, independently of his current focus, he was thinking of one thing.

This wasn't a game.

This was deadly serious. Those men searching for him now did not have his best interests at heart. They had three hundred billion reasons to want to find him.

62

HE was so close. Five more steps to go to finish the sequence. He'd already de-energized the grid. These were the last steps. Necessary to ensure he fully closed the loop.

The backups, all three sets of UPS units, including the APC Megawatt *Silicon 500s* were already initiating shutdown. In about seven minutes this entire facility would go dark.

Nervously, he looked at the FLIR. He wasn't going to make it. Those men would be here in moments. They were ignoring the alarms James had triggered. Guess they'd gotten tired of chasing phantoms. They had his number. Knew he was dialing those in to go off remotely.

Maybe Enrique had figured out how to get *Phalanx* working again. James looked up at one of the cameras. Maybe Enrique was looking at him right now.

He held up his middle finger to the camera.

Strangely, that didn't make him feel any better. There was acid on his tongue. Tasting like the bitterness of defeat.

Nix the psychobabble, you big baby. He wasn't done, yet.

This game wasn't over. He hurried up. Closed the last series of breakers.

The sounds the equipment were making were fueling his focus. He was getting there. This baby was going down.

Like the Titanic.

OOOOmmmmm...

Step 93.

Click, click, click…

Step 94.

His eyes flicked to the FLIR. Oh man, this was going to be close.

The step-down transformers were making a series of sounds. Clicks, whirrs, whumps and stutts…

He closed the last series of relays. The green LEDs blinked off. He was done.

In more ways than one.

He grabbed his laptop and duffel bag and ignoring the fact he had a bad ankle began to run.

63

HE could hear them behind him. That was the thing with metal grate floors. They made a helluva racket.

James ran down the corridor. He kept to the concrete areas, went down one of the aisles, took a left. Twenty yards down, he took a right and beelined for the stairs. They were just up ahead. He could still hear them, but their clanging seemed to be growing fainter. It gave him hope. He made it to the stairs and began to go up. There was a series of cutbacks. Huffing and puffing, he crested the top. Looked down. No sight of 'em.

He set the duffel bag down and plopped the laptop on top. He bent over and wheezed.

Jesus. He wasn't cut out for this. He closed his eyes. Took deep breaths. There was a strange sound, almost like a hum, then some rapid clicking.

His eyelids registered the loss of lightness. He opened his eyes.

Pure, absolute blackness. *Oh boy.*

The Vault had just gone dark.

He couldn't see a thing. He held up his hand. Waved it in front of his face. There was nothing. Not even a vague outline of his hand.

All light had just winked out.

This is what it must be like in caves. Catacombs hundreds of feet below the earth's surface. No light. Not even shades of it.

Absolute, complete blackness.

Right now those guys searching for him were probably shitting in their pants. Too bad this couldn't be drawn out a little longer.

Then again...

It was really friggin' dark.

James counted in his head. Any second now. The light meters were obviously picking this up. Sending very low-voltage electrical signals to the lamps.

Bingo.

The blackness changed. It was quick and sudden. An eerie blue fluorescence became the new absolute. All thanks to bugeyes with battery packs.

The emergency lights had just taken over. No way to shut those down. There were a few other auxiliary elements that should be functioning just about now, as well.

There were three sets of backups for the grid. He'd taken all of those offline. The fourth failsafe he couldn't touch. Not without going directly to the sources.

There were battery backups for the lifts, emergency lights, some fan units and certain servers, including those that ran the NAS gateway. Otherwise, this place was dead. The air handlers, chillers, high-density servers, every single piece of equipment in this facility had systematically turned off when he initiated shutdown. That was the reason for the complicated sequence of steps.

You couldn't just shut this place down with one switch. Too much of the equipment around here was too sensitive and too valuable.

That applied doubly for The Stacks.

He got his breathing under control. Relaxed, normal breaths. He picked up the laptop and checked the FLIR.

Then he began to move.

FIVE minutes later, he was in the place he needed to be.

The Stacks.

The area resembled a library, to the extent of how the servers were lined up akin to book stacks. Rows upon rows of high-density servers, which topped out just above head height, were tightly organized. Each of those servers—"racks"—housed a dozen thin server blades.

The place smelled metallic; that distinct smell of electrical equipment, which moments ago had been humming with all sorts of voltage. He was in an access aisle in-between two rows. The place, if it were able to be seen from an overhead catwalk, would have made an impressive sight. The footprint was about the size of a very large gymnasium.

The Vault contained twenty-eight more rooms just like this. Seven levels. Four quadrants to a floor. Taken together over ten football fields could fit down here. 520,000 square feet.

Daedalus's labyrinth had nothing on this.

The ceiling was twelve foot high in The Stacks. It still felt claustrophobic. He tried to ignore that feeling. It was distracting him.

He made sure he was in the right area. He checked the number on the rack. This was it. He pulled out the rack. The chassis had a slide-out mechanism that enabled individual server blades to be taken out for servicing or replacement. He found the one he needed and disconnected the blade.

It was a black unit with a circuit board protected by an open frame. The front face of the unit vaguely resembled a stereo amplifier—similar to a receiver, but without knobs or as many buttons. Like they used to have in the 80s and 90s, before things like iPods made stereo gear obsolete.

This little baby was his insurance, if he ever got out of here. Carefully, he stashed it in his duffel bag. It fit easily. Thing was less than a foot wide; about a foot and a half deep, and a little more than an inch in height. It weighed about twelve pounds, mostly because of the weight of the microprocessors and memory components contained inside.

He pushed the server rack back in place. He checked the FLIR again. So far, so good.

He took a seat and leaned his back against a rack. Not exactly comfy, but it would do. Time to check out some of those black holes. He had money to chase.

64

FIVE black holes. Five trails. Not much to follow. But enough…

He concentrated on the first.

The thing about Matryoshka dolls was even though each doll and face were different, they were still variations of the same. Each doll fit in the other. Collectively they were like a string. A sequence.

They weren't never-ending. Eventually you got to the last doll. It might take a while, but there was a finite element to the story.

That money wasn't gone. It hadn't vanished. It had been directed to go somewhere.

James retraced the tracks. The exploited vulnerabilities, the directives of the tertiary code… there were crumbs to follow, in the form of numbers. The internet protocol addresses couldn't be hidden. Those 128-bit numbers were telling.

A long, endless string of numbers. There were so many of them. Each a Matryoshka doll. Each with a "tell". In that number was contained both the location of the source and destination nodes.

Slippery buggers…

He followed the trail of the first. Find the end. Find the money.

The perpetrators controlling this monster may have hidden their exact origins, but their trails, based on their IP addresses and ccTLDs, (otherwise known as 'country code top-level domains'), could still be sniffed out.

It took a while as he ran it down. It was all over the board it seemed, but he got closer with each tap of a key. He paused for a moment as numbers, letters and symbols scrolled on his screen. And then there it was, near the end, standing out like red neon.

Simple. Unique. Just three characters. The 'period' being one of them. The country code.

.cn

China.

Ting.

James looked up from his screen. Had that been a sound? It was indistinct, like something very small and metallic being dropped. Far away. *Ting.* Again.

The noise stopped. James listened. He waited, but it didn't come again. He pulled up the FLIR and looked at the heat traces around his area. The servers, though off, were still emitting a good deal of residual heat. On the screen the colors looked like lava flows. He looked for anything else; an amorphous form that would signify a person.

There was nothing. Just the stacks radiating red and orange.

It was just nerves. The ting sound he'd heard was probably the stacks cooling, the metal chassis that housed the server blades contracting with the change in temperature.

James switched back and followed the second trail. Again, he had to dig deep. Past all the circuitous routes, the infinity loops and the never-ending series of numbers, letters and symbols that spilled down his screen.

He reeled it in. Followed it. And then the answer. Two in fact. Both of which meant the same thing.

.uk

.gb

United Kingdom.

This trail wasn't over. There was more...

He began to follow it. Another sound. Metallic. *Ting ting.* That was someone walking.

He quickly toggled to look at the FLIR. On the screen was a form. Amorphous. A blob of white, red and orange. And it was coming towards him.

65

JAMES closed his laptop. The amorphous form on the screen was coming down the aisle to his left, several stacks away. He picked up his duffel bag that held the server blade. He moved the opposite way, down the aisle. This was going to be close. He couldn't go too fast or he'd make noise.

Where had this guy come from? It seemed like he'd only just looked at the FLIR two minutes ago and at the time there was no one else on this level. Two minutes? Or had it been longer? He'd gotten deep into what he was doing. Time might have slipped away. It had a tendency to do that when he got too focused.

James could hear the man's footfalls. He was off the steel grate now and his boots were smacking. Was he running? Had the man seen him?

James scooted around the end of the stacks. He was in the opposite aisle now. The footfalls were loud. The man was running. His footfalls got louder... louder... then... they plateaued, receded. He must not have turned and come after him. James put down the duffel bag, flipped his laptop open and looked at the FLIR. There was the amorphous form. It confirmed what his ears heard. The man was moving quickly down the opposite aisle, away from him.

That had been close. He sucked in a breath and realized his laptop was shaking. The culprit was his hands—they were trembling.

Get it together.

His eyes went back to the screen. He watched as the guy entered another section. He was moving away.

James flipped to other views, making a quick scan. The man's compatriots were located in completely different quadrants. Nowhere close.

Okay. He had to be more vigilant. He'd gotten too sucked in. That couldn't happen again. He needed to make sure he checked the FLIR every minute, like clockwork. He'd use the calendar. Trigger a reminder to pop-up.

James moved into the aisle he'd just been and sat down to work. It took a few seconds to set up the calendar reminder. It seemed ridiculous, but he couldn't trust himself. He couldn't allow himself to be swallowed. Disappear down those black holes.

Not that these were proving to be any sort of challenge. There was plenty to follow. He went down after the other three. Soon he was clicking pop-ups like they were happening every second, not every minute.

Numbers, letters and symbols streamed. One at a time he ran them down.

.ch

Switzerland.

.us

United States.

.ru

Russia.

Strange bedfellows. This operation touched the corners of the globe. And they were feasting on ill-gotten spoils like a five-headed hydra.

James backtracked and took it to another level. It was one thing to follow. It was quite another to do what he soon did on his screen. His fingers were almost a blur.

It was all finesse at this point. Very soon the orchestrators of this operation were going to find wrinkles they hadn't anticipated. These types of games went both ways.

They were about to get a backlash, like water rushing back...

James in his role at ComTek dealt with all sorts of security attacks. He routinely rebuffed probing attempts from hackers, thousands of which came from IP addresses that originated around the world. He'd learned some inventive ways to send greetings back.

He normally went with proportionate responses. Right now five separate camps were getting just a taste. He reminded himself he shouldn't be enjoying this, but it didn't really register. It must be a character flaw of his. He needed to work on that.

With a few more clicks he was finished. James put his laptop in one hand and picked up his duffel bag. It was time to get out of here. He checked the FLIR for the hundredth time. The stacks were still radiating their residual heat.

He moved quickly, checking his laptop's screen every fifteen seconds now. He entered an area that was mostly red and orange. With the grid off the air conditioning had stopped. Even with the servers off, their residual heat had built up and created hot zones. This was one of them. The FLIR was useless in this section.

Based on what he'd seen moments ago, there hadn't been anyone close to this section. He moved fast, as fast as he could with his bum ankle.

He checked the FLIR. Still just lava flows all over the screen.

He was moving blind now. The next section was worse. The heat in here was intense.

James moved past more stacks. Up ahead was one of the open stairwells. He peeked through an opening. Not seeing anyone, he took a deep breath and stepped out into the main corridor.

He moved quickly, knowing he was exposed. He reached the stairwell. Now was the toughest part. Once he took to the stairs he'd be in plain view from several vantage points. He put his foot on the first step.

"Zhópa!"

The raised voice came from his left. James froze. He slowly turned. There, a few paces away, down a row of server blades, was a man dressed in a gray Security shirt. Whatever language the man had just uttered wasn't English.

James wasn't a linguist, but that voice had sounded Russian.

66

NICK Paulson would have made for a good poker player. His ridiculously handsome face had a sardonic grin that completely masked what was going on in his Machiavellian mind.

Some of this was expected.

The virus had migrated, infecting systems they hadn't planned on infecting. Security systems of correctional facilities, airlines navigational systems... the list went on. Aside from just banking institutions, the virus was causing quite a mess out there. The more the better.

Except it was causing some unexpected complications.

Paulson hadn't had contact for forty minutes, which wasn't good. He didn't know what was going on with either team. They hadn't anticipated cell phones not working. Everyone in the country must be trying to make a call. He kept pressing speed dial, but each time a recording just came on that said "no service, we are sorry, we are experiencing rather heavy volume at the moment, please try again..."

He tried again.

"No service, we..."

Click.

Fucking worthless.

Paulson leaned back in his chair and considered his options. This baby was supposed to be on automatic pilot, but until The Vault was taken out there was still one big loose end that could unravel everything. That along with James Kolinsky.

Like it or not, he was critical to their plans. A part of him felt a little sorry for the putz... for about one second. Once he looked at that enormous pile of dough at stake, he didn't give a rat's ass what happened to Kolinsky or his pathetic family.

Call it collateral damage... *whatever.* There were always a few saps that had to take it on the chin so the rest could go home blissfully happy. That was just the breaks.

His idle hands twirled his cell phone. He tapped speed dial again.

"No service..."

Click.

He had to give himself credit. Any other person would be sweating bullets right now wondering what was going on. But that wasn't the way he operated.

Right now he just wanted to do what came naturally to a good-looking guy like himself that needed some release. Call it an anxiety break... it had been three days that he'd been going nonstop with this deal and he was due.

He eyed Portino's assistant across the room. Alanna was sitting with her legs crossed demurely. The room they were in was in the south wing of Portino's estate. It was set up as an office—if a room sixty- by thirty-foot wide could be called that. This is what wealth bought. Ridiculous extravagance. The room was decorated with expensive furnishings. The desk Paulson was using—a glass top on a single-prop chrome engine propeller—was probably as pricey as a sport's car.

Paulson could appreciate it. It wouldn't be that long till this would be his own MO. Then he too could afford a yummy assistant like Portino's.

She was one luscious treat. Bobbed hair. A body snuggled into a trim pantsuit that hugged her ample curves. The soft swell of her breasts tantalizingly visible under her low-cut blouse. *Yowza.* He just wanted to rub his face in them and bite 'em. Her legs were disproportionally long for her body. Add those six-inch heels and that tight little ass…

Come over, baby, and bend over for me.

Paulson typed in a web address. He flashed a smile at Alanna. She didn't smile back. In fact, her fat ruby lips didn't even move, but Paulson knew the type. Under that haughtiness, she wanted it—that was just her game.

He surfed some good randy porn, checking out some lovelies. He clicked to a site called *Slovak bitches*. In no time, he found a girl that from the neck down resembled Alanna. He grinned; if he closed one eye she could have passed for her twin. She was taking it from behind from a large black man with a giant cock.

"Do you want to see something?"

She pretended not to hear him.

"Alanna?"

"Yes." There was chilly indifference in her tone.

Paulson's phone beeped. He raised his finger and gave her a wink. "Hold on a sec'." He picked it up. "What's up?"

It was Enrique. *About fucking time.*

What Enrique downloaded did not make him happy. They weren't done, yet. But there was some good news. They'd found Kolinsky.

"Get it wrapped, quick. This is taking way too fucking long. Next call I want to hear that it's done." He clicked off.

"Now where were we?" He gave Alanna his most winning smile. One thing Paulson could do was ooze the charm.

"What are you looking at?"

"Want to see?"

She walked over with a slight sashay. Now it was her turn to bring out the tricks. Man, Paulson thought, could he call them or what? She did want it. *Sassy bitch.*

He did a few clicks, as she approached. She sidled up next to him and looked at his screen.

"*Oh*," she said.

She had a great sexy scent. It made Paulson wonder what she'd smell like after a good in and out.

"Do you like that one?"

"She's so cute."

Paulson clicked to another puppy picture.

Alanna sighed.

That's it. The chillier they are, the more they melted.

Paulson's phone beeped again.

What the fuck—now everybody but him could make a call? Annoyed, he glanced at it, to see who was calling. It wasn't a phone call, but an email. The subject line said 'ComTek'.

He frowned and opened it.

[What's the status?]

Confused, Paulson looked at the sender's address. It had come from himself.

"Show me another," said Alanna.

"Hold on, darling." Paulson typed on the screen and opened his email box. It showed the same thing. Based on what it said, he'd just sent an email to himself less than a minute ago?

Paulson's brow furrowed.

Alanna pouted. "No more puppy pictures?"

Paulson lightly touched her thigh. "Sure, baby."

He minimized his email box and clicked to some more pictures. "Oh, this is a good one."

Alanna practically cooed.   Paulson glanced down at his phone, wondering…?

"You smell good," he said.

She raised a teased eyebrow.

"Is that perfume or just your natural scent?   Which I must say smells wonderful."

She pursed her lips, coyly. "I know what you're doing."

"You do?" He feigned innocence.

She smirked.

He smirked, as well. "I'm just a sucker for puppies." His eyes briefly flicked to her lovely ta tas.

"I could look at you all day."

She feigned annoyance. "Aren't you supposed to be working?"

"But I am working. Rex told me to find you a puppy. You do want one, don't you?"

She laughed and his eyes flicked to her puppies again, watching them do their delicious little jiggle.

He was beginning to forget all about that email.

67

THEY waited longer than they should have ~~of~~, not knowing if the men were gone. By the time they smelled the smoke, unknown to them, the fire had spread.

Hannah and Katie were pressed against their mother. Bob was looking at the metal pipe that tracked near them, in-between the joists. It wasn't insulated like the others. It was a gas line.

"They've set the house on fire," Sue mouthed to Bob.

He nodded. He gripped the pistol, which he'd taken from inside. "They may still be out there."

"What should we do?"

"We can't wait here."

They were deep under the house. They'd moved as far to the center as they could, so as to be completely hidden from sight. Stacked cinderblock obscured the view towards the front of the house. Behind them slivers of light from the late afternoon sun were coming through the latticework. It seemed very far away.

"Girls we need to go back to where we entered."

They started crawling. Black smoke was coming through the joists. The air was perceptibly becoming warmer.

Hannah whimpered, but kept crawling. "Mommy I can't see."

"I'm right behind you, baby. You're doing good. We're almost there."

A loud crash sounded and suddenly red flames were visible.

"Mom!"

"Katie, keep going."

Sue looked back and couldn't see her father.

Smoke was everywhere. It stung their eyes and hurt something fierce. Tears streamed down Sue's cheeks. She was forced to shut her eyes. "Girls, are you okay?"

"Mom?" Katie said, "It hurts, I can't see."

"Keep going," Sue said.

There was another crash. Closer this time. It sounded like the joists were caving in. A flash of heat like an oven opening blew over them. It made Sue gasp. She coughed. The smoke was thick and oppressive and cut off her air.

"Dad? *Cough...*"

No answer. Sue coughed some more and pushed her girls forward.

"Mommy, I can't go anymore," Hannah cried.

Sue tried opening her eyes, but the smoke was stinging and made her eyelids clamp shut. She pushed what must have been Hannah in front of her.

"Mommy? *Cough, cough...*"

Sue was moving blind. Her girls had stopped crawling.

"Keep going!"

Her girls still weren't moving.

"Help! I can't open it," Katie said.

Her girls must have reached the lattice.

"Hold on," Sue said coughing uncontrollably now.

She groped and found the lattice. She coughed, pushed, but it was no good. They must not be in the same spot they'd entered.

There was no telling which direction they'd gone. They couldn't waste time searching for the opening. The fire was too close. Sue could feel the heat.

She pushed harder. The wood slats, rough and splintery to the touch, bent, but didn't break. They were nailed to the posts and along the tops and bottoms. The trim piece on the bottom was just a few inches from the ground. There wasn't enough room to crawl under.

Hannah and Katie were coughing uncontrollably. Sue wiggled around. She positioned herself and kicked the lattice with her feet. She started to feel weak, dizzy, like she was going to pass out. She kicked again. Behind her there was another crash.

Her leg went through the lattice. She'd succeeded in breaking some slats. She felt the wood scratch and dig into her leg as she tried to pull it out. She had to maneuver and use her hand. She pushed the broken slats away. The edges, where they'd been nailed to the trim, had detached.

"Girls, see if you can get through."

She pushed the lattice forward, creating an opening. It wasn't much of one, but maybe it would be enough. Katie went first and was able to squeeze through. Hannah went next. Sue helped her, coughing. She was getting dizzy. She tried opening her eyes, but the terrible stinging from the smoke clamped them shut.

Hannah was through.

Now her turn.

In a daze Sue pushed the slats forward trying to make an opening big enough. It was too tight. The girls were so much smaller than her. She wasn't going to fit. She couldn't even get her head through.

She gasped. She could feel darkness closing in, her head getting tight. Not like this, she was thinking...

"Sue!"

Her name snapped her back from the abyss. The slats in front of her were wrenched away. There was the sound of slats breaking and wood being pulled off wood trim.

"C'mon!"

A hand reached in and grabbed hold of her. Sue pushed with her feet and was pulled through. She coughed, gasped. Large hands got hold of her and pulled her the rest of the way.

There was another crash. Sue blinked her eyes through the stinging pain and saw it was her dad pulling her.

"My girls?"

"Here, don't worry."

Sue coughed and looked back towards the house. Flames were licking the roof and coming out the windows. The heat was strong.

Popping noises were going off. A window upstairs blew out.

"Oh my God," Sue said.

There was a flash and then an explosion. Sue shut her eyes and saw red.

"Girls!" she cried.

"Mommy!"

68

Zurich, Bahnhofstrasse

THOUSANDS of miles away, a much more sedate scene was playing out. The world was not yet awake in this part of the hemisphere. It was the dead of night and most people were sleeping.

The corner office had a cold efficiency to it, which suited its owner just fine. The man was the no frills type. He had his blinds closed. They were always closed. Even during daylight hours, he kept them closed. Unlike others, he didn't care for the million-dollar view, which overlooked Paradeplatz, a famous square near the end of Bahnhofstrasse.

This area was known as the financial and banking district, and the headquarters of Switzerland's two largest banks overlooked the same square. The man had chosen this location nine years ago because it was the best. A prestigious address had done much to elevate his small, privately owned bank in those years. In a relatively short period of time—unusual in an industry known to move glacially where banks took decades, in some cases centuries, to make a name for themselves—his boutique bank had earned a sterling reputation for itself where it catered to an exacting clientele that expected only the finest customer service. Having offices here was considered de rigueur; there was no choice in the matter.

Only the best in the world. His clients were fussy creatures. He occasionally likened them to annoying insects.

His bank's vaulted lobby, which was just down the corridor, met his client's expectations to a tee, and during the day coddled them in the lap of luxury as soon as they entered through the arched paneled doors. It was not unlike an elite spa in some respects. Clients could work out and even take showers in the expansive men's and women's private adjoining areas.

He thought such expenses vexatiously frivolous. But he reminded himself that his bank's clients paid through the nose to have such fringe benefits. Let them eat the chocolate bon bons and confectionary treats in the lobby, which came from Confiserie Sprüngli just down the street. He would gladly take their millions and bilk them for all they were worth.

Of course he needed profits to lure ever more clientele and feed his bank's voracious appetite. And lately those profits were getting harder to come by. But that would all be behind him soon.

Gottlob!

His liquidity problems were about to be solved and then he could rid himself of the worries and demons that kept him awake at night and made him come into the office at all hours, like now, when most reasonable people were sleeping.

He was in the middle of typing an internal memo to his employees when the email came. He usually disregarded emails, letting his two assistants handle such perfunctory duties when they came in the morning. But this one caught his attention, as it came from his personal account, which his assistants couldn't access.

The email's subject line said: ComTek.

The hairs on the back of his neck stood up on end as he looked at the screen. He stared at the email and did not open it. This was not part of the arrangement.

There was to be no communication. Not for seventy-two hours. He stared at the screen for over a minute. Something must have happened, he realized.

With trepidation he clicked on the email.

[What's the status?]

London, Canary Wharf

NIGHT owls were abounding, and not just in Zurich. While night pressed its heavy blanket outside on the Thames, not everyone was gone from the shiny offices that overlooked the dank dark river.

The name on the faceplate outside the office was a common name. The man liked common. He'd selected such a name for that specific purpose.

Common was discrete. Common was anonymous. Common didn't draw attention, but blended like a dark suit at a funeral.

Common.

John Smith.

Name notwithstanding, there was nothing common about the man lounging in the sophisticated chic environs of his wall-to-wall glass office.

At one time he was considered a financial wizard, a master of the universe without peer. Back at the market's height before the crash, no one had been better at creating and moving structured instruments, CDOs, SIVs, you name it. He made piles of money. In one year he made more than the GDP of several small nations. The next year he lost twice as much when the market turned. Of course it was only investor's money; his money was safe. He was never obtuse enough to put his own money in the investment vehicles he spun to his clients. When he walked away from it all, he was a very rich man.

His name, however, was a little worse for wear. *The London Evening Standard, Financial Times, The Sun, Daily Telegraph,* and all the other arses out there that called themselves newspapers had a field day with him. Due to some trivial technicalities, such as investing in certain funds without his clients' consent, he was blackballed from ever working in finance again. That wouldn't have bothered him, except there wasn't any other profession out there that he enjoyed as much. So he got back into it. Only now he used an alias—*John Smith*—to match his new face.

He never thought he'd have the opportunity like the one before him. But fate was a strange lady. Some men were destined to be around money.

His was such a life, he firmly believed. He made money, moved money, and spent money. Money made his orbit. Just so long as he was around money, life was good. It's what he lived for.

That and a few other things.

Across from his zebrawood desk, on a floating island-wall, six 55" plasma screens were playing on mute. Each was tuned to a different news channel that was doing around the clock coverage of what was now a global crisis. He paid no attention to the newscasts.

He'd seen enough earlier and was bored with them. In an hour or so he'd leave his shiny office. At the moment, he was flipping through a leather portfolio for Gulfstream's latest private jet. Pictures of the beautiful craft showed its impressive attributes, its twin Rolls Royce engines, its technology-filled cockpit, its sleek refined lines. The craft had a top speed of .925 Mach and a range of 7,000 nautical miles. The price was only £45 million. A pittance.

He was looking forward to replacing his tired G5. The G6 was it. The new bombastic paradigm. It flaunted and pranced while others were left flat, their bubbles dissipating like left out champagne.

Coverage of a riot in LA flashed on one of his screens. People were breaking into a Walmart while the cops just watched. A news reporter in Shanghai was speaking with people worried about their savings who were standing in a line that went around six city blocks. A Japanese woman was covering what was happening in Tokyo. Young and old alike had taken to the streets. It was a big ugly mess.

And so blah, blah, blah.

In a few hours the world would be changed. *How droll.* A week from now all this would be over. And a scant month from then he'd have his G6 and would be able to look down on the world from 51,000 feet.

He smirked. He soon would be buying everything he wanted, just like he used to, except this time, there would be no budget, or island that he couldn't buy.

He would be flush. Richer than any fat Arab sheik. Able to thumb his nose at anyone or anything that stood in his way.

As he idly dreamed, the computer on his desk received an email. Oblivious, he kept reading his personalized portfolio embossed with gold leaf. He was envisioning being in those roomy seats that would be so much more comfortable than the ones he had now, looking out on that wide expansive ocean.

Ahh... he was so close he could taste it. It had the sweet taste of money.

Beijing

LO San had just finished beating an old woman. He'd left her for his men to finish up. It had been a while since he'd gotten his hands dirty. He'd forgotten how much he used to enjoy it.

He seldom took time for such small pleasures anymore. He was getting too removed from it all and not taking time for the little things. That was the problem with being the *mountain master*. As head of the most powerful Triad on the mainland, his life had dribbled down to endless meetings and fiduciary duties, which all swirled around the running of his holding corporation. And the bigger and more legitimate it became, the less he enjoyed running it.

He longed for the days when he was a young ambitious *red pole*, who'd risen from the gutter, and was making a name for himself with each contract killing. Everything was too easy now. His human trafficking business, counterfeiting, money laundering and extortion operations, and all of his lucrative businesses: toy companies, textile factories, software manufacturing plants... his entire empire... practically ran by itself.

Sometimes, when he was blind drunk on hundred-year-old cognac, he'd have strangely lucid moments where he felt like leaving it all behind and starting over. Getting back to where he had that true hunger in his belly again.

Perhaps someday he would, he'd ruminate as he'd have another glass.

But not today.

He flicked a piece of skin off his shirt's white cuff, which was now stained crimson red. Red was lucky. It was a good omen. It was going to be a good day.

A sixty-billion-dollar day.

Fêng!

His balls were large, like a bull's. He felt the winds of power coursing through him.

His phone interrupted his thoughts.

He had an email. The subject header wasn't in Mandarin, but English. He recognized the name.

ComTek.

69

"POÉKHALI!" Savic said. He cursed while the men finished their preparations.

Enrique looked at Savic with disdain. This alliance with their Russian partners was not to his liking. These guys were thugs and had no respect for the delicate nature of this operation.

If that wasn't bad enough—there was also the eroding situation in his own camp. Enrique had just gotten off the phone with Paulson. Paulson wanted things wrapped quickly—*as if he was calling the shots*. What an ass. He still didn't understand why Portino had insisted on using him again. The man was an arrogant prick, and Enrique trusted him about as far as he could throw him.

He began to regret the communication channels they'd pre-established. He was getting that itchy feeling that things were starting to slip. They were on their second audible call. It reminded him of the *MicroLan* deal in Germany they'd botched two years ago.

They were lucky that time. They were able to walk away when things got hairy. They wouldn't have that luxury this time.

Not with this. The American authorities were going to be all over this, shortly. And instead of executing, like they should be, they were improvising. Which introduced new variables. New variables introduced new risks... Enrique didn't like it.

Not one bit.

He chewed on his lower lip, as he looked around the service dock. The place was huge and vaguely resembled an airplane hangar, except that it was underground with a ramp that led up. The emergency generators were housed here. Big, freight container looking things. They filled the cavernous space with their thunderous noise. Near them was a large tank that said 'flammable' on its side in red cautionary letters.

Two identical white vans were nearby. The one near the tank was running. Yuri should have been here by now, Enrique realized.

Savic said something in Russian. His voice was a guttural slur of words all strung together. He even spoke like a thug, Enrique mused.

Enrique heard only static on his Bluetooth headset. They were all patched into the same frequency to hear each other's transmissions, but their reception was lousy. Much of their chatter was garbled static, and their cell phones had been working sporadically ever since they got here.

None of this boded well.

A few minutes ago Yuri had transmitted a short message saying he'd found James and was coming up. He definitely should have been here by now. What was taking him so long?

This whole operation should have taken twenty minutes tops. Eighty-six minutes later and they were still here, pissing away precious time trying to bottle James. How he'd managed to hide from them for this long he had no idea. This place was big, but still there weren't that many places to hide. Not when you had a dozen men searching.

To his manager's credit, the man had been resourceful. Too resourceful. There was no telling what he'd been doing for this span of time… that was something entirely else that worried Enrique. The man had shut down the power grid. What else had he done?

"We need to hurry."

Savic glared at him. "Don't tell me—" He stopped talking, as static crackled on the headsets. "Yuri?"

There was no reply.

Savic frowned. He looked at two of his men and gestured to Enrique. "Come."

"Where are we going?" Enrique said.

"To find him." Savic glared at Enrique. "This is your fault."

"My fault?"

"If you got cameras working we wouldn't be dealing with this. Come!"

Enrique bit back his tongue. He followed Savic and the others back into The Vault.

70

AS the elevator stopped, the man ripped his headset from his ear and cursed. Even though he couldn't hear what was being said in the man's molded earpiece, James had an inkling what had the man incensed; the man was only getting static. The Vault's two foot thick concrete walls made reception spotty down here; they must be in one of the dead zones. Either that, or the man was using a bad frequency. The shielding used for the equipment down here could affect transmissions.

Enrique wouldn't know that. That was more trivia James had learned from Jerry. There was shielding down here to protect the servers from EMI (Electromagnetic Interference). It must be affecting his Bluetooth.

The man motioned with his gun for James to move forward. Duffel bag in hand, James limped off the platform.

They'd just ridden the lift up three levels. It appeared the man was leading him towards the service dock. They were taking a circuitous route, definitely not the most direct way. They had already backtracked twice.

The guy had most likely gotten lost. It was confusing down here. Even some of the guys that worked here every day joked about getting lost in The Vault anytime they were late for a shift. If you weren't familiar with the place, the place could overwhelm you.

Over half a million square feet—if you plotted your path right, you could walk for miles down here and not once redouble your tracks. The place was laid out in a grid, all modular bays. It wasn't difficult to navigate once you understood the logic of the place and how each quadrant was identical to the one above and below it. Yet for newbies, it could feel like walking in a maze. Each of the stacks looked the same. Row after row. Entering another quadrant just to see a repeat of what you'd just seen.

"Stop."

James looked back.

The guy pulled something from his pocket and glanced at the directional signage on the wall. To the uninitiated it might as well have been Greek he was looking at.

02-DD-884120-AZ <

02-DD-758916-AZ >

The first two numbers let you know which level you were on, the following two letters corresponded with the quadrant and the next batch of numbers and letters were specific to the servers and told you which servers lay which direction. Based on this guy's expression this guy didn't have a clue where he was.

"Where are you trying to take me?"

"Shut up." The man motioned with his gun for James to move forward again.

"My ankle hurts."

"I said shut up."

"What are you going to do with me?"

The man's face contorted. He had one of those faces that didn't seem quite to go with the rest of him. It was round with soft cheeks. The rest of him was a beast. Nothing soft about him. The gray Security shirt barely fit him. His entire body looked to be rock-hard muscle. Tattoos tracked up his neck. He towered over James.

The man pointed his gun. "Say another word and I shoot your ear off." His accent was thick and Slavic.

The man was Russian, James was pretty sure of that. The guy had spoken a few words in his native tongue into his headset a couple of minutes ago. From all the info James had uncovered earlier on his laptop there was no doubt in his mind he was looking at a guy that had every intention on killing him. The fact he hadn't done so, yet, didn't give James reason to hope. The guy was probably just waiting for the right time and place to dispose of him.

James adjusted the duffel bag on his shoulder and shuffled forward. The Russian followed. In another minute or so they'd be at the service dock. James knew he was running out of time.

"*Ahhh!*" James stumbled. The duffel bag fell from his shoulder. He grabbed his ankle and his face winced in pain. He sat down and cradled his ankle.

The Russian looked at him in disgust. He tucked his gun in his pants and cursed. He grabbed James by his arm. "Get up. *Tëlka.*"

James felt himself being lifted.

"Hold on. I'm getting up."

The Russian stepped back. James winced again. He looked at the Russian, who was still slightly stooped over. The position of both their bodies was just about right. They were facing each other. James began to get up.

But instead of standing upright, James dipped his head and shot forward. His arm went through the man's open legs and powered-up into the man's groin, grabbing a meaty hold on the back of the man's upper leg, right on the hamstring. At the same exact moment, his other hand grabbed the man just above the elbow. He had two holds, wrists locked. James pivoted ninety degrees while bent at the knees and slammed his shoulder into the man's stomach. Simultaneously, he pulled down hard on the elbow and torqued his body, flexing his knees double and falling sideways.

The entire thing was one seamless motion. It was called a fireman's carry. And it was all about leverage. James was falling and the man had to come with him. Only in the man's case he was heading head first towards the concrete floor. The man had no choice. The way he was going gave him no control. He flopped over like a two hundred and thirty pound fish, crashing hard onto his back.

It was an ugly sound. An experienced wrestler would have anticipated what was happening and would have tucked his head. But not this guy. He'd tried to resist the entire way over. He never fully tucked in his head.

Big mistake. The guy's noggin had hit hard and he was out stone cold.

James wiped the sweat from his brow and drew in a breath. He still had it.

Kind of hard to believe. James was in the worst shape of his life. He barely worked out anymore, and his eating habits were terrible. But that hadn't always been the case.

Back at Penn State, twenty plus years ago, he'd wrestled in the 157 pound class. Had come one victory away from winning an NCAA title his senior year. Back then get him on a mat and he was a force to deal with. Used to have a washboard for a stomach. Ran six miles a day and that didn't include the miles of wind sprints he routinely did in practice.

He wasn't that young buck anymore in any shape or form. He was probably pushing 200 plus now. Not quite this guy's weight, but close.

Granted, in James's case his girth wasn't rock-hard muscle like this guy. A lot of it was flab. But those extra l-bees did come with a benefit. It upped his weight class. Gave him a lot more leverage than he used to have. He'd taken out a gorilla. Up close the guy was scary looking, just slabs of muscle. James was stunned how easy it had been. Even with his bum ankle, he'd had no problem executing a highly technical move he hadn't tried in years. It was still automatic.

He checked the man's pulse to make sure he hadn't broken the man's neck. There was a pulse. The man was breathing, just unconscious. No doubt with a fat concussion.

James rifled through the man's pockets. There was nothing in them. He had no form of ID. He retrieved the pistol the man had been carrying. It was a few feet from him. It had fallen out of the man's pants as James had flipped him over.

The pistol didn't appear to be damaged. He was lucky it hadn't discharged when it hit the floor. James examined it. He wasn't an expert, but he'd handled a gun before. He'd learned to shoot when he was thirteen. His dad had taught him; the first time out in an abandoned field. His dad hadn't owned one of these. This one looked like a semi-automatic.

There was some writing on it.

Austria. 9x9. <u>LOCK</u>.

A circle was around <u>LOCK</u>. He realized that circle actually formed a "G".

Shit. This was a Glock. That was a firearm that James had heard about. They came with a lot more rounds than the .38 revolver he used to shoot with. Something like fifteen, he seemed to recall.

James checked for the safety. There was a trigger safety and it seemed to be off. He switched it on, testing the trigger slightly to make sure he got it right. There was resistance. The safety was on. With some reluctance, he pocketed the piece. As much as he wanted to, he couldn't take the high road here. He was past that. He knew the stakes. These men were armed.

James left the man on the floor and picked up the duffel bag. The emergency lights were casting their blue haze. He went down some stairs and found a niche behind some equipment. He needed to see where the others were.

He opened the duffel bag and pulled out his laptop. With dismay he saw that it had been damaged when he'd dropped it. The server blade was badly damaged too. There was a big scratch and a wedge-shaped dent on its electronic circuit board. Pieces were broken off.

Shit.

This was supposed to be his insurance. He had pulled data off the main servers and stored it on this blade. That data would help clear his name, if he ever got out of here. He looked at the blade and examined the full extent of the damage. There were more than just a few pieces broken. It was destroyed.

James opened the laptop. Worthless too. Its screen was cracked. So much for using the FLIR. He wasn't going to be able to see where the others were. He was in their shoes, completely blind.

Not good.

He chewed on his lower lip. He couldn't get out of here. Not yet.

What he needed was another laptop. He needed to be plugged in. And not just because of the guys roaming The Vault looking for him. He needed to see if his first salvo—*what's the status?*—had hit any targets.

He left the niche and headed to a lower level.

71

Moscow, Russia

MIHAJLOVIC roused from his rumbling slumber. His heavy-lidded eyes took in the blonde hair splayed on the pillows next to him. He glanced, disinterestedly, at the naked back, the silken sheets hanging off his latest *Krasivaya*. He raised his portly fat frame, his powerful arms propping himself up like a sitting bear.

"Time is it?" he grunted.

"Three thirty." The man standing by his bedside was thin with effeminate features. He gave no look towards the beautiful naked girl.

"Better be good. Spit it out."

"You need to see."

72

JAMES found another laptop in the same room he'd gotten the first two. He didn't stay there, but plugged in long enough to do what he needed to do. FLIR gave him the edge. This time those men weren't getting close to him.

He steered far from the hot zones, where FLIR was useless. That kept him well clear of The Stacks. It was too risky in those areas. There were other areas to hide. Other areas where he could be dangerous.

Dangerous. That was a strange term to use. He didn't dwell on it for long. There was work to be done.

In one of the mechanical rooms he found a spot to sit down. It was tucked behind some ductwork. There wasn't the normal *WHOOSH* sound to contend with. The air handlers were off. He could hear his thoughts.

Focus. Get down to business.

His initial forays, reverse-stream phishing, had some hits. His first salvo, simple emails on the surface with the subject header: ComTek, had done better than he could hope. Contained within the bodies of those emails—*what's the status?*—was an imbedded malware program.

Nothing needed to be opened; the email didn't even need to be viewed. It just needed to find their inboxes and slip past their spam filters. Seemingly harmless…

James had spent a good chunk of his life learning about viruses. He knew the most successful ones were the ones that never made the news. They always intrigued him the most. A virus in some ways was a beautiful thing. Perfectly constructed, it was not unlike a snowflake.

Snowflakes.

For some reason he always saw the correlation. Beautiful. But perhaps another analogy would have been more appropriate, such as the white and pink blooms of Wisteria. Equally beautiful. Each bloom a variation—like a snowflake—different than the next. But those sweatpea-like flowers were no gentle lady. Their vines could choke and kill. Wrap around trees. Their green leaves waving in the breeze, taking over. Sucking the light and life, squeezing trees' limbs.

Pine trees were no match for Wisteria. The vines of Wisteria crushed the soft wood. Made the cambium layer unable to bring up water. Squeezed those trees to death.

Beautiful, but oh so deadly.

Viruses were no different. There was elegance in their construction. Beauty in the brevity of their code. Some were just a few bytes. Too small to produce any harm.

Or so it seemed.

There were reasons virus definitions had to be constantly updated. Viruses propagated themselves, they multiplied endlessly. It took nothing to create one. Particularly the simplistic ones. A two-second tweak of the source code, and what was once a prehistoric—at least in Internet years—*Sasser Worm* or *Mydoom virus* became something else, a new variant that could slip past updated antivirus measures.

The best viruses in James's opinion were the ones that didn't draw attention to themselves. The ones that did nothing on the surface, but allowed computer systems to work as seamlessly as before. The ones that simply infiltrated and observed.

Shoots of Wisteria, spreading its feelers…

It was all about finding that initial crack in the door. No matter how slim or slight, once that was found, from that point on it was just a matter of time before vulnerabilities could be exploited.

James followed up his first salvo with a second and a third. He was shooting in the dark at first, but with each salvo he was able to shed some light on who he was dealing with. He infiltrated and observed, doing it all with speedy surgical precision.

The puppet masters behind this couldn't cleanse everything about themselves. They needed a link; a means to orchestrate what they were trying to do. He followed that tendril, that common byte connecting them. He peeled back those Matryoshka dolls and used their own aliases—those masked TCP/IP addresses—against themselves.

The money wasn't hidden. Far from it. It was right out in the open.

James had found it. Now it was just a matter of letting the Wisteria take over. Embrace it. Let the arms of the vine show its unrequited love.

73

AGAIN, he was on the move. This time he was determined to find a spot he could stay a while. He should have thought of this spot the first time.

It was near The Stacks on Level 3. Far enough away that the migrating heat hadn't taken over. It was a large room. Like a proscenium with a stage and seats that fanned out.

This room was no longer used. Its walls were unusual. They were designed to attenuate sound. Keep sound in, and keep sound out. They were of double-walled construction, and there were access panels. Some of the cavities in the walls were large enough for a person to fit.

It was claustrophobic, but James was getting a handle on facing his fears. So far he was managing that rather well. It all had to do with his frame of mind. James should have learned this trick a long time ago.

He also just realized something. He had other tools at his disposal. Not just the regular suspects. The Web was the whole wide world. Reach out and touch somebody.

He pulled up Skype. There was a free download available. Skype was a software application that enabled persons to make voice calls over the Internet.

He had a call to make.

74

THE flames rose. It was a spectacle. Neighbors, who'd not shown their faces when the gunshots had gone off, now came out of their homes, stood in the street, and watched.

Sue, her face streaked with dirt and soot, had a drawn haunted look on her face. Pieces of the house caved in as the fire consumed and greedily ate everything that meant something to her family. Years of memories.

Inside that house were photographs, homemade Christmas ornaments, the girls' baptismal dresses, their first baby shoes, the artwork they'd done over the years, the antique hope chest that she and James had bought at a flea market when they first got the house. In that chest Sue had tucked special items, such as James's poetry he'd written her in college, their passports they'd used only once, their marriage certificate, the handmade quilts that had been Sue's great grandmother's who'd lived in Poland...

Their home.

The joys of becoming parents had occurred within its walls—walls, which were now burning cinders and glowing embers.

Sue hugged her girls. Their faces were puffy from crying. It was about being alive, Sue knew. What had happened was like a bad dream. Men had tried to kill them. She was still in a daze, as if the heat coming off the house was giving her sunstroke.

They were alive.

That was the important thing, the only thing that mattered. *Material things could be replaced.* That was a phrase she'd heard and it rang true.

Still… she could see the pictures and memories swirling in the flames, dancing away forever.

Bob touched her arm. "We should go."

Soot blackened his face. He was standing rigid. There was a strength that radiated from him, which gave her comfort.

Comfort. That's not a feeling she'd ever associated with her dad before. He had saved her twice. Saved her girls.

He'd also had the foresight to save his truck. It had been parked far enough from the house and hadn't been damaged from the initial explosions. That truck was now running, waiting to take them from here. Far from this…

"Oh my God."

"I've tried calling, but I can't get the Fire Department."

The neighbors were chattering in the background. Sue barely heard them. Some of them had come up and expressed concern, while others were just frantic, worried about their own houses catching fire too. A few minutes ago she'd overhead someone exclaim that Sue should be doing something. As if the fire was her fault and she was supposed to put it out.

"…don't care, just do something!"

Voices swirling, dancing with the flames. Sue took one last look at her home. The once pretty yard that the girls loved to play in. The grass that James agonized over every weekend, pulling weeds, adding fertilizer every spring and fall, and kept looking so green for his girls.

It was gone. Pitted with small fires that were now smoldering. Pieces of burning house and their minivan, which had exploded, littered the yard.

But they were alive. That's what mattered.

Sue turned her back on the depressing scene and helped Hannah and Katie into the truck. Bob helped buckle them in. There were no toddler or booster seats for the girls, and they did their best to latch them tightly.

"Ready?"

Sue nodded. She felt so drained. So spent.

They drove away. Past more neighbors who were coming to see the spectacle. Some glanced at them with curious or alarmed expressions, while others strode forward, their eyes fixed on the flames ahead.

Some houses down they passed a black sedan that was parked along the curb. Two men were sitting in the car. One of them looked right at her. Sue shrugged off a sudden chill.

"You okay?" Bob said.

A vibration trembled her leg. It took her a moment to realize what it was. She shifted in her seat and pulled out her cell phone.

Her brow knit.

"Someone calling?"

"Yes."

"Don't answer."

But she had already clicked to accept the call.

She tried to keep the emotion from her voice, but it was no use, it came out in just one word.

"James!"

75

"GET it?"

"Yeah." Denis finished jotting down the number.

"Antique plates."

"Yep."

Peter took a drag from his cigarette.

"That file say anything 'bout the family?"

"Not much. Wife, forty-two, girls three and five."

"That it?"

"Yep."

Peter flicked his cigarette out the window. He looked at the burning house and pulled their sedan into the street.

76

JAMES felt like he'd been working for hours, but looking at the computer's clock he realized it must still be daylight outside. The emotions inside him—like steam in a boiler—were so intense he was afraid if he didn't keep channeling them, they'd take over and he'd explode.

They had tried to kill his wife and girls.

They'd burned his house down.

This wasn't just about him. They'd gone after his family.

His wife and girls.

By downloading Skype on his laptop, he'd managed to get a call through. At first it hadn't worked and he'd had to download it a second time. When he finally got it set up and got hold of Sue, she'd relayed what had happened in a voice that trembled with emotion.

Men had broken into the house. They spoke Russian. They'd meant to kill them. Sue gave details. How they were tied up and their girls almost suffocated. How Sue had managed to cut through her constraints and take the girls to the garage. How her father had saved them.

She'd called him "Dad". His wife had no relationship with her father, and now she was with him, calling him *Dad*?

Their phone connection was terrible. The static on the line made it hard to hear everything, but James heard enough. He asked to speak to Hannah and Katie and he told them he loved them. He could hear them cry, "Daddy!"

His heart had cracked. He wanted to be with them. To hug them and keep them safe.

These monsters had tried to kill his girls.

He had to channel that anger… that terrible caustic energy. If he didn't, he knew it would consume him instantly. *These monsters.*

He had to focus.

To detach himself.

It took effort this time. It was like shutting out a thousand voices yelling at him at once. Somehow, he was able to do it. His mind was wired differently than some people. It was almost like he had an on/off switch inside his head. It was probably what allowed him to do his job so well. He could flip that switch and laser focus for hours. Others, if they were put in this situation, might get overwhelmed, or just completely shut down.

Sue sometimes said he was so distant. It used to worry her, particularly when they didn't have kids and he devoted so much time trying to make his startup work. The weeks, months, years on end he'd work straight, with hardly any rest.

He was an odd bird, he realized. His family was what grounded him. Kept him normal. Kept him sane. If he didn't have them, there was no doubt he'd still be holed up somewhere trying to make another startup work. Trying to do the improbable or impossible again. Make an altruistic concept monetize. *Green.com SecondChance.com*

Pipe dreams. So much energy expended. So much time working on failures. Fourteen years of his life.

Fourteen years hitting the wall. He'd failed so many times that eventually he began to lose faith in himself. Eventually it was hard not to think he was a loser. He'd had a losing streak for so long it instilled an almost defeatist attitude beneath his optimism. As paradoxical as that was, it described the tug-a-war inside him where the losing side had won.

He'd created these concepts, packaged these ideas. The software he designed. The algorithmic innovations he'd painstakingly done to make things work better. Faster.

He'd poured his heart and soul into it all the way down to the web design. How the user interface was intuitive. How it gave a service that people might want. Might enjoy using. Might be the next big thing.

But when he was out there trying to make a go of it, he never had any takers. Could never get in front of the right people that could see his vision. Could take it to the next level with just a little funding.

All the VCs he'd managed, finagled a way to get in front of—even if just for two minutes—had turned him down.

Not for us.

No thanks.

Try the boys on the hill.

Good luck with this.

Every no, every rejection, eroded his confidence. It changed him. He'd begun with unlimited, unfettered enthusiasm. When he was in school, he had these grand ambitions of how he was going to make a mark. Do something big with his life. Really make a fantastic life that he could share with Sue, where they could travel, afford the nice and finer things in life. Would not have to worry about money. Would not fret about paying the bills, or wonder how they'd fund retirement.

In his mind, he was fighting for freedom. Fighting to not have to work where he answered to someone else. Where he could be his own boss. Could make his own rules.

It didn't take long—it's amazing how quickly years can fly—until he was like some poker player so in hock he couldn't even afford the air around him to breathe. He was beaten. He'd put it all out there and come up empty. That internal drive, that positive attitude, which carried him even on the bad days, was gone.

He felt lucky to get a second chance; to get a job. He'd still spent some time working on stuff on the side, but in truth, he was done.

That man—the one he'd become—that worked for ComTek—made for easy prey. He was beaten by failure. Put in his box. Accepting of whatever they gave him. He was afraid... afraid of losing his job.

That beaten man made for a prime target. These people—whoever they were—had picked carefully. They'd taken his money, his job, his home, and were about to take what little freedom he had.

Still they wanted more.

They'd gone after his girls.

It was like coming out of a bad dream. James straightened and lost the slouch. He knew what he had to do. He wasn't just going to take this. He was going to use the skills he had. *Shoo away the lotus-eaters...* He wasn't going to quit.

He tackled this thing from a purely objective standpoint, as if it was any other professional exercise he might undertake, except in this case he decided to throw out the rules. Rules are what put him in his box.

Small good those rules had done him. He'd always been playing by someone else's rules; going upstream. Expending so much energy trying to carve out a better life for his family, working a job he didn't like, hoping beyond hope for that promotion that never came, answering to a company that saw him as just a worker.

These people that targeted him thought even less of him. They thought they'd picked on a weak, easy target. A man that wouldn't fight back. Wouldn't even know what happened to him, until it was too late.

They thought they had the perfect fall guy. Had planned the perfect heist.

What was one man's life? What did his family matter? Just erase them and be done. Cold and efficient. That's probably the lens with which they saw the world.

Okay.

That's the way they wanted to play it.

The rules had just changed. From now on, there were no rules. He wasn't that old James anymore. This was the new and improved version. James 2.0. They hadn't seen nothing, yet.

He took a deep, calming, channeling breath and went to work.

He had a large toolbox to pull from. *Trojans, backdoors, sniffers, rootkits, exploits, buffer overflows, SQL injections...* Those were just a sampling.

Till now, he'd kept the kid gloves on with everything he'd been doing. That stuff was mild with what he was about to unleash.

Proportionate response. Too gentle for them. Time to ratchet things up. The gloves were coming off. No prisoners. No hiding place.

What is yours is mine.

He'd only been *footprinting*. Gathering information. He was done with that. Now was the time to turn those aliases—those masked TCP/IP addresses—against themselves. Let the cannibals eat their own.

The IP address in Moscow received an email from its counterpart in Beijing. The IP address in Switzerland, likewise received an inquiry from its partner in London. By the fifth and sixth salvos, which James kept unseen, he had accessed their networks. His imbedded program provided the key, the back door entries he needed.

In no time he commandeered their websites, which were indirectly linked to those IP addresses. A Moscow-based company that specialized in wheat commodities and futures trading. An investment holding company in Beijing. A third, which was a private equity bank located in

Zurich. A fourth entity, which was owned by a financier in London. As for the fifth one, that led him to ComTek—ending with an anonymous IP address that originated from one of ComTek's routers.

Anonymous soon to be eponymous.

Somewhere, halfway around the world, a person was looking at Mickey Mouse on their home page. Another in Beijing was seeing a text message scroll across their screen, behind which, as a background, a soviet-era communist flag with the hammer and sickle was waving in an imaginary breeze.

These monsters weren't anonymous anymore. One by one he'd found them. Found where they lived.

They'd turned his world upside down and now he was returning the favor.

He clicked a third stage of instructions and outside his hidden niche the lights fired up. The Vault was back online and didn't need the emergency generators anymore. The equipment in the entire facility began to hum.

Chained exploits.

He was adding to his chain. The shutdown he'd initiated was only temporary. All part of his grand plan.

Set things right.

He took a deep breath. A few more clicks and he was done. Least for now. Once they reacted, tried to bite back, he'd drive his spear right into their hearts.

James crawled out of his hiding spot from within the wall cavity behind the raised dais and looked around.

A proscenium, like a small theatre or stage.

No one to witness his dramatic production. *Aeschylus* would have been proud. No one, just empty chairs, fanned out.

This room didn't see much use anymore. It never really had. It was one of those anachronisms. Out of place even here, in The Vault. A place that seemed to project and embody the future. A grim future, below ground. What things might look like if everything topside just went to hell.

This room, even more than The Vault, was ahead of its time. Playfully nicknamed the 'Jedi Mind Room', it was a three-dimensional holographic video conferencing room. This room could link up with Central IQ, any of ComTek's regional offices, or any businesses out there that employed the same technology. There weren't many. Not many businesses could afford this setup.

The system was cutting edge, literally Star Wars like, and cost a small fortune to install all the components that comprised the room. It allowed someone to project a high definition holographic image of themselves, which could be viewed in an almost identical chamber that could be located anywhere, be it halfway around the world or two blocks away— just so long as a company set up the technology. The image was lifelike, you could actually see perspiration on the forehead, it was so crisp.

ComTek had developed the technology a few years ago and had done an aggressive sales campaign to sell it to Fortune 500 companies. But it had proved to be a tough sell. Too tough in the end. The whole project had gotten shelved.

Not many companies wanted to pony up two million dollars just to have a better video conferencing system. It was ahead of its time, perhaps doomed, like so many innovative concepts out there. One of those ideas that almost made it.

A living, breathing anachronism.

James could relate, if he'd taken the time to reflect on it. Not that those thoughts were on his mind right now. He looked around the room. The place had served its utilitarian purpose. It had hidden him long enough to do what he had to do.

Somewhere, out there, he'd just made several people very unhappy.

77

BLOOD was coming from the man's nose. He looked fearfully at Semion Mihajlovic with the one eye he could still open. He didn't have the answer his boss wanted. "I don't know where it's gone." His hoarse voice was but a whisper. He bowed his head and waited for a shot he felt certain would come.

Mihajlovic spat on the floor and cursed. His eyes, beneath hulking brows, looked one by one at the other men in the room. Each of the men withered under his gaze. Mihajlovic, like a great bear, walked around the room. The banks of computers were a cold backdrop.

Mihajlovic gestured dismissively with his gun. "Out!"

The men scrambled out like cockroaches, as if someone had just turned on a light.

Mihajlovic stood there. His enormous chest heaved. His eyes, getting blurry now, looked at the computer screens.

Numbers.

His shares in *AngelGuard*, of which he was the primary stakeholder, were now gone. Shares that on paper had grown to a billion American overnight.

The other screens, which tracked his other investments, told an even more inconceivable story. His personal wealth, which had stood in the billions of euros just yesterday, was now liquidated. Transfers and trades he never authorized were shown on the screens.

How?!

No answer. His men had no explanations. They had cowered like worthless curs.

Today should have been a day of great victory. A day of wealth heaped upon wealth. Sixty billion dollars was to be his!

But instead, he was looking at this…

This?!

Mihajlovic's face contorted into an inscrutable snarl. He bent his head back and screamed.

78

LO San was not amused. He looked out on the city of Beijing. His palatial office had a seventieth floor view. A thick haze of pollution, draped like a mourning veil, hid the sun.

Skyscrapers, gleaming dully, broke the horizon. Cranes, moving ponderously, were in the distance. Lo San looked beyond, past where his sight could see. He was deep in thought, still digesting what his CIO had not wanted to tell him.

One hundred programmers, culled from top engineering universities, were busy at work just ten floors below. They were doing their best to combat the DDoS (distributed denial-of-service) attack that had paralyzed the network. Lo San's CIO had given the details. He called it a *ping of death.*

It was a tactic that hackers sometimes used to bring down networks. A ping was normally 84 bytes in size. Computer systems could not handle ping packets larger than a certain IP packet size, which was north of 65,000. Sending a ping packet that exceeded that number could crash a system.

Apparently this attack had slipped through the firewalls because it was fragmented to appear smaller than its actual ping packet size. A buffer overflow had occurred, which resulted in a temporary network system collapse.

As soon as they got the network back up and running, a second ping of death had taken it down again. Then a third, then a fourth... They were facing a ping flooding situation, where pings were causing normal traffic to not reach the system. It was a coordinated DDoS attack.

His CIO had said it was preventing his men from following through on their operation. It had caused an untenable situation. They couldn't initiate any wire transfers. They were shut down. Unable to function. Unable to carry out the necessary steps required for the operation to succeed.

"I have failed you," said his CIO.

Lo San glanced at his desk. His screen saver showed a Russian flag waving in the breeze. Across his screen scrolled a continuous text message.

Nyet. I've taken everything... Ha...ha...ha...

Lo San's face was as rigid as steel. The only perceivable chink in his armor was the slight twitch happening right below his eye.

Nyet. I've taken everything... Ha...ha...ha...

79

IT was a Bangkok cluster fuck. Paulson's head was wound like a noodle. Portino's comment irritated him to no end.

"Where were you?"

He was gone for ten minutes, tops, and that's the grief he got.

Across the room Portino was issuing orders to his head of security. Outside the estate's gates an explosion had gone off. Vandals were looting the neighborhood.

Vandals?! *Jesus fuckin' Christ what else could go fuckin' wrong?*

"Why are you still here?" Portino demanded from across the room.

"I'm almost done," Paulson said. He resisted the urge to tell him to fuck off.

He couldn't believe what he was looking at—the system had gone haywire. Every time he tried to log on, he was getting a different error message. He needed time, time he didn't have, to sort this out. There was still no word from Enrique. Portino was griping that his partners were trying to contact him.

His partners.

The man still was keeping everything close to his chest. He wasn't letting him in. Guys like Enrique and himself had done all the heavy lifting, and this was the thanks they got.

"Where were you?"

He'd wanted to snap back at the sonofabitch, *I was fucking your assistant in the ass,* but damn that bitch, he never got the pleasure. Asking for seven thousand. For what? For him to dribble down her leg?

Don't flatter yourself bitch. Once this was done he'd buy twenty Alannas. There was nothing worse that he hated than a tease. Getting him rock hard, then pulling that shit on him. He should have thrown her against the wall and raped her on the spot. Wouldn't be the first time. Fucking had blue balls now.

Paulson grabbed his keys.

"Take my men," Portino said.

The SOB was still giving orders. *But what was he doing to fix things?* Paulson walked out the door. Portino's head of security followed behind.

"Boss wants me with you."

"No, we're taking two cars."

"That's fine. But I'm coming with you."

That SOB didn't trust him. Sending his muscle to keep him in line. Paulson bit back the bilious taste in his throat. *If this ship even gives the hint of going down...*

Paulson tossed his keys. "If you're coming—you drive."

He took a seat in the back and looked at his iPhone. He skimmed the emails again. Who the fuck was sending these?

80

THE office was closed and dark. The shades were drawn and the furniture was sparse.

"Can we validate it?"

"No."

"Where did it come from?"

"We're working on that—I don't have an answer, yet."

"Go check it out."

"It may be another rabbit hole."

"Understood. I want you on it."

"Got it. I'll take Martinez and Chambers."

"I want a status update when you get there."

The man nodded. He went out the door.

81

RANDOM thoughts. Memories. Some recent.

James recalled his first and only camping out experience with his girls. Hannah and his wife Sue had taken to it like ducks on water, while Katie and he had been miserable. They'd spent half the time worrying about the dark and fretting about the noises. Out in the country at night there weren't the city lights to illume the sky. The darkness became complete and almost swallowed you.

It wasn't James's finest hour. He wasn't the stalwart dad, the white knight, protecting his girls. He was as scared as Katie, who was four at the time. Sue, more than a year later, still hazed him about what, no doubt, would be their one and only camping trip.

It was an odd thought to pop in his head. Random. Or maybe not.

One thing that tied the thought to his situation right now was that James was used to being uncomfortable in new settings. Change tended to frazzle him. Anything new or different could put him on edge. He was good at hiding it, and feigning composure, but the reality inside was a different story.

He'd been known to have the periodic panic attack when work just became insane. It'd usually hit him at night, right before he was trying to sleep. He'd be processing all the work he had to do and challenges he faced the next morning. The running monologue in his head could keep him up for hours.

James was all about routine. When things got a little out of whack, or were different, he didn't function well. It shook him up. Put him off balance.

Right now, considering what was going on and all he'd been through, James should be a basket case. But he wasn't. He had no explanation for it. Men were searching for him right now, with intentions to kill him, and James was okay with that. He hadn't shut down. He wasn't a victim of self-imposed paralysis. He was thinking, moving on his feet.

In fact this entire day, James had operated that way. Since this morning at ComTek when he covered his tracks by breaking into the system and altering the memory matrix. To how he stepped up to rescue that poor girl Taneesha from getting raped. To pulling that woman out of that burning car.

Every bizarre string of events that had happened to him today should have completely thrown him off his game. He should be a mess. Ready to be locked up in the funny farm in one of those padded rooms.

But he wasn't. He'd been so pushed out of his comfort zone it was as if his body had reset, somehow compensated, found a new equilibrium. Instead of being off-balance, he was measured and dare he say it...

Calm.

That was not a word he would have ever used to describe himself, even in a peaceful setting. He was Type A, high anxiety, a chew his nails sort of guy. He used to get the worst butterflies before he used to wrestle. Even with all his wins, every time before a match he'd throw up because of nerves.

None of that was happening right now. His mind was strangely lucid. Seeing things from different vantage points. Omniscient like.

At this exact moment, seven men were triangulating on him. They had him boxed in. James had already backtracked. It was as if they knew he was in this area. They were closing in on him. There wasn't anywhere for him to go. They would find him in the next few minutes. Find him and kill him. He had one gun; they had seven, and they were killers. He wasn't. But for some reason James wasn't afraid. He was ready.

Calm.

It belied explanation.

82

THE news on the TV was merciless. The newscaster was going on about the disruption in phone service. How server networks around the US were affected by the virus, which they'd dubbed the '*GreedKills*' worm.

Tell me something I don't know. Enrique was past the point of screaming. His throat hurt from earlier outbursts.

He'd been trying for over an hour to get in touch with Paulson and Portino, but none of their communication channels were working. His Bluetooth Signal Scrambler and cell phone were worthless. Emails weren't an option. He was shut out from the system.

When they began this operation, Enrique had been given clear directives, and one of those was that James was to be removed from The Vault. That was critical. He was not to be left or disposed of at The Vault. The set up with family… the places and times… all the necessary coordination pieces that had to fall in place to convincingly sell what they were trying to do was dependent on making sure James was served up at the right place, at the right time.

That little directive, thoroughly imbedded into his head, was now holding everything up. Things had gone south since then. Way south. The milk had soured and the rank smell was getting worse.

A little over an hour ago, they'd found Yuri. The man had been knocked out. He'd finally come around. James had pulled some time type of move and taken him down. It didn't make any sense. James was a middle-aged engineer with a dough belly. He sat at a desk for a living. How in the world had he taken Yuri out? Yuri was enormous and built like a tank.

Enrique looked out on the humming servers. They'd been activated and were doing their thing. *What was James doing?* Enrique had tried to get back on the system, but was unable to do even the simplest operation. James had outmaneuvered him. Enrique was locked out. Every time he tried to log on, he got an error message.

Littered on the floor behind him was a broken monitor. Enrique had thrown it in a fit of pique. He couldn't figure out what James had done. James had revoked his security clearance. He couldn't access the NAS Gateway. He couldn't even access the Internet. He kept getting the same message:

Please type in your pass code.

It was enough to make him want to pull all his hair out.

His Bluetooth crackled. "Enrique?"

Enrique tapped his ear.

"Paulson!"

"Where are you?" Paulson's voice sounded far away.

"I'm at The Vault."

"What?! It's still there?"

"There's been a complication. We can't find James."

Static crackled. Paulson said something that Enrique couldn't hear.

Savic walked into the room. "A car is at the gate. Three men. We may need to take them out."

Enrique tapped his Bluetooth. Still only static. He looked at Savic. "Wait, hold on. What did you say?"

"A car is at the gate. Looks like authorities. Cops... maybe feds? If they try and enter I'm giving my men the order."

"No, that's the last thing we need to do. Let me handle it. If they come through, I'll go out and talk to them."

267

Savic raised an eyebrow. "And say what to them?"

"I'm going to explain everything is cool. Get them to go away. Last thing we need is for them to call for backup. You said one car right?"

"Yes."

"Then they're just fishing."

Savic looked annoyed.

Paulson's voice interrupted. "Enrique!"

"I can hear you. Can you hear me?"

"Yeah. Why the fuck is The Vault still there?"

"Listen. I need you here."

Enrique started talking quickly. Paulson took charge of the conversation, as he was prone to do.

Enrique nodded, grimly agreeing to the new plan. "Got it. When you get here." He looked up at Savic, but Savic was gone.

Oh fuck, he better not be...

83

THEY had him. It was certain this time. This insect that had been biting them under the collar was about to be squashed like the insignificant gnat it was.

Savic's men converged. They'd worked together for years. The Solntsevskaya brotherhood in many respects had more discipline than special branches of the Russian military, such as Spetznaz.

They'd been hardened with death and cold steel. All of them had seen hand to hand combat. Using knives or shivs was something they'd done at an early age. The streets of Moscow were an unsympathetic mother. They'd suckled its teat. Learned the ways of cruelty and iron will.

They knew how to hunt and kill. Whatever the directive. They would carry it out with cold efficiency. The Solntsevskaya brotherhood had many rules, which kept its members in line. To a man, they would not hesitate to take someone out. Whatever was asked of them they'd do.

Rape. Maim. Dismember. Whatever. It was all the same to them.

These men were not married. Marriage was forbidden. Children were forbidden.

They could have mistress, but their family was the brotherhood. Women were only to meet their basic carnal needs. Love was not something they knew. Love was considered soft. These men were not soft in any way. They saw the world through a much different eye.

A man was only as good as his reputation. Any erosion of his strength, any perception of weakness was anathema to each of these men.

Such was Yuri's world.

He was near the front. His head still throbbed with tightness and pain from being knocked out earlier. He was not in a pleasant mood. He'd been humiliated by a *súka*. A *blován*. He was not about to let this one go. This man was nothing, and had invited scorn and ridicule on Yuri.

Yuri seethed.

His comrades and he entered a large room. There were banks of seats, arranged almost like an auditorium, fanning out from a small raised platform. On the raised dais was their quarry.

This nothing of a man. Yuri's jaw tightened.

The man had a gun. The same gun he'd taken from him. The man's soft face had a look of surprise. Not fear, which was unusual.

The man put down the gun. He raised his hands slowly. "I give up. You have me. Take me..."

Yuri sneered. *Fuck instructions.* He unloaded his gun, firing multiple shots at the puny *súka* in front of him.

Blam! Blam! Blam!

More gunshots. His comrades opened fire, as well.

Hot steel. The wings of death flew. They hit their mark.

The noise was deafening.

84

SAVIC'S right hand man, a man named Motka, screamed, trying to be heard above the din. The gunshots in the enclosed space were amplified and created an unbearable noise.

"*Ostýn!* Hold it! Hold it!"

The men stopped firing, but it was too late. A barrage of bullets that would have taken down a rhino had already been unleashed.

Motka knew what this meant. This was not good. Savic had been very stern. The man was to be taken alive. Alive! He was not to be killed.

Motka looked at his men. He cursed. But it was too late to take back what had happened.

He looked at the man who had been shot. *Da nu!* The man was still standing.

He blinked, and the man had a gun in his hand. Motka fumbled for his weapon, but the man was already setting his pistol down.

The man raised his hands slowly. "I give up. You have me. Take me to Enrique."

What?

Motka walked up to the platform. He put out his hand and it went through the man. The man wasn't real. He was...

A ghost?

No.

Something else.

"What is this?"

Motka looked up at the ceiling towards a series of bright colored lights. They were all focused towards the same spot; exactly where the man was standing. The lights were creating a three-dimensional holographic image.

Lípa. What type of technology was this?

Motka frowned. "Fan out... find him. This time keep him alive, or you answer to me."

85

THE noise could only be one thing. The Vault had thick walls and thicker insulation. Though faint, those were definitely gunshots.

Enrique was not worried that the noise would transmit outside. But it no doubt meant they'd found James. Enrique pulled off his disposable scrubs. He was in the DECON chamber. Nothing had gone as planned.

He finished lacing his shoes. Savic, after a brief disappearing act, had informed him the men outside were using a bolt cutter to snip the chain.

"My men will be ready when you give the signal."

"You need to make sure you get your men out of here."

"We'll do our part," Savic said.

Enrique's jaw set. He went to greet their visitors.

86

THE ruse had worked. It provided the distraction he needed. When the men started shooting James slipped away. They had him bottled and now they didn't.

He'd known these men's intentions, but it didn't hurt to have it spelled out with bullets. It removed those remaining barriers in James's head; allowed him to go where he needed to go. Put this in its proper context of black and white. He wasn't a big fan of capital punishment. He thought it unnecessarily cruel, but he acknowledged that killing did have its place. There were evil people out there. These people certainly fit that bill.

These men and the ones who had gone after his girls were working for a pretty despicable outfit. James had seen enough when he'd worked his back door magic. He hadn't connected every last dot, yet. But he'd painted enough of the picture to know who he was dealing with.

The Russian connection in this operation was *Semion Mihajlovic.* He was one of the Matryoshka dolls. James had followed his cyber trail to the end.

It was just a name at first, but a quick Internet search had told him the man's character. Russian newspapers called him untouchable. He was a ruthless mob boss, head of an organization called the *Solntsevskaya bratva.*

Before James had unleashed his dogs, he'd done the five-minute skim, reading the various recent articles.

Just a sampling…

[Prostitution ring of young kidnapped teens attributed to the *Solntsevskaya bratva*. // Car bombing of a judge and his family—the signature killing style of the *Solntsevskaya bratva*. // Nuclear fission material gone missing, rumored to be the work of the *Solntsevskaya bratva*.]

Two hours ago, James had never even heard of such an outfit. Wikipedia had brought him up to speed in a hurry.

Man, he sure knew how to pick his enemies.

James headed towards the loading dock. It was time he got out of here. The neighborhood had gone to hell.

87

THE car was a boxy, late model, American made sedan. The three men each wore dark blue suits and white shirts. Each was fit looking.

Enrique met them at the front gate. They'd just finished cutting the two chains that Savic's men had used to padlock the outer fence.

"Are you police? Did Paulson call you?"

The man flashed his ID. "No... FBI. Agent Hockney. These are my colleagues, Agent Martinez and Agent Chambers."

"Thank God you're here. I haven't known what to do." Enrique did his best to look frazzled, which considering the circumstances was not a problem.

"Calm down, son. What's going on?"

"He's inside. He doesn't know I'm out here."

"Who is inside?"

"My boss. He made me come here." Enrique looked at the cut chains. He needed to be convincing. "Isn't that considered illegal? Can you guys do that?"

"Article 16, the Patriot Act gives us the right..."

The sound of vehicles approaching interrupted them. The men turned. A white Cadillac Escalade, followed by a black Suburban was coming down the drive.

"Are you expecting visitors?"

Enrique nodded. "I called one of our engineers."

The man seemed to hesitate. The two vehicles were about fifty yards down the drive. He gave a look towards his colleague who had his phone pressed to his ear.

His colleague nodded back. "Gotcha, Mac. But I'm not getting any service here. Thought you should know."

Agent Hockney grimaced. "Stay alert." He looked at Enrique. "Don't move. I want you where you are."

"Sure," Enrique said. He stole a glance at his watch. The sun was going down and the pole lights around them were firing up. Enrique watched as Paulson's car pulled up and came to a stop.

This was it. *Paulson, you fucker, you better pull this off.*

88

HIS Tyvek® pants had ripped. They weren't made for the type of use James had put them through in the last few hours. The rip was on the inseam and was causing his boxers to poke through.

James wasn't too concerned. It wasn't like he was going to get cited by the ComTek clothing police. He had bigger problems on his hands, like getting out of here in one piece.

The Vault was in the middle of nowhere. It was a good twelve miles from the outskirts of Raleigh. He could walk a mile in any direction and still have another mile or two to go before he saw so much as a house or trailer.

The location was chosen deliberately. The Vault was all about being under the radar. It was out of the way, and didn't have any close neighbors. Even for the few that were around, the topography was ideal to keep the place out of sight, out of mind. A thick tree range ringed the place, past its outer perimeter fence.

James might be able to slip out of The Vault, but it was going to be a tougher proposition actually making it to the woods without being seen. Bright LED pole lights lit up the grounds. There was little to no cover for at least two hundred yards any direction. The place might as well have been a prison.

There were two options that James could think of—one was to sit tight and wait till they left and the other was bolder and held more risk. James was all about sitting tight, except for one small problem.

Click.

Make that two small problems.

James heard the man before he saw him. He thought he was alone in here—he'd checked the FLIR a minute ago—but he wasn't. The man was getting inside the van. The one that James had been admiring. The one that had been left running with its driver's door open.

"Ta-Boom!"

"Ha ha."

Words that James had overheard between two of the men, not less than three minutes ago.

James looked up the ramp that led towards daylight—actually it was night at this point, but with those lights out there, small difference. The ramp was a good seventy yards stretch, if he ran it, which wasn't really an option with his ankle.

Meanwhile, those two men he'd overheard were presumably setting charges that would blow this place sky high.

James sucked in a breath. So much for choices. Stay here and die? Or try and make it out there where they'd see him for sure and plug him with holes?

Whatever happened to option C?

None of the above.

89

PAULSON handed his card to Agent Hockney. "Nick Paulson, Director of Information Security."

Agent Hockney frowned and looked at Paulson's security detail behind him. He glanced at the card. "You work for ComTek?"

"Yes. We just discovered the breach. An employee of ours has wreaked havoc with our systems. We're just getting our hands around it. I'm glad Rex got hold of you."

"Who is Rex?"

"Rex Portino? Our COO. He should have called you. Isn't that why you're here?"

"Let's back up a sec'," Agent Hockney said. "We're here because we received some correspondence that came from one of your employees. A James Kolinsky."

"But he's the man responsible," Paulson said, letting his jaw drop. "He contacted you?"

"Kolinsky is my boss," Enrique interjected. "He's the one that's inside."

"Calm down," Agent Hockney said. "One at a time."

"Responsible for what, exactly?" Agent Martinez piped in.

Agent Hockney gave an irritated look at his colleague.

"Everything that's going on now." Paulson realized he needed to rein this in quickly. *Fuck. Kolinsky contacted them?* "Kolinsky works for us. We just recently detected some illegal activity on his part. He was going to be fired this Friday."

"Going to be?" said Agent Hockney.

"You know HR. Friday is the day they do it. But what we detected was minor. We're just discovering what he was really doing. I can only guess that he must have discovered we were going to fire him, and sped up his plans."

Paulson launched into it. He'd been rehearsing it in his head on the entire ride over here. He kept it loose; he didn't want it to sound rehearsed or canned. "...he's worked for us for eleven years. He knows our systems better than anyone, including myself. He knew exactly how to bypass our internal filters, all our security measures, safeguards..."

Paulson tried to read the agents' faces, as he spoke. But they were inscrutable. All three of them looked like they had sticks up their butt. Rigid posture, necks hardly moving at all. One of them was taking notes.

"As for why he'd do it, I have no idea. I believe he was undergoing psychological counseling. I may be wrong on that—but it was in his file," Paulson said.

"I think he was having problems at home," Enrique said.

Agent Hockney looked at Enrique. "Why do you say that?"

"I know I shouldn't just throw this out, but he may have been having an affair."

"Did you see him with another woman?" Agent Martinez said.

"No, but a couple times I overheard him tell his wife on the phone that he'd have to work late, and then the guy would just leave."

"Leave the office?"

Enrique nodded. "Yes."

"And he was to be fired this Friday?" Agent Hockney said.

"That's correct." Paulson bit his lip. The men seemed to be buying it. He looked at Enrique and gave him the signal. Enrique put his hands behind his back, which was presumably the signal that Savic's men were looking for. That was it. They had two minutes now.

It wasn't the original plan, but it was stitching together. They almost couldn't ask for a better wrap. Paulson made sure he didn't smirk as he grasped his phone. It hadn't gone off, but these men didn't know that. "Excuse me."

He pretended to click his phone. "This is Nick." He paused, as if hearing some news. "What? When? You're kidding. I'm here now."

Paulson nodded and looked up at Agent Hockney. "We just looked over some video footage. It isn't good. James Kolinsky apparently has a van parked inside. It could have weapons, I don't know."

"A van?"

"Yes."

Paulson said some more words and pretended to click off the phone. He shook his head. "He's already done enough damage. Why would he come back? It doesn't make sense."

"Can we go this way to get inside?"

Paulson looked up. Good, the man's face told him everything. He was buying it. "Yes. We can head towards the service entrance. It's around back."

Paulson's phone vibrated, for real this time. Agent Hockney looked down.

"Phone call?"

Paulson frowned. "Yeah, sorry." He quickly clicked to answer it.

"This is Nick."

"We need him alive," said the voice on the other end.

"Rex."

"The money is gone. What the fuck is going on? I've just spoken with two of our partners."

"Gone? That's not possible."

"Alive! Keep him alive."

Paulson's hand dropped.

A gunshot rang out.

The FBI men quickly turned and drew their guns.

"That came from inside."

Paulson felt sick. He was going to throw up. *The money was gone?*

90

JAMES stomped his foot on the accelerator. The van let out an ear-shrieking whine and propelled itself up the ramp. He tossed his pistol on the passenger seat.

He'd left behind a man prostrate on the concrete. His shot had communicated his resolve. He was just glad he didn't have to actually shoot him. Bad guy or not, killing someone was not something he was quite ready to do.

Up ahead, however, there were bound to be men that felt differently and would have no such constraints. He prepared himself to duck down. The van reached the end of the ramp. He eased on the accelerator, but it wasn't enough. He was still going too fast. The van hit the bump and almost launched into the air. There was a resounding thud of objects shifting in the cargo hold. James glanced at the rearview mirror, but his attention quickly ricocheted to men up ahead. They were by the other van.

He saw several of them. By quick count... six. They were by the van's open side door. The vehicle was near the back gate, right in the middle of the lane. It effectively cut him off from heading that way. They'd riddle James's van with bullets before he got halfway to them.

James made a split decision. He turned the wheel and floored it. The van was sluggish, but it picked up speed. He headed around the building towards the front entry.

He expected to hear bullets popping and hitting his van, but the men didn't get any shots off. In another second, James was in the clear. He turned the corner, his wheels screeching.

He went through the parking lot. Off to the side was Enrique's car, parked where they'd left it. Up ahead was the front gate. His heart shot up to his throat. There were four vehicles past the guard house.

Shit.

He saw men standing. He kept going. Some of them had guns drawn. It was too late to turn around. The wooden drop-down barricade was drawn across the lane.

James blew through it and the guard house rushed past. Twenty more yards of asphalt and the chain-link gate came up fast. The men pointed their guns at him. The gate was partially open.

The men jumped out of the way. With a crash James hit the gates. They blew outwards. James saw a blur of vehicles and men. He pressed the pedal to the floor.

His eyes darted to his side mirror. The men and vehicles behind him got smaller and smaller. The lights of the facility became just a glow behind him. No cars were following, yet.

He'd done it!

His euphoria was short lived. The sloshing sound coming from the back drew his attention. He glanced back in the cargo hold. There was something back there.

He looked at the dash, trying to find a switch for a light. It took him a second—he found a knob and pulled. A light lit up the back and he looked in the hold. It was packed full with huge hundred gallon drums. There were electrical wires connected to the tops of each.

His eyes went wide. The cargo hold was one big bomb.

91

"THIS is Agent Hockney, we're in pursuit of a suspect. Believe it to be James Kolinsky."

Agent Chambers was driving. They'd jumped in the car, as soon as the van raced past. The boyish-faced Enrique had said it was Kolinsky driving the van. The man named Paulson had yelled something that Mac Hockney hadn't quite heard.

Mac Hockney was a thirty-year veteran in the FBI. His two compatriots were wet behind the ears compared to him. They, however, had understood what the heck that guy Paulson had been talking about when he got into the technical mumbo jumbo.

Mac wasn't a computer whiz. Tech lingo was as foreign as Swahili to him. He always thought life could throw you some strange curves, none more so than where his career had gone. Two years ago he was installed as team leader within the FBI's Cyber Warfare Unit.

Since then he'd had a crash course in everything from computers to blogospheres. But it was like trying to teach an old dog new tricks. It was this stuff that Mac was good at.

Chasing down perps. Doing field work. Running down the bad guys.

"I see him!" said Agent Martinez.

The guy had ditched the van, leaving its headlights still on.

"Jam it, jam it!" yelled Agent Martinez.

Even the lingo his team used was too hip for Mac.

Agent Chambers braked and came to a stop behind the van. The three of them piled out and began to run after him. The guy had made it to the tree line. He wasn't running fast; seemed to have a bum leg.

"Freeze!" Mac yelled.

The guy didn't stop. He was moving slow.

What was the guy thinking?

Mac had on his most comfortable shoes. He could run a marathon in these go fasters. He jumped over a fallen tree branch and reached the tree line. A noise, too deafening to even calibrate on a decibel meter, blasted the air.

Mac didn't have time to blink. The world around him was suddenly a burning inferno of hell.

92

THE concussion wave of the blast threw James to the ground. Tops of trees suddenly lit up like matches. James must have blacked out, because when he next opened his eyes a tree was lying near him. Branches had hit his leg. He crawled out from under the coniferous mess.

James looked at the circumference of the tree. Another ten feet his way and he'd have been crushed. He was in a daze as he looked at the scene around him.

Other trees were down. Some branches were burning. The smell of something acrid was in the air.

James stumbled and walked towards where he'd left the van. Beyond the outer ring of trees was a desolate scene. Blackened landscape, downed trees, burning grass and shrubs. Past it all, he could barely make out what appeared to be a crater where the vehicle had once been.

Jesus.

The other car was gone too. The one that had stopped. Before the explosion, James had heard someone yell at him. He looked for those men, but only saw scorched earth and small pitted fires.

He needed to get out of here. There were other cars he'd passed when he'd bulled through the chain-link gate. Those men might get here any second.

Just as he was about to head back into the woods, he saw a glimpse of something in the dirt. It was a man. Face down.

You need to go, said that voice in his head.

He ignored it. The man was hurt. He went over to see if he was alive.

The man had a pulse, but appeared to be unconscious. Less than a foot from him a downed tree was burning. James hesitated. He needed to go. But there was that other voice in his head that wouldn't let him.

He grabbed hold of the man and pulled him gently to an area where the fire couldn't reach him. The man moaned.

"Are you okay?" James said.

The man didn't reply. He was dressed in what James realized was a suit, which was now blackened and torn.

"Are you hurt?" James said.

The man looked at James. He seemed disoriented; eyes not focusing. James heard a vehicle approaching and saw headlights. He couldn't stay here.

"Who are you? Are you police?"

The man closed his eyes. James saw something shiny clipped inside the man's jacket. It was an FBI badge.

The headlights were getting closer.

93

"GODDAMNIT!" Paulson felt his world sinking. He slowed down when he saw what was ahead.

"*Wow*," said Portino's head of security.

"What's wow about this? This is fucked up."

The explosion had been like a small quake. When it went off the ground had shaken. Paulson had held his men back. He didn't want to be driving after that thing when it went off.

The Feds had raced ahead. Paulson saw what looked like their vehicle. It was upside down and burning. It was about a hundred feet from the crater. They must have reached the van or been close behind when it exploded.

Paulson eased to a stop. He left his headlights running and stepped from his vehicle.

"Give me your gun."

"What?"

"Just give it to me."

Reluctantly the guy handed it over. Paulson checked it. He pulled back the slide and loaded a bullet in the chamber.

He surveyed the scorched ground and started walking. With the van blown into smithereens they were going to have a hell of a time taking out The Vault. *What the fuck were they going to do?*

"Goddamnit!"

His world was collapsing. Three hundred billion dollars gone? How was that possible?

"Goddamn you Kolinsky!"

He was going to find his charred body and plug every fuckin' bullet he had into his dead carcass. Then he was going to piss on his skull, right where his eye sockets were!

He walked towards the crater. He could feel the residual heat coming off the ground. The explosion had incinerated everything a good hundred feet from the blast point.

Gasoline and fertilizer were a toxic mix. He didn't see any of the remains of the van. It was completely gone.

Paulson wasn't going to get the privilege of seeing Kolinsky's remains. He was probably all over the ground. Dime-sized pieces of him littered like pieces of bird poop.

Goddamnit!

"Found one!" yelled Portino's head of security.

Paulson took his eyes from the crater.

The other men, including Savic's, had arrived and were getting out of their cars. Portino's head of security was about seventy yards away from the crater, near the tree line.

Paulson walked over. It was one of the Feds. The man was still alive, barely.

"Here's another."

Paulson looked up. The second was about ten yards away. They were nowhere near where their car would have been. These men had gotten out. They'd run all the way over here?

Why would they do that? They wouldn't have known there was a bomb in the van. Unless...

Unless they had been chasing someone.

Paulson smacked his palm with the butt of his gun. Kolinsky was alive!

"He's around here," Paulson said. He yelled instructions to the others for them to start searching. "We need him alive. Alive!"

"What should we do with these guys?" Portino's head of security was looking down at the second guy. The man, like the other, was still breathing. His face was all burned up. The man was trying to say something, which was more just a mumble.

Paulson walked over to him. "What did you say?" He pointed his pistol straight at the man's face. *Blam!*

"I'm sorry, I can't hear you."

Paulson strode over to the other guy. The guy was trying to get up. *Blam!*

"Jesus, man! That's my gun," said Portino's head of security. "Why'd you do that? These guys are Feds."

"Fuck 'em. We'll just tag Kolinsky with this. Like everything else."

Paulson looked around. "Anyone?"

"Not yet," someone said.

"Start searching the woods! What are you fuckers standing around for? Find him!"

94

NOT more than thirty yards away, James and the FBI agent were screened by a burning tree. Otherwise they'd be in plain view.

"Can you walk?" James said, barely a whisper.

"He shot my men."

"I know. We need to go. Can you walk?"

The man tried, but could barely stand. James knew he couldn't leave him here. Those men—that had been Nick Paulson's voice!—would shoot him for sure.

"How much do you weigh?" James said.

The FBI agent looked at him, confused.

James looked out on the field. The men, including Paulson, were walking towards the woods.

"We can't stay here," James said. "I'm going to carry you."

James bent down and picked him up. *Jesus.* The guy weighed a ton.

Getting his balance, James began to hobble with the man slung over his shoulder.

"I'm sorry," James said. The man had to be in pain, but didn't cry out.

"I'm James."

"Mac," said the man. "Thank you."

James picked up the pace.

Hold on ankle. Hold it together.

Fighting back the pain, James, laden down like a pack mule, headed deeper into the woods.

95

THE darkness was thick as soup. James couldn't see a thing. He had no idea if he was walking in circles, or if he was heading in a straight line.

For the first twenty minutes he didn't think they were going to make it. Every step he took he expected to hear a shout, signifying they'd been seen. A few flashlights had come close to being shone their away, but Mac and he had somehow avoided detection.

It certainly wasn't because of James's speed. He was walking at a snail's pace. Branches kept scraping him. Mac moaned once or twice, but otherwise he was a silent package on James's back.

James was still processing what he'd seen. That had been Paulson who had done the shooting. *Nick Paulson.*

James knew the guy was a certified asshole, but a cold-blooded killer? If he hadn't seen it with his own eyes, he wouldn't believe it.

"How are you doing?"

Mac didn't respond.

James set him down. The man was in bad shape. He needed medical attention. James hoped he hadn't done the wrong thing moving him.

As he second guessed his actions, he had to remind himself that the man's two colleagues had been shot. He couldn't have left him. That wasn't even an option. But now that they were away, out of immediate danger, he wondered if he was doing the right thing carrying him.

"Can you hear me?"

The man looked at him listlessly.

"I'm going to get help for us." *Should he leave him here?*

The man didn't respond, but closed his eyes.

Shit.

James had no idea what to do. With the darkness and expanse of the woods, he wasn't sure he'd be able to find him again. Leaving him now might be leaving him to die.

"Thank you," Mac said.

James turned his head. "I was getting worried about you. You still with me?"

The guy raised his thumb.

"Good. We're getting out of here. Think you're up for one more go on my back?"

"I don't know how... how you carried me this far."

"Me either." James managed a laugh.

"You're James Kolinsky?"

James nodded.

"We intercepted some emails from you. You sent them off..."

The man trailed off and his eyes closed.

"Mac?"

Mac opened his eyes back up. "If you got it in you, I'll go along for the ride."

"Alright." James ignored what his body was telling him. He picked him up, worked through the pain, and continued on.

96

THEY drove up the drive.

"This is your home?"

Bob nodded.

The place was definitely out of the way. It had taken them a while to get here. The traffic on the road had been terrible. There were cars left abandoned without any gas and people were walking on the side of the road. They'd gone through one road block. The National Guard was screening cars. Around them it seemed like chaos was breaking loose. There were lots of fires.

A guardsman had told them a curfew was in effect. He'd let them pass. The last road to Bob's house was a curvy country lane. His place was in the middle of nowhere it seemed.

"Neat," Katie said. "Is that a barn?"

"I see horses!" said Hannah.

Sue was amazed at the spread. "Is all this yours?"

"It's about two hundred acres, more or less. Do you like it?"

Sue looked up at the house. It was enormous. The type of place you'd call a manor house or an estate. It was lit up and looked beautiful.

Bob parked his pickup in the circular driveway. A man came out to greet them. "This is Lewis," Bob said. "He lives here and helps me run the place."

The man had wrinkly skin and looked ancient. "He's part Navajo," Bob said. "Doesn't talk much. Kind of like me. We're just a bunch of old guys out here waiting to die."

"Don't say that," Sue said.

"Sorry," Bob said. "Didn't mean it that way." Bob looked at the girls. "Do you want to see your rooms?"

The girls looked excited. "Can we see the horses?"

"Tomorrow girls," said Sue. "It's getting late. We need to eat and get to bed. It's nice to meet you, Lewis. I'm Sue. These are my girls, Katie and Hannah."

The girls ran inside with Tigerlily.

Sue looked at her dad. "This is really nice."

Bob gave her a warm smile.

Sue touched his arm. "Thank you for taking us in Dad."

Bob's eyes seemed extra shiny. "Of course. Let me get you something to eat." He turned quickly and walked inside.

97

"CASH reward," Paulson said. "Call this number if you see them."

"Phone ain't working, so well," said the man. He was dressed in just his underwear and a dirty tee shirt. The room they were in smelled of cat urine. "What I do if it don't work?"

"These are dangerous criminals. I'd protect yourself as best you can. Do you have a gun?"

"Does a pig shit?"

Paulson nodded. "Then I'd suggest you use it then, sir."

"Ain't that illegal, Agent—what you say your name was?"

"Chambers."

"*Right*. Chambers. You saying I can just shoot 'em?"

Paulson feigned a look of deep concern. "These men just killed two federal agents and blew up a facility. They will kill you in a second. I'm just saying… if it was me, I'd have my gun loaded and ready if these men came anywhere near me."

"How much that reward, 'gain?"

"Fifty thousand."

The man whistled. "Does it matter if they're dead?"

"No, it doesn't. Take care of yourself, sir. Sorry to disturb you this evening."

The man shrugged. "Hell, I might just get my dogs and find 'em myself."

"Good night, sir." Paulson left the trailer and looked at his two men.

"Next house."

One of them was holding a map. "We've hit the three that are in this area. Savic's team has this area covered. Next plat is over the ridge, but that is a good four miles away—you think they'd head that direction?"

Paulson got in the car. "How the hell should I know. Was this trailer shown on the map?"

"No. Just the plat."

"Fuck." Paulson started the car. These places were dirt holes. These people were disgusting. They lived in abject filth. He needed a shower just to get the stink off him. "Have you been able to get Enrique?"

"Not yet. Our service out here—"

"What was that?"

A deer had darted across the road. Paulson cursed as he almost went into a ditch. "Dammit!" He picked up his phone.

Enrique you better be making progress.

Paulson glanced at his watch as he called Enrique to check on the status of things. Manually doing what the bomb was supposed to do was not going to be easy. They were running out of time. The Feds could show up at The Vault any minute.

"No service, we…"

Fuck!

Paulson shifted into third gear as they raced against the clock.

98

"WE'RE not getting a reading. It's off the grid."

"What do you mean?"

"I mean it's gone. Their car is no longer there."

Special Agent in Charge Wiseman looked around the room. "How about you Kulnich? Pulled anything up?"

"Negative. Still trying... having issues with connectivity."

"Keep at it." SAC Wiseman frowned. He raised his voice. "We're going to work all night, people."

"Got something!"

"Spit it out, son."

"James Kolinsky opened up a new Amex account three months ago. I've got several purchases here. There is some interesting stuff you're going to want to take a look at. Just this one here, *ammonium nitrate...* that is common grade fertilizer. I've got several purchases. Each were too small to trigger a watchdog alert. This one here from 'Drag Racing Depot'. *Nitromethane.*"

"Jesus."

"That's not all. I've been working with the ComTek representative, I told you about. Have clearance to the top. Their COO is fully cooperating with our investigation and has given us special access to their records. They sent over some more info regarding Kolinsky. Kolinsky signed off on *seven* new corporate Amex cards in the last six months."

300

"Have you run that info down?"

"All different names, sir. But he may have been using those cards."

"Purchases?"

"Looking into it right now, sir. I should know in a few minutes."

SAC Wiseman was not liking this one bit. They were playing catch-up on a cyber attack of seismic proportions. And this was in his team's sandbox. His home turf.

And then there was Mac. He hadn't called in.

He'd known Hockney since the Academy. This wasn't like him. Last call they received was going on two hours. Wiseman could only think the worst. And to top it off, their systems were working like they had molasses junking up the works.

They couldn't pull up *Skyview*—couldn't even pin down where Mac, Martinez and Chambers were last. Right now a kid was rifling Mac's desk looking for a hand scrawled note... anything.

It was amateur hour. And it was happening on his watch.

Wiseman picked up the sheaf of papers, which he'd already read twice.

James Kolinsky.

This guy had been under the radar for forty-two years and now he decides to become public enemy number one?

Wiseman looked at the printout Mac had given him before he went down the rabbit hole. This didn't line up with the rest.

Wiseman rubbed his temples. It was going to be a long night.

99

JAMES heard dogs barking. There seemed to be several of them and they were wound up. He was too exhausted from carrying Mac to think anything other than the noise was a good thing.

It meant that up ahead was a house. A house meant people. He needed to get this man help. He was in bad shape. He wasn't responding anymore when James spoke to him, and James had given him an earful.

Each time they'd stopped, he told him a little more what had happened. How he'd been set up. What was really going on; the players involved. But he wasn't sure if any of it got through.

Not that he could blame the guy for not listening. The guy was barely hanging on. James had tried to attend to the man's injuries the last time they'd stopped, but what the man needed was to be taken to a hospital. Mac had told James to leave him, but James couldn't do that. "We're going to get through this together."

For some reason saving this man he didn't know was important. James was not about to leave him. He'd carried him this far. He could carry him farther.

It was his oar, his special burden.

His oar...

His mind was wigging out a little as he placed one foot in front of the other. James had been a fan of *The Odyssey* when he was a boy. He'd read the book over a dozen times. Right now he felt an intimate affinity for the storyline.

Odysseus, after the ten-year siege of Troy, had endured all sorts of horrors and pitfalls on the journey home. *Polyphemus, Charybdis, Scylla...* When he finally returned to his rocky homeland, twenty years since he'd first set sail, he discovered his house had been taken over by rogues. His wife and now grown son were at their mercy, being eaten out of house and home. Odysseus, older and gray, not the young warrior he used to be, was able to fight off the rogues and rescue his family.

Peace would not come to him easily, though. During his journey, he'd angered Poseidon by blinding *Polyphemus*—the Cyclops—and Odysseus was destined to not rest until he carried a heavy oar on his back and wandered the ends of the earth until he found a land where the people didn't know what an oar was.

James had his oar. He needed to get that oar to a hospital. *Somewhere in there that thought actually made sense to him.* Yeah, he was losing it. "Mac, you with me?"

No response.

James staggered and caught himself. The noise of dogs barking, once a terrifying sound to him, wasn't fear inducing anymore. They were like sirens luring him in. He went forward, urged on, brain dead from weariness, lack of food and water, oblivious of any of the voices inside him that might suggest caution.

"Mac, we're almost there."

James could see that the trees thinned out ahead. He made out what looked to be a trailer. Lights were on.

He was just about to step into the clearing when he saw the van.

There was a man standing next to it, smoking a cigarette.

100

THE girls were squared away in their room. They'd wanted to stay in the room with matching beds and the bearskin rug. Sue had tucked them in. She was finishing singing them a lullaby.

She hardly sang to them anymore. She used to sing to them all the time when they were babies. But they'd gotten older and she'd stopped at some point. After what they'd been through today, Sue wanted to give them something familiar and comforting. They needed that—or maybe it was her that needed to remember what it was like during a gentler time.

Sue touched their heads.

"Mommy, is this our new home?"

"Where's Daddy? Is he okay?"

"I love you, girls. I told you, Daddy will be with us soon. We're going to stay here with Grandpa for a little while."

She kissed their little heads. "Goodnight. Sleep tight."

"Don't let the bed bugs bite," Hannah said.

Sue smiled and shut the door.

Bob looked up as she walked down the massive wooden stairs. The room was one of those great rooms with cathedral ceilings and large wooden beams. She walked across the Aztec-patterned rug.

"Are they okay?" Bob said.

She sat in one of the comfy chairs by the fireplace. "I think so."

She closed her eyes. She felt so tired. James still hadn't called. She had no way to reach him. When he'd called he'd told her he was using

304

Skype—talking on the computer. It wasn't a number she could call back. *James…*

When she opened her eyes she found that Bob had put a blanket over her legs. "Did I doze off?"

"You were beginning to." He looked at her tenderly.

"Dad…"

"Yes?"

Sue smiled. "Nothing." She felt so out of sorts. Competing thoughts drifting in her head. She looked around the house. It was even more beautiful inside. During dinner Sue had asked him about it, wondering how he could afford such a place.

Bob had told her the stock options he'd gotten over the years when he was in management—overseeing rigs out at sea—had allowed him to retire with quite a nest egg. "I never thought those things would ever amount to much. But the oil business had some good years. I wish…"

He drifted off and Sue had thought he'd lost his train of thought.

"I wish I could have provided a house for your mother like this." He'd seemed sad, but his face brightened a moment later. "It's so good having you here."

Sue was surprised at her own feelings. She'd hated her dad for so long that she didn't think it possible to feel what she was feeling now. As much as she didn't want to admit it, it felt good to be here. The place was like a pair of well-worn jeans that fit just right. Even the chair she was sitting in felt like it was made for her.

Granted, the place was definitely a bachelor pad. Not much of a woman's touch, but it was comfy. Their food had been simple fare. Cold cuts and a warmed can of beans. As hungry as they were, it had tasted good. Sue had loved the kitchen.

"I love this setup. Do you think I can cook something for us tomorrow?"

Her dad had smiled when she said those words. She had actually smiled back. It felt more like a dream…

"Mommy?"

Sue looked up. Katie had come out of her room and was standing at the top of the stairs. "What is it honey?"

"I'm scared."

"Baby, there is nothing to be scared of. We're safe here."

Hannah joined her big sister. It was a touching scene, the two of them standing there.

Sue got out of her chair. "Do you want me to sing to you again?"

They nodded and Sue walked back upstairs.

"Goodnight Grandpop," said Katie. Hannah gave a shy little wave.

"Goodnight you two," said Bob. "Love you."

101

JAMES felt like he was leaving a long tunnel. He'd been so focused putting one foot in front of the other, closing his eyes every time he sensed or felt branches scraping him, that he had entered some type of wake/dream state. It was as if the weariness had sapped the blood from his brain.

James found a spot to put down Mac. A stone's throw away was the same van he'd seen at The Vault. Identical to the one he'd taken before it had blown up. The man standing next to it was presumably not alone. Judging from the lights and the shadowy silhouettes he'd glimpsed, the others were inside the house. If it could be called that—the house was more some combination of lean-to and trailer.

What were those men doing? Looking for him and Mac? Or maybe this was their home? Doubtful, but there was no telling.

James looked down at Mac. The man was in bad shape. He was still breathing. Still alive.

James knew this was not a moment for him to be indecisive or afraid. He'd done it once. He could do it again. Now, before those men came out and it was too late.

"Do you have a gun?" James said. The one he'd had, he'd left in the van. It had fallen to the floor when he'd braked. He hadn't taken time to find it before he ran from the van. He was regretting that decision now.

Mac didn't seem to hear him. James already knew the answer to his question. Still, he lifted the man's jacket. The man's holster was empty.

James knew he would have felt the gun when Mac was slung on his back.

And he hadn't.

James sucked in a breath. This was going to be tough. *And if he didn't go, this man would most likely die.*

Mac grabbed his arm. He looked at him—didn't speak. He pointed to his leg.

"What is it?" James said.

Mac lifted his pant leg. He was wearing an ankle holster. "Take it." His voice was hoarse.

James retrieved the gun. It was a compact piece with a snub barrel. The textured grip was cool to the touch. James examined the pistol in the poor light. It didn't have much heft and looked to be a .22 caliber. Not that he was sure; it could have been a 9 mm. "I'll be back. I'm not leaving you."

Mac nodded and his eyes closed. James took another breath and started towards the clearing. He didn't see how he was going to surprise the man. There was no cover to hide behind. The dogs had stopped barking. If they started back up, they might alert the man. James steeled himself.

He was going to have to be ready to kill this man.

He said a prayer as he moved forward. He reminded himself that these men had shot and tried to kill him earlier. They were criminals. Killers. They would show him no mercy. He needed to do the same if he was to survive.

The light coming from the house spilled into the yard. James stayed low, keeping in the fingers of the shadows. It had been over twenty years since he'd held or shot a gun, with the exception of earlier back at The Vault.

He had very little experience shooting pistols. The shooting he'd done was mostly shotguns and rifles, and he'd never been exceptionally good at it. He could appreciate guns and admire old shotguns, but handguns he didn't particularly like. They scared him. It was as if he could feel the death in the metal.

Like now. Cold. James could almost feel the black tendrils wrapping around him.

Lord forgive me.

James approached from behind the van. The van partially screened him. The dogs were still silent.

The man took another drag on his cigarette. His face was briefly profiled in the light. His face, neck and shoulders—all one mass—cut a hulking profile. James recognized him.

It was the same man he'd taken out at The Vault.

The one he'd done his fireman's carry on. James eyed the man's bulk. The man was considerably larger than him. James remembered seeing the man close up.

This guy was a beast.

James felt a cold sweat come over him. His hand was sweating. The pistol was unsure in his grip.

Easy.

James was fifteen yards away. He moved to the right so that the van fully screened him. He moved closer. He was just an arm's length from the back of the van when his feet disturbed the gravel.

Shit!

James stopped. Had the man heard? James readied himself. He listened intently.

"Grolsch?"

James bit his lip. *Darn it.*

He stepped from behind the van and pointed his gun. "Don't move. I don't want to shoot, but I will."

The man was framed by the light behind him. James couldn't read the man's facial features. He was just a mass of black.

The man dropped his cigarette. For a split second, James's eyes went to the movement. The man took advantage of the moment. He moved forward, covering the five feet in a rush.

James pulled the trigger.

Nothing.

Fuck. The trigger was stuck. Oh my God, he'd left the safety on.

102

"LINE three, *señor.*"

Javier stood stiffly, waiting. "Shall I say you are unavailable?"

Rex Portino waved his hand. "No." He picked up the phone.

The annoying drawl of his boss filled the other end. *"Rexie baby. Man, am I glad I gotcha."*

It was Scooter, CEO of ComTek.

Scooter. The name was fitting. "It's a little late, Scooter."

"Is it? Hell. It's only five o'clock here."

"You're out of the country?"

"Last minute thing. Woulda told you, if I knew the damn world was going to hell in a handbasket. Jesus. You believe this? Just got the news a few minutes ago. What the hell's happening out there?"

"You just got the news?"

"Out of pocket... you know. Doing wheeling and dealing—trying to get our stock up."

Portino smiled, snidely. He was well informed regarding Scooter's itinerary. Including the fact right now the man was out of the country on a pleasure trip with his mistress.

"But hell, man. Tell me you got this?"

"Have what Scooter?"

"Have what! Dammit man, you been watching the news?"

"At the moment... no. But we are dealing with the crisis, if that is the question."

311

"Shooo. That's what I wanted to hear. You scared me for a second, buddy. Don't do that. Tell me how you got it?"

"We're working on several concurrent issues. I have our best men making sure we root down the infiltration points, reset systems, ensure database integrity…"

"'Nough. That's all I wanted to hear. You got this. That's my boy. You need me back? Or are we good?"

"In an hour or so, we hope to have everything…"

"Shit. Tell it to me straight. Are we good?"

"In an hour… yes."

"Alright then. That's the reason I hired you. Don't let the house fall down while I'm gone." Scooter gave a nervous laugh. Portino could hear what sounded like a woman's voice chittering in the background. *"Listen Rexie, I gotta go. You pull through on this, and you just earned yourself a big bonus. I'll make sure the board knows what you did. Got that?"*

"Completely."

"Alright, buddy. I'll see you back on the home front soon."

103

THIS was not proving to be easy. Enrique was out of his league.

Savic had left him two of his men. Each knew how to rig explosives, but they didn't have enough of what they needed to get the job done. They hadn't come prepared for this, they told Enrique in their faltering English, cursing and pointing fingers at each other. The van, which James had stolen, had the punch to do the trick. But the little C4 they had was barely enough to blow up a car, let alone a facility the size of The Vault.

Even by shaping the charges and using the propellant in the fuel tanks they were going to come up short with the sort of blast they needed to bring the house down. Enrique was going to have to use other options. None of which could be done in the time frame he was being given.

The best Enrique could hope to accomplish was to stagger a series of charges, combined with downloading a cyber cocktail, equivalent to antifreeze, into the system. The problem with that, as well, was he needed time. And time was not being kind to him. He'd spent the last hour just trying to get back into the system.

It had taken forever to figure out what James had done with the security interface. And when he did, it was not what he'd expected. Enrique had no idea how James had pulled off this sophisticated blend of subterfuge and sabotage in the compressed time frame he would have had.

The guy, he hated to admit it, was brilliant.

Enrique navigated the NAS Gateway. Finally, he was going to be able to see the full extent of what James had been up to. Around him The Vault was humming. It was like the engine was revving at 8,000 RPM. Something was happening. With a few more clicks, Enrique discovered exactly what James had done. What he had set into motion.

His jaw dropped. Enrique stared at the screen. This was not happening. He shook his head.

"No! No, no, no!"

Enrique screamed, ripped out the monitor and threw it against the wall behind him.

104

JAMES didn't have time to react. He was suddenly airborne. He landed hard, in the dirt and gravel. The pistol flew from his hand.

The man wasn't done. He came at him, picking up James like he was a sack of potatoes. The man was huge. And powerful! Holding him one armed, the man wound back to take James's head off.

James moved, but it wasn't fast enough. He saw sparks.

Bright white!

James squirmed, as the man landed another shot. It wasn't full on, but still rung his bell. James staggered backwards. The man had let him go. The dogs were barking.

"Bljad!"

The man advanced with a snarl. Fists raised.

"Zatknis!"

James's head was still ringing. He was disoriented, feeling his knees going weak, all blood rushing from his head, things getting fuzzy.

This was not good. Not good…

The man was coming at him. Smiling cruelly now… "I piss on your grave. You got lucky last time, this time you're mine."

He jabbed, hitting James on the jaw. It snapped James's head back. He was having fun with him now.

Futilely, James brought his hands up. The man swung again. James barely avoided the blow. The man had left himself open. James feinted with his left and connected with his right. The man stepped back.

"Ha! So you box, do you?"

The cobwebs were clearing; James was still standing. The man stepped forward to finish him off. This was it, James realized. He would not get another opportunity; if he took another hit he wouldn't have the legs. As the man swung, James went in and closed the distance; he felt the rush of air as the man's punch just missed him. He kept going, grabbed the man around the middle and drove forward with everything he had.

The man was surprised; he hadn't expected such a move. He tottered, and James had the momentum; he kept driving, his lower center of gravity working in his favor. He shoved the man into the side of the van. The metal bow flexed inward.

"What?!" The man cursed and cuffed James, but didn't have a good angle. The punch just grazed James's shoulder. James dug his head into the man's body, protecting it as best he could.

The man punched him again, landing a shot on the side of James's head. James let go, and the man sensed that James was crumpling, but that wasn't it. James changed his tactic and grabbed the man's wrist. With a solid hold on it, he turned, all in one fluid motion, like a running back doing a spin move around a defender, he got behind the man. It was a Greco-Roman wrestling technique. Use the man's own body against himself. He still had hold of the man's wrist; the arm was torqued and bent. The man yelped, as James pushed the man's elbow past its pressure point.

This was where James would have stopped, back when he'd been on the mat. It was a submission hold; the point where one's opponent had no choice but to yield. But this wasn't playing by rules; this was a fight for survival; a fight to live. If he let go, the man would kill him for sure; all the wrestling skills in the world wouldn't save James from that grim end.

James didn't hesitate, but drove with everything he had. He had the leverage. He'd never pushed to this extent, but he knew what the result would bring. The man's arm was essentially a fulcrum. Tissue and cartilage… it wasn't going to be pretty. With a sickening sound, the man's shoulder popped out of its socket like a chicken wing being twisted. The man screamed. A door slammed. The dogs were in full howl.

"Yuri!"

Men emptied from the house.

James let go of the man and pushed him away. He yanked open the van's door. The interior light came on. James went for the ignition, but the keys weren't there.

He looked again, blinking. The keys were definitely not there!

Through the windshield, James saw men running down the steps. He got out of the van. He looked on the ground for the gun he'd dropped.

He didn't see it. His peripheral vision saw something and he instinctively ducked. Yuri lurched past him, swinging with his one good arm. His dislocated shoulder made his other arm look obscenely positioned. James saw the gun he'd dropped. It was a few feet in front of Yuri; closer to James. Yuri saw it too.

James went for the gun. Yuri tried to pull his own from his shoulder holster, but his holster was rigged for his other arm. The man fumbled.

James got to the gun and flipped the safety. He looked at Yuri.

The man was leveling his gun towards him.

Blam! Blam!

James waited for the pain, but it didn't come. Yuri went down, slowly, like an oak felled from a saw. James's gun was smoking. The shots had been his, not Yuri's.

James stood up from his crouch. The men were fully out of the house now. Gunshots rang out. James moved and hunkered behind the open van door.

Bullets hit the van. *Pop! Pop!*

James glanced in the van. Something caught his attention. The keys! The keys were on the coin tray!

James jumped in—shut the door, grabbed the keys and fumbled with them. Bullets hit the windshield. *Krak! Krak! Krak!* The noise was deafening. *Holy shit!* Glass went over the dashboard, onto the seats.

James put in the key…

Pop! Pop! Pop! Pop!

Staying bent down, he started the van. The van fired up. He put it in reverse. He hit the gas and the van took off backwards.

James looked up. The men were running now.

James looked in the side mirror, but it was blown off, barely hanging on the side of the door. James looked backwards. The van hit something, went over it and bounced. James hit the brakes… slammed it back into Drive. He hit the gas again and did a tight one-eighty.

Bullets raked the side of the van as he completed his arc and got back on the single track. James kept going. Up ahead, about forty yards, was the spot he'd left Mac. He'd left him on the side of the road, tucked from sight. James saw the big rock, hit the brakes, and scrambled out of the van.

"Mac!"

Mac was lying on the ground. James picked him up under the armpits. He dragged him to the van and opened the door. He shoved him in, pushed his legs up and closed the door. He ran back around the van.

Gunshots—*Pop! Pop! Pop!*—punctured the van.

"Mac, you okay?"

"Mac?"

James hit the gas and tore down the single track.

105

REX Portino had not gotten where he was by being sloppy. He thought things through. He'd learned long ago it paid to be prepared. All avenues had to be explored. Do it first in the head, so when faced with a choice there was no wavering on what to do.

Some called that leadership. No hesitation. Firm decision making.

To Portino it was just common sense. Like breathing. It was just something he did. Like every thought out exercise, if and when the final phase was complete, there may have to be alterations to the plan.

Worst case: his shock of white hair was going to have to be trimmed and dyed; his face, which over the years he'd grown attached to, was going to have to be altered yet again by the finest underground surgeons that money could buy.

Twenty-eight years ago he'd started over. He could do so again. Of course, back then he'd had the luxury of time being on his side. It had allowed him some flexibility, which may not be an option this time. Back then only his imagination stood in the way from creating the person he wanted to be. He'd reinvented himself. The prestigious credentials, university degrees and doctorates, doctored transcripts, falsified records, fraudulent work experience; everything that had set the foundation for the man he later became was based on *constructive liberties.*

Some might call them lies. They were the narrow-minded ones that had no vision. Shackled forever in cages of their own construct.

Throughout his career Portino had learned that if he could imagine it, then he could become it. Each time he'd parlayed what he had into something bigger, something better. The companies he'd worked for, some real, some not, all went to create the illusion of the man he was.

The cultured persona. The pedigree. The reputation.

It had taken him far. Farther than he would have ever imagined when he was just starting out on his path of deceit.

He was a top executive at a billion-dollar company. It should have been enough. But like every grifter, it was never enough.

The paradox of his gilded life. He lived beyond his means. Always had, always would. The baubles and toys, the young boys. The lifestyle, both the hidden one and the projected veneer, required an insatiable mouth to feed. The creditors, liens and bankruptcy that perpetually waited in the wings. Always one misstep away. One wrong move waiting to happen.

This job was to be the big fix. The one time score that allowed him to walk away from everything. To live beyond his dreams forever.

Sixty billion.

He would have been king.

That may still happen, but that reality was slipping away each hour.

He'd finished packing. *Just in case.* His passport and visa were in his pocket. Two hundred and twenty million might be his take.

His partners weren't happy. They all wanted more. Course they did.

Everyone always wanted more.

106

"KILL the lights," said Paulson. He was in the passenger seat, watching the unraveling scene in front of him.

Savic and three of his men were in a car behind them. They'd just gotten word that the other crew was stranded. One of Savic's men had been shot. The van had been taken, presumably by Kolinsky.

Paulson, steely eyed, looked at the rest of the bad news. He could see it from a mile away. Cars, a line of them, were streaming down the road heading towards The Vault.

Feds.

Enrique had run out of time. He better have gotten the job done. Paulson had no intention of staying around to verify.

"Let's get out of here."

"What about Enrique and Savic's men?"

Fuck 'em, Paulson thought. He said it more tactfully, "What about 'em?"

"We can't just leave them."

"Sure we can. They knew the drill. They should have been out of there by now."

Paulson chewed on his remaining options. The noose was tightening. Everything had crumbled. Kolinsky—the key to this—had slipped their grip. Enrique, if he was captured, might cop a plea and implicate the rest of them. Of course he would never be allowed to live that long. Still, it was going to get messy. The Vault, if it wasn't taken out, meant that everything they had planned, everything they had done... could be undone.

Three hundred billion dollars, gone. All because of Kolinsky not going with the program. He grit his teeth. *Kolinsky.*

His thoughts were interrupted. Savic was rapping on his window.

Paulson rolled his window down. "What?"

Savic handed him his phone. "Listen."

Annoyed, Paulson took it. "Yes?"

"He wants twenty-five thousand," said a voice on the other end.

"Who the fuck is this?"

"It's one of our men," Savic said. "Listen."

Paulson did. His frown was soon replaced by a cruel smile.

No, this wasn't over. *Not yet.*

107

HE hadn't slept for over thirty-six hours. He was on his third shift. Manuel Escodoba, M.D. had never seen anything like this. And that was saying something.

This place being in the inner city saw more than its share. On a bad night he might see victims of gang attacks with multiple knife and bullet wounds. A few head trauma cases: caused by hit-and-run, an angry housewife who'd hit her husband with an iron, a construction worker doing the night shift who'd put a nail through his eye.

Those nights, the worst of them, were bad. The staff, ever since the latest round of budget cuts, was way too lean to handle the volume this ER unit saw on a regular basis. On nights when things spiked, everyone was just running around trying to keep up. Staunch the bleeding. Addressing the worst patients first.

They always managed... somehow. Manuel worked with some good people. They were all stressed, but they did their job.

But they had never seen anything like this.

Manuel was exhausted. Beyond exhausted. He'd seen more patients in the last twenty-four hours than he'd seen in two weeks. It was standing room only at this point.

Manuel felt like a pinball, ricocheting from one patient to the next. A father with his young son who'd both been injured during a human stampede. An older man who'd been shot for five dollars. A woman who appeared to have been beaten... with a bat. The list went on; each case seemingly worse than the next.

As the night had progressed it just seemed to get worse. This night was going to go down in the record books. They'd never been in this position. Not even on the worst nights had they ever considered what Manuel was seeing happening right now.

He didn't believe it at first.

He walked straight of purpose toward the doors. It was never an option. Turning away a dying man or woman, a bleeding child? It was counter to everything Manuel believed in.

"What are you doing?" Manuel said to the guard.

"I'm locking the doors."

"You can't do that."

"I'm sorry, sir. I've been instructed."

"Who told you to lock these doors?"

"I'm sorry, sir. I'm just doing my job."

Manuel looked around the jammed ER unit. It was like a terrible dream. People were bleeding on the floor. There were screams, crying. Attendants and nurses were completely overwhelmed, outnumbered ten to one.

Manuel looked outside. More were coming. A man was stumbling, carrying another man.

"Don't lock it... yet."

The guard looked at him.

"Let these last people in. Then do what you have to do. This is only a temporary thing, right? People are going to be directed to the next hospital?"

"Sir, I'm just supposed to lock it."

Manuel looked at the guard. He was just a kid, he realized. "Then don't lock it. If anyone asks, you can tell them I told you so."

The kid nodded. Manuel held the door open for the two men coming in. They both looked terrible. It was hard to tell who was in worse shape. The man stumbling or the man being carried?

"Can you help me?" the man said. His face was beaten up; there was dried blood caked around his nose. Around his neck was more dried blood, and there was dirt all over him. His clothes—if they could be called that—were torn to shreds. Had those been hospital scrubs at some point?

Manuel looked at the guard. "You and me, we're going to carry this man. Find him a spot to put him down."

The guard nodded. The three of them made their way through the crowd.

"What happened to him?"

"It was a bomb explosion."

"Bomb?" Manuel saw some blood on the man's torn clothes. "Are you okay?"

The man nodded. "I'm fine. He's an FBI agent. Can you help him?"

Manuel nodded. "Don't worry. We'll take care of him." They navigated through the morass of people and found a spot in one of the corridors. There was an open stretcher past some double doors. "Put him down here. Now where was this bomb? Can you give me some more details?"

Manuel looked up. "Where'd he go?"

The guard looked around. "I don't know."

Manuel looked around, but the man was gone.

108

JAMES hated to leave like that, but he wouldn't have been much good to anybody. He certainly was no doctor, and he didn't want to be signing any forms or answering any questions. With what had happened it was best he cleared things up on his own terms. If the cops had arrived, and anything had been found out, they might have taken him in.

Besides... that man was FBI. He would have friends. And if they came it would have been worse.

No... he'd done the right thing. He was just lucky it worked out.

Earlier, at a checkpoint, two National Guardsmen had seen the bullet holes and riddled windshield and had raised their weapons. "Step from the vehicle, sir." He'd tried to tell them he was trying to get an FBI agent to the hospital. If Mac hadn't roused himself to flash his badge and tell the men to let them pass, things could have gone much differently.

He didn't want to think about it—it was time to put this behind him. Time for him to get home. Except home wasn't there anymore.

James took a deep breath as he started the van. His nose hurt and was probably broken, but that didn't matter. He focused on the positives.

He was alive. Sue and his girls were safe. Hearing Sue's voice again a short while ago had kept him going. To know that soon this would all be over.

He'd used Mac's cell phone. After a brief emotional exchange, Sue had told him to call her back, saying her cell phone was about to die. She had given her dad's number. He was concerned he wouldn't be able to reach her again with phone service being so spotty.

She'd said "don't worry, I'm watching the news. Everything is getting better now."

Getting better…

Hard to believe it, but she was right. He got her back with one try. "See," she said. She told him the girls were sleeping. She'd described her dad's place. "It's so nice. I can't wait for you to get here." She'd given him the address and told him directions. "I'll wait up for you."

"Don't. You sleep."

"No. Call me when you're close. I'll be here." Her voice was so beautiful to his ears.

He could almost hear it now. He couldn't wait to get back to her. To his girls.

This day, this night… had been a nightmare.

But it was over.

109

IT was over.

It could have been an echo, but the meaning held different connotations for Rex Portino. *Finito. Ich Bin Fertig.* Done.

Almost, but not quite. Least not yet. Paulson may just surprise him and come through, but the odds at this point were against it. The Vault was still there. Kolinsky was still at large.

Their perfect fall guy had proven to be not so perfect.

Portino smiled ruefully. Lo San and Mihajlovic were not the type of men who took failure well. Portino was still taken aback by some of the correspondence he'd seen.

What's the status?

Why is the money not there?

Answer me!

Ingrates. Was it so much to ask for seventy-two hours that people just shut up?

Alanna entered the room. "Rex, someone is at the front door. I can't find Javier anywhere. Should I answer it?"

"Who is it?"

"I don't know."

"How did he get past the front gate?"

"I don't know."

"What do you know?"

"Rex, I'm sorry, I was doing what you asked me to do. Do you want me to get the door?"

"No. I'll do it."

Rex went to his desk and pulled out a revolver. He was surrounded by morons. He glanced at his watch. It was after one AM. A little late for house visits. He walked through the house and into the dark foyer. The lights were off inside, but outside, the landscape lights were still on. He could see the person outside the glass. It was a guy in a chicken suit.

What in the world?

He tucked the gun under his shirt and opened the door. "You've got two seconds to tell me what you're doing here, before I shoot you for trespassing."

"Sorry to bother you, but…"

The man in the chicken suit didn't finish. He pulled out a gun and thrust it in front of Portino's face.

"Simeon Mihajlovic wanted you to have this."

Blam!

110

1:40 AM

THE thrumming of crickets filled the night. The house with its gables and wide porch was lit by uplights. The sky was dotted with millions of stars.

That was the setting outside. Tranquil.

Inside was something else. Sue looked at their captors. There were nine of them. Three were nearby.

"How long you been married?"

The man that spoke hadn't given his name, but he didn't seem to fit with the others. He was handsome in a rakish sort of way. Angular cheekbones; his hair was slicked back. Maybe it was his hair, but he reminded her of that actor Christian Bale in one of his earlier works where he'd played a stockbroker who just happened to be a serial killer. Like that stockbroker character, this man standing, looking down at her, seemed evil. As if it radiated off him.

"Fifteen years."

The man smirked. "That's a long time."

Sue got a sudden case of the willies, like snakes were crawling on her skin.

In the other room, where she could barely see them, were her girls, her dad and Lewis. They were on the kitchen floor, tied up. For some reason they hadn't tied her.

"What do you want?"

"I already told you, your husband."

"Why do you want him?"

"He has something of ours and I intend to make him give it back."

"What could he possibly have of yours?"

The man laughed. "You ask a lot of questions, don't you?" He leaned in and spoke softly. "My turn now."

She met his gaze, looking into those cruel icy eyes. Women probably thought those eyes were dreamy, but Sue saw only depravity in them.

"Mind if I sit down?" He still had the smirk.

She didn't answer, but looked away.

"I'll take that as an invite." He sat next to her and she could feel him looking at her. "Mmm... I wouldn't have thought James had it in him."

She could smell him. He had the scent of old cologne mixed with rank onion undertones of faint body odor.

"I'll tell you what. You answer some of my questions, I'll answer yours."

Sue hugged her knees tighter, hoping he'd just leave her alone.

"No—don't want to play that game? Fine, I'll ask my questions, anyway."

He leaned closer, almost touching her now.

"Which way?" His voice was soft and low. "Because I must say, I can't see James being all that great under the sheets. He probably prefers missionary, doesn't he? Two minute guy?"

Sue's body tightened.

"Don't be shy. I want to know. On top? Or do you like it from behind?"

"You disgust me."

"Do I? Don't tell me after fifteen years you're not bored out of your mind. Probably haven't done it for weeks, have you?" He touched her hair. "How about we rectify that and go in the back room? I'll do you in the ass first. I always like that way best."

He laughed. "Don't worry, I understand. I know your head's probably not into it right now. This will be for me this time."

He leaned back and put his hand on her thigh and began to move it down.

She elbowed him right in the face, catching him full on the mouth.

It took him a moment to recover. "*Nice.* Not quite the reaction I was looking for." He touched his lip and his tongue went over his teeth, checking them. "If you wanted rough, you should have said so."

She clenched her teeth. "Get away from me."

He stood up. "This could have been so much easier for you."

He looked at the two men nearest him. "Take her to one of the bedrooms. You hold her for me. Then she's all yours."

The men, heavy-browed and sullen, flashed thin smiles.

Sue closed her eyes.

111

AS the two men grabbed her arms and pulled her off the couch, a phone rang. The noise split the air. All eyes went to the coffee table.

The man she'd just hit picked up her cell phone. His lip had blood on it. He looked at the touch screen.

"*Honey?* I presume this is James? Or is this your fuck buddy?" He pointed his finger at her. "Careful how you answer—don't make me jealous." He handed her the phone. "Keep it simple. Say anything you shouldn't and you'll regret it. I have your girls."

Sue took the phone, but he held on to it. "By the way, how old is she? Your oldest? She reminds me of you."

The phone continued to ring.

"Understand?"

Sue nodded and he let go of the phone.

"Put him on speaker. Get him here."

Sue clicked the phone. "Hello?"

"Hey, it's me."

"James?"

"Yeah, who else? You expecting another call?"

Sue heard him chuckle. Across the coffee table, the man glared at her. He pointed towards her girls.

"Sorry, I nodded off honey." Sue wanted to warn to him, but couldn't think how. She looked across the table at the man watching her. "How far away are you?"

"Almost there, but you won't believe it, I just got a flat tire. Listen, I know your phone is about to die. I'm just down the road. I think I can see your driveway up ahead. I'm going to walk the rest of the way. I'll see you in a bit. Okay? Love you."

Click.

The man across from her smiled. "Scintillating." He took the phone from her and looked at the two men. "Tie her up for now. Put her in the bedroom, and don't start without me. I've got dibs."

He snickered and walked towards the kitchen. "Savic! How about we go get our boy?"

The two men grabbed Sue's arms again and hoisted her up. As they walked by the fireplace mantle, one of them picked up some rope.

"You have knife?"

"*Da,*" said the other.

"Should we wait?"

The man said something back in Russian and they both laughed.

112

PAULSON took in the night air. It tasted sweet—wet and fresh. The dew had made everything glisten.

His anger was about to have an outlet. He decided when they nabbed Kolinsky he was going make him watch. Then, after he was done with his wife, he'd threaten to do the same to his girls. That should make the guy cooperate.

Right now he was on that razor edge, where only violence could appease him. They might salvage some of this fiasco. All that money couldn't be gone. Kolinsky had gotten in and done his tricks, but whatever he'd done he was going to fix.

One way or the other.

Even with The Vault still up, they'd have a few hours till time worked against them. In all likelihood the money was just hidden in plain view, or diverted. With what Portino had told him, their Swiss and London partners had said the money was there. They just couldn't access or move it. To Paulson it sounded pretty simple—an administrator glitch or shade operation. But Portino said they'd tried everything so far. It was something else.

Well… they'd soon find out what that little something was.

He'd sacrificed two years of his life for this and there was no way he was coming up empty. No way. He was due.

"We'll take him here."

Portino's head of security nodded.

Savic grunted. "Looks good."

They had a view of the dirt road. They were behind a large clumping of rocks that hid them perfectly. Paulson didn't want to risk that Kolinsky might see the extra cars. They'd tucked them out sight, parking near the barn. Still... he didn't want to take any chances. They'd grab him here, where Kolinsky would have his guard down.

Paulson looked at his watch. 1:56 AM.

James Kolinsky was expecting his wife's open arms.

The man was in for a disappointment.

113

Forty minutes earlier

1:16 AM

THAT was the time on his digital watch. James looked at the flat tire. *Everything happens for a reason.*

An odd time for that trite phrase to pop in his head, considering his last sixteen hours of hell. He reflected on it—there was the gas station—back at the beginning—before everything bad started to happen. If he'd had money in his wallet he would have been able to fill his tank, or at least he would have been filling his tank right about the same time there had been that shooting. If that had been the case, he might have been shot.

Then later, when he'd run out of gas in that bad neighborhood? As bad luck as that was, it had led to him saving Taneesha from being raped and maybe killed. Perhaps he was meant to be there to do that exact thing? Maybe she was meant to do great things with her life, or her child was meant to have a mother and grow up being loved?

As for the boys jacking his car that were shot, it was hard to see any value in that outcome. It only seemed bleak and meaningless. But maybe their path was leading them to choices of destruction that would have meant death and harm for others?

Reading too much into things like this always made James feel out of his element—as if his thoughts were going on hopeless tangents. He wasn't what he'd consider a religious person. He went to church, but it wasn't often. He looked at scripture with a skeptical eye and thought much of it dated and no longer relevant. But there was a side of him that did pause when strange events happened. On those rare occasions his mind tended to delve into things he could and would never understand.

When he considered the ramifications of his car running out of gas, he couldn't help but think of what didn't happen. He didn't go home. He didn't join his family. The men waiting for him? The men that had tied up Sue and his girls? Their plans went awry. Things might have gone much differently—not in a good way—had he come home like he was supposed to.

And to add something else...

Perhaps those men that had killed those boys jacking his car had really meant to kill him? His car running out of gas may have saved his life... twice?

So many loose ends. If, perhaps, when, maybe.

A part of him wanted to shake this off. Ignore this clutter in his head. But today, with what had happened, he felt strongly was not a day to ignore. There were too many signs and coincidences to chalk them up as happenstance, or random chance.

His car being stolen, which had led to him pulling a woman from a burning car? He couldn't shake the eerie feeling that somehow, someway, he was placed in that situation on purpose. As horrible as it had been, particularly for the woman who'd almost died, he'd come away from that stronger. He'd faced a fear and tackled it head on. He'd gone in a burning car. The James of last week would never have done that.

As for the woman—there was no telling how that event might impact her life. Hopefully she'd move on to have a greater appreciation for life. To live a richer, fuller life.

Yes, the optimist in him hadn't died. Strangely, that part of him felt revived. Stronger.

James had gone through so many tests today. For a while there, he felt like Job in the Old Testament. Losing everything: his identity, money, car, house, facing the loss of his job, and then the prospect of going to prison when he discovered he'd been set up to be the fall guy for a cybercrime of gargantuan proportions.

And how had he faced those tests? Only he knew the answer to that. But hopefully when he looked back on this day, he'd have no regrets. He'd stood up for himself. Stopped those men from doing what they were trying to do. Even—to add another coincidence—when he stole the van with the explosives. That random event had prevented them from destroying The Vault.

Another coincidence?

He didn't know why, but he always felt there was no such thing. That everything did indeed happen for a reason. He'd heard the flip-side arguments, ones which said coincidences were inevitable. Mathematically it was nothing unusual. In fact, it was mathematically improbable—no, make that impossible—for coincidences not to happen. Mathematically coincidences were going to happen every day to someone out there.

Somewhere right now, somewhere in the world, a sixteen-year old was finding sixteen cents, euro cents, or pence, on the ground at exactly sixteen after the hour. A person in a casino was doing the same thing, except instead of being a sixteen-year old they were an elderly person that was married on January 16th, and instead of finding sixteen cents they were winning sixteen tokens in a casino slot machine at this exact time.

1:16 AM

It wasn't fate, grand design, or a divine sign. It was just random coincidence.

James was still looking at his flat tire. Of all the times to get a flat. He couldn't be less than a mile from where Sue said the house was. It might

340

be further, but if he'd followed the directions right they were just ahead, up over that knoll.

He'd already gone in the van and found where the spare was, except it wasn't there. The spare tire was gone. *Just one more crappy thing to add on top of everything else that had happened today.*

James took out his phone—or rather it was Mac's phone, which he'd never returned. He was going to call Sue to tell her he'd had a flat and would soon be there, but he paused. He looked at the phone. He looked at the flat tire. He looked at the empty wheel well inside the van.

Everything happens for a reason.

What was that on the floor, under the seat? He bent down and picked it up. It was a bible and Old Testament.

A chill came over him.

In the Book of Job, Job lost everything, including his wife and sons.

1:16

Please don't be…

He started flipping pages.

114

HIS heart was up in his throat, almost choking him. He rifled through the bible, looking for the scripture. There were several with those numbers.

In the poor light from the van, he read each one, his eyes scanning over the text. He looked at each passage, each reference...

None were the Book of Job. He double checked, just to make sure. The last one he read one more time.

Romans 1:16.

For I am not ashamed of the gospel, for it is the power of God for salvation to everyone who believes, to the Jew first and also to the Greek.

He immediately felt relieved. His mind had been going so fast, already going there to that awful place he never ever wanted to find himself. His family...

He could lose everything, but not them. Not his wife and girls. They were what made him get up every morning. Look at each day with shining eyes.

With a heavy sigh, he put the bible down.

Thank you.

He could feel his blood pressure, the beating in his temples, the drumming incessant, *thrum thrum...* feel it subsiding. Everything inside him had spiked, like a car's engine redlining. The red haze receded from his eyes.

"Thank you." He said it out loud. He didn't want the big guy up there to have any doubt of what he was thinking.

He looked at the bible. His eyes lingered, not looking away. That last passage, one word in particular, stayed with him.

Greek.

That was a peculiar word. He shook his head. Again, his mind was going off on another tangent.

Greek.

Another damn coincidence. Would they never stop? They seemed to be everywhere. He thought back to his bout of delirium when he was carrying Mac earlier. When he'd thought of an oar and felt a kinship for the tribulations of the Greek hero, Odysseus. James knew this was borderline crazy.

No. It couldn't be.

Salvation for everyone who believes.

He had a flat tire. Here was a bible spelling it out for him.

Greek.

That word was intentional. He was meant to make some sort of connection. To revisit his thoughts.

The Odyssey, written by Homer. One of his favorite books. Like the sightless seer who penned it, he knew the storyline blind. Odysseus, upon returning to his homeland Ithaca after being gone for twenty years, had found his home beset with rogues. His wife and son were their prisoners. Odysseus, with Athena's help, had disguised himself as a beggar and dressed himself in rags.

This was crazy. He knew it as he was thinking it, but then he glanced down at himself and saw the remnants of his paper clothes. *Dressed in rags...*

Maybe this was all nonsense. His head finding parallels in anything and everything, going off on crazy tangents. But James suddenly felt a higher power speaking to him. It was almost like he could actually hear words being whispered.

Don't call Sue.

He gripped the cell phone. His knuckles turned white.

He closed the door to the van and began to hike up the road.

115

IT was more than a mile. It might have been two, but it felt like forever. He wanted to run, but couldn't with his ankle. When he saw the address that Sue had given him, his spirits lifted. He realized that his crazy imagination was just that. Crazy. Delirium caused from exhaustion.

But as he walked up the winding road, a tightness lodged in his chest. There was the lit house, as Sue had described. But it wasn't the house that drew his attention.

The road dipped and peaked. In one spot, as the road turned, he was given a glimpse of one of the outbuildings. Near it were parked several cars. There was barely any moonlight to see by. But there it was, glinting faintly from the house's floodlights.

James stopped and looked hard. The vehicle catching the light was a white SUV. It was a Cadillac Escalade. That was the same vehicle that Nick Paulson owned.

James drew in a breath and it hit him, like a thunderbolt, the epiphany of all epiphanies. He believed, and the feeling washing over him wasn't fear and it wasn't panic. He knew what this was.

He believed.

He was going to get through this. Somehow, someway, he was going to save his family. Just him. Odysseus, his childhood hero, had done it. Though he was helped by Athena, it was by his own power that he survived and saved his wife and family. One man, using his wits.

I hear you.

James left the road. He hunkered down to lower his profile. He went down a gully and then climbed a small bluff. Using his hands and stepping carefully, he navigated the rocky terrain. There was a fence. It had those old-style wooden posts. He got down on his belly and slipped under it.

His nostrils, even with his nose broken, flared from the scent of manure. It was pungent; just inches away was a patty. He rose to a crouch. His hands were wet from the dew; dirt and wetness clung to him. Off a ways he saw shapes in the darkness.

He froze and lay still. The shapes were silhouetted. Those were cows. They weren't moving; just sleeping.

His eyes scanned the entire horizon. He took in everything. The lone tree on the gently rolling hills. The dark shapes of clouds in the starry sky.

His ears...

The thrumming.

The crickets reminded him of servers humming. Constant. White noise that receded to the background, till he didn't even hear it. He looked towards the house. It was large and had several levels. There didn't appear to be anyone on the decks.

He looked hard. There may be men outside. Perhaps someone smoking; a guard? But he didn't see anyone.

He moved, keeping low. The house was lit up and gave him a clear view of its entire perimeter. At its rear, it had expansive windows. As he got closer, he saw people inside. Too many people.

Yes, they were here.

He found a spot on a knoll that was slightly elevated. There were some rocks. He got down on his belly and moved forward, crawling. He was soaked and his face was buried in the grass. The blades of the grass seemed like razors. He could feel them slicing and cutting his face.

He paid no attention to it. His eyes were laser focused on what was inside. He could see faces and people moving. Then he saw her. Sue. His heart skipped a beat.

He looked into the other rooms. There… that was Katie. Just the top of her head, but it was her. He didn't see Hannah, but she was probably next to her.

His eyes went back to Sue. She was with someone. He sucked in a breath, tasting bitterness on his tongue. It was Paulson.

His emotions flared. Not now, he couldn't get distracted. He looked around. There were the cars; a barn, another outbuilding.

All he had was his phone. Mac's phone. He'd left the gun with Mac. Dammit.

He took out the phone and dialed 911. His eyes were glued on Sue. He got a busy signal, gnashed his teeth and tried again.

Busy.

Okay. Stay calm.

He looked around. His eyes went back to the barn. There would be something there he could use. Slowly he made his way towards it. He didn't risk getting up. Even though his progress was immeasurably slow, he didn't want to take the chance that someone inside might see him.

As he got closer he saw gravel towards his left. He stayed in the grass. There was a pile of wood on the side of the barn. Next to the wood was a tool of some sort. Something leaning.

He looked back at the house. Still no one outside. He slithered forward and reached the wood pile.

The thing leaning against the barn was a shovel. Rising to a crouch, he retrieved it and then slunk back into the grass. He stayed on his feet this time and didn't crawl back. It would be too difficult to do that and hold the shovel, and a part of him was afraid he might be running out of time.

Sue was okay for now. But for how long? And his girls?

Let them be okay.

He gripped the shovel. It was a heavy one. The heavier the better.

His eyes and ears took in everything. Night sounds; the thrumming of crickets came to the foreground. They seemed intensified, louder. They were building to a fever pitch inside his head. Vibrations of millions of wings rubbing.

He got back to the clumping of rocks. Some of the men inside the house had moved into other rooms. He could see Paulson clearly. He could see his wife. They were next to each other on a couch.

His wife elbowed Paulson in the face. What was happening? He watched, transfixed, afraid of what would happen next.

Some words were exchanged. Two men came over and grabbed Sue. Oh no. Think James. Do something. He pulled out his phone and quickly dialed Sue's number.

"Hey, it's me." He tried to keep his voice calm.

James? Her voice betrayed emotion. She was hiding it, but he knew her too well.

"Yeah, who else? You expecting another call?" He forced a chuckle.

Inside, Paulson appeared to be speaking to her. He heard Sue's voice again.

Sorry, I nodded off honey. She paused; it was as if he could hear her thoughts. I know baby, you want to tell me, but you can't. *How far away are you?*

"Almost there, but you won't believe it, I just got a flat tire. Listen, I know your phone is about to die. I'm just down the road. I think I can see your driveway up ahead. I'm going to walk the rest of the way. I'll see you in a bit. Okay? Love you."

Click.

He sucked in a hard breath. He'd done it. His voice hadn't cracked. He'd gotten through that, and now he had to wait.

He didn't have to wait long. There was lots of movement. Paulson got up and spoke to some of the men. There were words being exchanged. If only he could hear what they were saying.

Please.

Then…

They bit the bait.

The men, including Paulson, spilled from the house. He counted them. Some stayed. Three. There were still three in the house. One was in what looked to be the kitchen. That man was with Katie. Two men were with Sue. They had hold of her arms and were taking her into another room.

I'm coming, baby.

With his shovel, James moved quickly towards the house.

116

THE men threw her in the room. Sue stumbled and barely managed to keep from hitting the baseboard of the four poster bed. It was a massive bed made of hewn logs. She had a feeling of utter hopelessness come over her. She reined it in.

"You don't need the rope," she said. "I'll do what you want."

Inside, she was biting back bile. She did her best to keep those emotions from reading across her face.

"No tricks," said the largest.

"Or we break your face."

"No." She shook her head. "I'll do as you say."

"Course you will."

The other one laughed.

These men were monsters. Where did people like this come from?

She inventoried the room without moving her head. There, on the wall, were two rustic design elements. A wooden pitchfork with rusty steel tines and an old wooden shovel. They were about six feet from the bed.

"Can I be with just one of you? It'll be better. You can both have me, but it'll be easier for me if it's just one of you."

The men paused.

"Please? It'll be better that way." She backed up to the bed and looked at the larger of the two. "How about you and me first?"

"No!" said the other man. "Both!"

But the larger man said something in Russian. They started to squabble. Sue tried to read their faces. They seemed to be arguing and their voices raised a notch. The smaller man glared at her. He spit on the floor and didn't argue anymore.

The larger man grunted, "Wait outside." He'd won.

Sue said a prayer. She was going to get through this. She forced a smile at the man who remained. "Do you have protection?"

The man laughed, cruelly.

"It'll help me… help me not focus on other things. Please?"

The man laughed again. "Shut up and strip."

Sue dropped her head. *Lord help me.* She started to unbutton the shirt her dad had given her when they arrived here. The man watched like a slobbering dog. From what she could tell his gun was tucked in his belt.

A part of her now just wanted to break down. To cry and scream. To make this go away. But she knew that was not going to happen.

Outside were her girls.

She needed to get him undressed—get that gun away from him.

"It's not exactly fair." She took off her jeans. "I'm almost naked and you have all your clothes on."

The man grunted and leered. He pulled out his gun and bent down to untie his boots, not taking his eyes off her. Next, he undid his belt and let his pants drop. He motioned with the gun. "Take rest off."

She unhitched her bra and let it drop.

The man ogled. "*Kátit.*" He set his gun down at his feet and went to pull up his shirt.

Sue waited till the moment his shirt was going over his head, then she ran over to the wall.

117

JAMES made it to the house in record time. He went to the closest rear door. He got a break. The door was unlocked.

He slowly pulled the handle and slipped inside. The room wasn't lit, but there was plenty of light to see by. He scanned the room quickly. To his left there were boots lined up on the floor. The floor was worn tile. Clothes had been tossed haphazardly on a wooden bench that was on his right. Some shelves and curved metal hooks just above head height lined both walls. The walls were made of white beadboard.

He was in a mudroom of some sort. The space was long and of generous width, and appeared to lead to the kitchen. He moved quickly, but carefully so as not to make any noise.

The shovel felt solid in his hands. He paid attention to the distance to objects around him. It wouldn't do to knock something over, or brush the wall with the shovel's blade. He needed the element of surprise. There was a cased opening up ahead from which light spilled. That had to be the kitchen. His pulse started to race.

He paused and forced himself to take deep, calming breaths. He reminded himself that this was for his girls. It didn't matter what happened to him. Just so long as he saved Sue, Katie and Hannah. Right now he was giving himself the mother of all pep talks. Drilling one point home. One sole objective.

This was for them.

What he did now only had to accomplish one thing. One very important thing. Save his girls. And he wasn't going to fail.

It had its desired effect. At the moment, he firmly believed he could take a bullet right now and just by will alone force his body to keep going. He was going to save his girls, and heaven help any person that tried to stand in his way.

He moved forward the last few steps, towards the light. Through the cased opening there was a small foyer. On another beadboard wall was hanging an old antique sign. It was a picture of a little girl with black locks bringing something up to her mouth. *Chocolat* in italic letters was on top. Beneath the girl was the word *Suchard.* She was smiling.

James took another step forward. He wanted to run in, but there were three men and they likely were armed. One step at a time. He reached the cased opening. Through it he could see the extent of the foyer. There was another door to his right. It was partially open. That probably led to the garage. He needed to peek the other way, into the kitchen, see where the guard was.

He moved slightly, tilting his body. He could see a counter and glimpsed what must be a stainless refrigerator. He couldn't see anymore; his vantage point was restricted. He needed to be on the other side of the cased opening.

He reminded himself to breath. One big step. Now.

He moved across the cased opening and made it to the other side. He saw a blur of shapes and the rest of the kitchen. There were people on the floor.

No shout, no noise. He waited. Still nothing. He hadn't been seen.

From his new spot, James had a sliver of a view into the space. There were cabinets and a kitchen island. On the floor were two men tied up. One he didn't recognize. He was older with lined skin, sitting in an uncomfortable position with his hands tied behind his back. His legs were also tied. Next to him he recognized Bob, Sue's dad. His head was drooped and there was a large knot on his forehead and what looked like dried blood.

James looked for the guard, but couldn't see him. He looked for his girls. When he'd seen Katie from outside, he could only see the top of her head. She had to be on the other side of the island.

A small movement made James key on Bob again. Bob's head had moved, just slightly. James watched as Bob's eyes opened and flicked around. A grim expression was on his face. His eyes were observant, calculating. He was okay. James then noticed that Bob's hands were moving. He was working on the ropes, trying to free his hands.

He stopped. There was some movement off to the side. James saw boots and a man's leg. The cabinets on the wall prevented James from seeing anymore. That had to be the guard.

James gripped his shovel. The man standing took another step.

"What are you doing?"

The man partially filled James's view. His back was to James.

If James stepped forward now he could get him. But he realized the space he was in was restricted. The man was too close. There wasn't enough room in the foyer to swing the shovel. Not with the cabinets, the wall and the overhead cased opening.

He choked up on the shovel like a ballplayer might do with a bat. No, it still wasn't good. Choked up on the shovel like he was gave him less to swing. He might not be able to bring the man down with it, and if he didn't, the man could yell and bring the others.

"I said what are you doing? You think me stupid?" The man kicked Bob with his steel-toed boot. He had an unlit cigarette in his hand. He pulled a lighter from his pants. He didn't appear to be armed.

James carefully turned, leaned, and set the shovel lengthwise on the clothes on the bench. He moved his torso back to how he'd been standing and took one small step so that he was fully tucked from sight, tight into the corner. The man was just a few paces away.

He could move out now and with one grab to the neck, pull him down. He'd have to make sure he grabbed the neck just right and silence him, prevent him from yelling. James edged his head sideways till he could see the man again. The man was raising his lighter's flame to his cigarette. The man's head turned abruptly.

There was a blur as something streaked across the floor. It was a cat. It darted into the mudroom and raced past where James was standing.

Halfway into the space the cat stopped running. It stopped almost mid stride. The cat was a calico with a mottled black and brown coat. It stood stiffly, then took two minced steps forward and glanced back with an irritated look, as if to check if it had been followed.

James knew that cat. It was Tigerlily. Tigerlily's green eyes appraised the guard with a look of disdain. She shifted her eyes slightly and they alighted on James.

A subtle change occurred. The cat recognized him instantly. Although she was Katie's and Hannah's cat, she periodically deigned to show James traces of affection. She liked to rub against his leg when he was sitting on the couch. And occasionally, when she really wanted to bestow a gift, she'd sit and fall asleep on his lap. That was usually on rare occasions when Sue and the girls were away.

Of course, those thoughts were not on James's mind right now.

"Meow."

James pulled himself tighter into the corner. Tigerlily meowed again. It was loud. She had the loudest meow of any cat James had ever heard.

"What are you meowing at?" The guard stepped into the mudroom. He strode forward a few steps and Tigerlily arched her back and hissed. The guard stopped. He looked at the cat and cursed something in Russian.

The man's head tilted. James eyes went to what had drawn the man's attention. There on the worn tiles were footprints.

James's footprints.

Wet tracks leading to where James was standing. Right to his corner.

118

SUE grabbed the pitchfork and pulled it off the wall. Like a bare-skinned Amazon warrior, she turned in a flash, pitchfork pointing out like a lance.

The man had just finished pulling his shirt over his head. His eyes went wide, seeing Sue with the weapon. He looked at the three steel tines with their sharp points, then his eyes briefly flicked to the pistol at his feet.

Sue lunged forward, not giving him a chance to reach for it. The man jumped back, but his feet got tangled. They were still partly in his pants. Just as it looked like he would fall, his right foot tore free from his trouser leg. He jerked and caught himself; his legs splayed, like a man doing some crazy dance. He kicked his pants off his other foot.

With both feet free, he looked at Sue. She had pushed him back towards the other side of the room. Away from the door, away from the pistol. The pistol was now closer to her than it was to him.

She feinted with the pitchfork and went for the gun. She had to take one hand off the pitchfork to reach for it. The man wasn't about to let her get the gun. He went for it too.

Sue checked herself and grabbed the pitchfork with both hands again. She went to stab him, but the man leapt clear of the points. He swiped with his hand, trying to grab the shaft of the pitchfork. Sue was quicker and pulled it back.

They stood there, eyeing each other. Two stripped-down combatants. He was muscled, dressed only in his underwear, which looked like some tight red bathing suit hugging him obscenely. A smirk came on his lips.

He eyed her nakedness.

"Svlad! Bit' baklúshi!"

He was calling for his partner. Sue's eyes flicked to the door.

The man seized the opportunity. He dove for the gun. Sue was slow to react. As the man's hand touched the gun, Sue stabbed with the pitchfork. The steel tines dug deep into the man's arm, into the meat of the triceps.

The man howled and shrank back. There was blood on his arm. Two of the points had gashed his skin.

He hadn't retrieved the gun. It was still on the ground. The man touched his bleeding arm and cursed.

The smirk was gone now. The man yelled something else in Russian. Sue looked at the door with fear. She had to get the gun before the man's partner came in.

She lunged for it. The man went for her. She saw him moving and swung the pitchfork, but she was holding it with only one hand and it was a slow swing. He easily dodged and kept coming.

Sue screamed as the man grabbed her arm. She tore away from him, and scrambled to get clear. She butt his head with the pitchfork, using its back end. He snarled and swiped for her face.

Stumbling back, she crashed into one of the log posts of the four-poster bed. It hurt. Somehow she managed to keep hold of the pitchfork.

The man had pushed her far enough away. He went to grab for the gun. Sue jumped forward with the pitchfork. She gave it everything she had. She caught him in the side, digging into flesh, hitting hard into bone.

The man grunted. He clawed for the pitchfork with his free hand. Sue stumbled. He got a grip on the shaft. He ripped the points clear and then with the strength of a bear, he swung her around. Sue tried to hold on, but he was too strong.

She was whipped around. Her legs and body smashed into the bed's footboard and the pitchfork flew from her hands and sailed from his. The man howled in triumph.

Rising to a full stand, eyes blood-crazed and ablaze, he came towards her.

119

JAMES launched himself as the man started to turn. His arm hooked the man's neck. His momentum almost made them both topple. James was behind him. Spinning, they smashed in the wall, bounced off and tottered like two drunks in a drunken brawl.

The man jerked back with his elbow, but James was pressed against him tight, and the blow barely landed. James shot his other arm under the crotch of the man's arm and put it behind the man's neck. His cupped fingers pushed down.

It was a combination of a chokehold and a half nelson. He applied force, pulling back on the man's neck and pushing down on the head at the same time. The man's windpipe was cut off. He couldn't yell and couldn't breathe. The man clawed at James's arm. He kicked out with his feet.

James let go with the half nelson and swiped the man's leg, using a sweep. It brought the man down. James landed on him, making sure the man took all two hundred pounds of him.

The man wheezed. James had just collapsed the man's lungs, expelling his remaining breath. The man squirmed and tried to move. James wrapped his legs around the man and immobilized him. He took a quick second to adjust his grip. He locked his arms. This move was illegal in collegiate wrestling. On WWF they faked using this hold.

They called it the sleeper. It was very effective. Particularly when it was applied for real. James squeezed the man with everything he had, using both his legs and arms. His legs alone, back in the day, could do a number on his opponents. He'd won many a match by squeezing a guy till the guy just quit.

James upped the pressure. He was bending the man, contorting the man's body like a pretzel. The man couldn't breathe. His windpipe was collapsing. James had taken every bit of oxygen from the man's lungs. The man kicked the bench, limply. Tried to claw James's arm. Two more futile kicks. Then...

Ten seconds later it was done.

James kept squeezing for another full minute, just to make sure. Then he released and got up. Panting for air, James staggered into the kitchen. He was afraid to see... afraid the noise had drawn the other two.

There was a yell; a man howling in pain. James cringed, expecting to see the other men storming in with guns. But there wasn't anyone. Just Bob and this other man tied up on the floor.

James went around the island. There was Katie and Hannah. They were on the floor tied up. Their eyes were closed. Oh please, merciful God...

He saw Katie's chest rise. She was breathing. Asleep... just asleep. Hannah, as well. His babies. His little girls could sleep through thunderstorms. *Thank god.*

He pulled a knife from the chopping block. There was a scream and his blood curdled. That scream had come from Sue! For a second he was torn on what to do. Race towards her or free his girls? He made a quick decision. He bent down and quickly sliced the rope that was around Bob's wrists. He gave the knife to Bob. "I've gotta go."

Bob nodded.

James went into the mudroom and grabbed the shovel. Bob was cutting through the rope on his legs. There was another scream and James looked at Bob. Their eyes locked for a brief moment and Bob, his eyes wet, motioned with his hand.

"Go! I'll untie the girls."

120

SVLAD cursed and hiked up his pants.

Can't a man take a shit?

He hastily fastened his belt and grabbed his gun. He heard the woman scream again, then Boris yelling. That wasn't fucking. That was something else.

Toilet paper trailed him as he left the bathroom. With his peripheral vision, he saw something to his left. It was movement, coming down the corridor. Something… make that someone running...

He turned his head and saw something, which was just a blur. Something being swung.

121

"BLJAD! Kudá namýlilsja?" the man yelled. "Where are you going?" He grabbed her by the waist and tossed her on the bed like she was a little girl.

His face contorted into a snarl.

"Menjá nadúli!"

He picked up his gun and strode towards the bed. He towered over her. His muscled torso and arms were covered with black tattoos and smeared with blood. There was blood oozing from the gashes on his arm and side.

He thrust his pistol in her face. "Mouth on it!"

Sue shrank from it, pushing back with her hands, till her entire body was against the headboard. The man laughed. "Not so tough now, are you? Put your mouth on it!" He shoved the gun closer. She turned her face and he dug her cheek with the barrel.

He grabbed her breast and squeezed hard.

She kicked out with her legs and he grunted. She bit down on his hand.

"Súka!"

He stepped back and yelled towards the door. *"Kakógo chërta!"*

He kept his eyes on Sue as he backed towards the door. "Are you sleeping?!" He turned and yanked open the door.

Sue could only see the man's back. The man's head snapped back. It was like whiplash. His knees buckled and he toppled backwards, falling with a thud onto the floor.

A man entered with a shovel. His face was bloody and bruised. The clothes on him looked like rags.

"Sue!"

"James!"

122

SUE threw her arms around him.

"Are you okay?" he said.

She started crying. He held her tight.

"Baby, are you okay?"

She blubbered, "Yes, I'm fine." Her body tightened. "Our girls?"

"They're fine. They're with your dad."

James picked up her shirt and put it around her.

"There are more men."

"I know," James said. "I saw them go down the road."

He explained as Sue put the rest of her clothes on. How when he called, he'd been outside and could see everything through the window.

"I wanted to warn you," she said. "But I couldn't." She put her hand to her mouth. "Your face…" She started to cry again.

"It's okay, baby. It looks worse than it is."

A moment later, they joined their girls in the kitchen. Bob had untied them and the older man, and was loading one of his shotguns.

Katie and Hannah ran over and grabbed his legs. "Daddy!"

James hugged them. The scent of their hair sent a wave of emotion washing over him. He didn't want to let go, but knew they weren't safe, yet.

"We need to go," James said. "The others will be coming back."

"It's better we stay here," Bob said. "How many did you take out?"

"Three."

Bob nodded.

James looked at Sue.

"Mommy?" Hannah said.

Sue seemed frozen. James saw what she was looking at. The man he'd just hit with the shovel had walked into the room. He was holding his gun.

123

"SOMETHING'S not right." Paulson looked at his watch.

"Should we walk ahead, check it out?" Portino's head of security said. "You sure he parked just up the road?"

"That's what he said. But this—"

He didn't get to finish before he was interrupted by the sound of a gunshot. Next to him Savic frowned. Savic looked at his men and pointed to his eye. The men nodded.

The six of them raced back to the house.

124

JAMES watched as the man fell down. Bob said something unintelligible. His shotgun was smoking.

"We need to get these lights off!" Bob moved fast. "Lewis, Suzy, take the girls downstairs to the cellar. Lock the door. We'll be there as soon as we can." Bob motioned to James and spoke quickly.

James nodded, listening. He didn't like Sue and the girls leaving, but they didn't have time to waste.

"They'll be okay," Bob said, seeing the look on James's face.

They moved quickly through the house. Bob used the breaker panel to turn the rest of the interior lights off. The house was pitch black, but James's eyes had already adjusted. In his hand he had the gun he'd retrieved from the man Bob had just shot.

"Outside," Bob whispered. He pointed towards the windows. The floodlights, which illuminated the perimeter, were still on. James saw men running towards the house.

"How many do you see?"

James held up five fingers.

"There should be six." Bob bolted the front door. He opened a panel on the wall and armed the security system. "That'll tell us where they try and come in. You ready for this?"

James bit his lip and nodded.

125

BOB had been in these situations before and knew how they could end. It was almost forty years ago, but time collapses when certain events trigger memory. He could still remember the fear in his belly the first time he was out on patrol. Knowing there were men out there who wanted to kill him.

He had given James the best advice he could. He didn't like they had to split up, but knew with just the two of them this was the best way. Staying together made them ineffective. They became one easy target. Split up they might stand a chance.

There were six killers out there. Bob had told James he shouldn't hesitate. Shoot at the biggest target, and then follow-up with the kill shot. Just squeeze. Don't think.

This wasn't a time for indecision or for doing things halfway. He'd seen men go down and with their dying breath take out friends that were right next to him. A man was dangerous till the very end... and even then he was still dangerous.

A river of memories washed over Bob. His emotions right now were opening the deluge. Even though he was calm on the surface, on the inside he was eighteen again.

He could still recall the face of the man he'd first killed. It had been with a knife. No one should ever have to do that.

He still had nightmares where he was struggling with the man, both of them not wanting to die. That struggle repeated itself in a never-ending loop. But in his dreams it wasn't him holding the knife, but the other man.

Sometimes, even when he awoke, he was convinced that his life all this time had never happened; that he had died in that miserable place and never come home.

There were plenty of memories to join that one. Bob reminded himself that it wasn't Vietcong out there. These men had probably never been to war. They may not know the psychological part of this. It was usually the mind that kept you alive. The fear that made you step into the fire.

Bob took a deep breath. He tapped a code into the security system and opened the door. This was the most dangerous part. He was on the south leeward side of the house. Just a few moments ago, per his instructions, James had killed the floodlights.

The men were out there. It was impossible to know where exactly. A minute ago he'd seen them go around the other side. The men had been together in a pack. Bob could only hope they were stupid enough to stay that way.

Okay. Into the fire.

Bob gripped his shotgun and ran out into the dark.

126

THE house was deathly quiet. It was unnerving in its silence.

The sounds of the night, which had been so loud when James had approached the house, were completely turned off, as if a switch had been flipped. It was as if all the crickets were listening, waiting for something to happen.

Listening...

To his steady heart.

James realized he was not afraid. He believed. He was going to save his family.

James got to work. Those men would be coming soon. Any moment now. He needed to be ready.

127

THE men were huddled. Packed together. Bob wished he had an M60 right now. He'd be able to take them all out with one short burst.

He was flat on his belly to keep from being seen. The men didn't seem worried in the slightest they might be visible. They were standing there talking.

Bob considered taking them out with his double-barreled shotgun, but he'd never be able to pump fast enough to take them all out.

His thoughts were forceful. Disturbing. But he realized their cause.

These men were trying to take his little girl from him. While she may be grown now, it was the same thing to him. His little girl was inside. His granddaughters were inside. And because of that… because of these men's intentions… these men were all going to die.

It was coming back in a rush. The man he became in 'Nam. It had changed him then and he was changing now. Bob could feel his finger getting itchy. They were so close together. If he just got closer, got off two quick shots, reloaded in time.

No. Patience.

The shotgun spread would hit most of them, but it wouldn't kill all of them. Two, three, maybe four would still be alive. He couldn't risk that. He needed to cut down the odds. Pick them off one by one.

He waited.

It didn't take long. The men split into two groups. Five headed towards the house. One headed towards the barn.

That worked.

He followed the solo one. He'd double back once he took him out.

The man loped over and entered the barn. Inside were the horses. *What was he doing?* Bob soon found out. The man had found the hay area. He'd taken out some matches.

What a coward. It would kill the horses for sure. They were in their stalls. The man knew this, and here he was lighting his match.

The man cursed; seemed to be having trouble. The hay was probably wet from the nighttime dew.

"Hello."

The man turned. Bob jerked with the stock of his gun. It caught the man on the bridge of the nose, smashing and splitting it like a banana's ripe skin. The man staggered and Bob hit him in the face again.

The man fell back.

He was dead before he hit the hay.

128

IMPATIENT, not waiting for the wanted diversion, they shot out the windows and entered the house. Four of them went in at once. Paulson held back. Let them be the first to get shot.

He didn't like this. The men hadn't listened to him. He told them they needed James alive.

It's too late for that, Savic had said in his guttural pig voice. *Fine*. Kill them all. What the hell? Who cared about the money?

Paulson was not happy. This game was over and he was just now realizing it. Portino probably thought the same thing. Asshole was probably packing his bags right now. He hadn't answered any of Paulson's calls.

Damn them all. Least let the woman live. James's wife. He wasn't getting zilch out of this. Of course it wasn't going to make up for the lost billions. But at least he'd have someone to take his frustrations out on. She wanted rough; he'd give her rough.

Paulson looked on as the men entered. Before they took out the windows, they were able to see James and the old man. Both were so stupid. Hiding in plain view, just visible, peeking over the couch.

Savic and the others entered quickly. They were shooting as they moved. Bullets riddled the old man and James. Paulson saw both their bodies go down.

Except...

The men stopped shooting.

It wasn't the old man and it wasn't James. The two blockheads they'd left to guard the captives, fell down, twice dead. Someone had propped them up to make it look like…

Shots rang out. Savic and another man went down.

Shit.

The two men standing returned fire. Paulson looked on as one was hit; he spun, was hit again… went down. Just one left. Paulson didn't stick around. This was over, but he didn't have to witness it. He ran towards his car.

BOB heard the shots. He was too late. He'd seen the men entering the house.

He ran across the field. In the dark he tripped and went sprawling. *Dammit!* His shotgun flew from his hand. He got up and looked for it. As he did so, he suddenly noticed a man less than fifty yards away. The man noticed him too.

PAULSON squeezed off two shots. The man went down. *Not bad.* So much for the old man. He went to his car and started it. Live to fight another day. He looked in the rearview mirror. The barn was right behind him.

Well fuck.

Paulson quickly backed up. Can't just leave like this.

He put the vehicle in park and left it running. Inside the barn were the horses. The shooting had spooked them. Two of them whinnied and snorted at Paulson. They were digging their hooves in their stalls.

The place stunk of manure. Paulson looked for what he needed. Hay bales. Perfect. They were over by the far wall. Near them, on the ground, was Savic's man. He was laid out on his back. Blood had pooled around the man's head. He was dead, lying in his own filth.

So much for doing a simple job. He was supposed to light a fire and create a diversion. Guess that old man had mucked things up and gotten here first.

Paulson pulled out a lighter. If you want something done, do it yourself. The hay was wet. It lit, but not fast enough.

Annoyed, Paulson looked around. He walked past the horses. They were making more noises, kicking the stalls now. Stupid animals.

He didn't have time for this. Just as he was about to cut bait, he spied a riding mower. There, near it, was just what he needed. A fuel can.

Wearing a grin, he carried it back towards the hay. He splashed liberally all around the hay bales, on the walls, making sure not to pour the gas directly on the sputtering flame.

He winked at the horses on the way out. "Goodbye, ladies."

He heard the whoosh of flame as it lit the gas. *Now that's what I'm talking about.*

He got in his car, passed the house, and gunned it down the lane.

129

JAMES hunkered down as the men pumped bullets into their dead compatriots. He'd propped them up, made them appear alive. The darkness had misled them. They thought they were shooting at him.

James was up on the second-story landing. His elevated position gave him a direct bead on those below him.

Go for the biggest target, Bob had told him. James followed the advice. He rose just enough to get the right angle. He aimed for their chests. A dad's voice in his ear. *Breathe. Easy son. Slow squeeze.*

One.

The man with the gray cap splayed backwards like a rag doll. With a steady hand, James oriented on the man in the black Windbreaker. The man was looking at his compatriot fall.

Two.

A thump in the chest. The man slumped and fell. James moved from his position, backwards, out of their range of vision. He scurried ten feet, got behind a flower pot.

The third and fourth were firing. They were shooting everywhere. They obviously didn't know where James was.

James took a deep breath and moved just enough to get an angle. The man was arcing his fire. His bald head looked like a cue ball. Slow squeeze.

Three.

The man spun. The shot had tagged him on his right side. James squeezed again, three dots centering on the target. The man doubled over and then crumpled to the floor.

One more.

The last man standing didn't run. He was in this till the end, squeezing off every shot he had. He still didn't know where James was. His eyes began to scan the stairwell... looking up near where James was on the landing. His shots were going errant. The man paused... out of bullets... he frantically reached for another clip.

Lord forgive me.

Four.

The man's face twitched to an expression of permanent surprise. He fell. It was over.

The Feds arrived minutes later. Talk about timing. The rest was a blur.

James was hugging his girls again and not wanting to let go. He kissed and hugged his wife. It was a tender moment cut short.

A barn was burning.

Later, he remembered one of the FBI agents telling him that Mac Hockney was in stable condition. "He sends a hello and a thanks. Good thing you had the guy's phone. Otherwise we couldn't have tracked you."

Somewhere in the mess, as the fire was being put out and horses being saved, they found Bob. Two men had to hoist him up. He refused to have a stretcher.

"What happened?" James said.

"I think I hit my head."

"You're bleeding."

"Just a scratch, guy barely tagged me. Dumbass self did the rest. When I fell I must have hit a rock. The girls?"

"All okay."

Bob smiled. "Let's go see them."

130

"MOMMY, don't watch this! Dora is on."

"Grandpop, can I sit with you?"

"No let me!"

James took his eyes from the family scene in the living room as Sue flipped the channel. They'd watched too much news in the last few weeks. It was good to see the world returning to normal. There was hardly anything today about the *Billion Dollar Four*.

That's what they were calling it.

A week ago they'd made another arrest. This time in Belize. A Swiss banker who was one of the masterminds. The week before it had been Cairo: a London financier arrested in his underwear trying to flee through a window.

And the weeks before then were Moscow and Beijing. The Solntsevskaya bratva and Chinese Triad, now household names, each day for weeks were having firefights with each other and Russian and Chinese authorities. The two criminal outfits were being outed just as they tried to go even more underground. Their leaders were known and it was just a matter of time until they were caught. Hundreds had been arrested so far. Their criminal enterprises were suffering setbacks on all fronts.

The Russian mob and Chinese Triad were turning each other in, in places they didn't even have competing interests. Rumor was they were in a turf struggle, each vying for what the other had. Each ruthless in trying to take the other out.

Lo San and Simeon Mihajlovic were being painted as the Al Capones of the computer age. Every watch list had their pictures front page and center. It was a media feeding frenzy. The audacity of a billion-dollar heist. The public loved it. Lo San and Simeon Mihajlovic were bigger than rock stars.

And that wasn't even what they almost made away with. The world watched as the global net tightened. Every government it seemed wanted to be the one to find where they were hiding—to make the arrest of the century.

James was done with it. It was old news. He turned on the TV in the kitchen to see how the weather was going to be today. Later, he wanted to go for a run. He was getting back into working out. He'd even lost ten pounds.

As the TV came on, he realized perhaps he'd been hasty with his thoughts. There was still some coverage. One of the business channels just couldn't seem to get enough.

"...at no point were the companies we protect ever in jeopardy. We kept our eyes on the ball. Finger on the trigger. Investors realized the value of that. In today's uncertain world a firm, strong company is what people want to see—particularly when it comes to their money. We certainly didn't get to where we are by being doggone complacent..."

James clicked the TV off. That was the CEO of ComTek. He was still making the rounds. The man was loving this. Stock was at an all-time high. In eight weeks the company's value had shot up to $23 billion.

Six weeks ago that very same CEO had flown James out to his spread in Aspen. The CEO—who'd been on vacation at the time—had fetched him using the company's private jet. James was treated like royalty. They put his family and him up at a five-star hotel. They spared no expense. A limo had taken James to the CEO's lavish residence at the top of the mountain.

The CEO had a million-watt smile. James was called by his first name. *Sort of.*

"Jimmy boy, so glad you could make it. Aspen treating you well?"

The small talk soon segued to the purpose of the trip. The CEO wanted to offer James a promotion. "Really wanted to do it personally. Just to show my appreciation and all. You really stepped up. Company owes a lot to you."

The CEO didn't mince any words.

"How does ten thousand sound to you?"

That was to be his bonus. Ten thousand dollars. And his promotion was to be from manager to senior manager with a ten percent raise. "That's another seven thousand dollars for you. Not too shabby, huh?"

There was only one small catch. James had to sign a confidentiality form, which in a nutshell said he'd never speak of his role, what had really happened, or what he'd done. The FBI, NSA and all the other outfits knew the full story, of course. But in the interest of national defense and maintaining the integrity of the financial system, they were going along with the spin. All the way down to it being organized by the Russian and Chinese mobs. There was no mention of Rex Portino's involvement, only that the COO of ComTek was an unfortunate casualty in a nefarious operation that failed to infiltrate ComTek's impregnable safety systems. Paulson and Enrique were not even brief mentions.

As for everything James had done, including the last phase he'd initiated before he left The Vault, none of that was being aired. He was privately praised for his actions. The detailed instructions he'd sent out to every ComTek customer telling them what they needed to do to restore their databases and purge their systems of virus threats had essentially allowed the financial markets to return to normal.

Those instructions were the same that Mac Hockney and the FBI had intercepted. James had single-handedly saved the free markets. Because of him the amount of monies that were lost went from three hundred billion to one billion.

The few banks that didn't utilize The Vault were the causalities in this drama. All the other banks and financial funds came out spades—they didn't lose a cent. The official publicity release was that The Vault had done its job in sterling fashion. And because of those automated systems, *"which operated flawlessly"* (a phrase repeated ad nauseam by the CEO), ComTek was the latest darling on The Street. Investors were rewarding the company handsomely. The company was on a roll.

James thought back six weeks ago. Looking the CEO in the eye.

"I don't know. I'm thinking the ten part sounds good. But you seem to have left a few zeroes off. Don't you think ten million might be more appropriate?"

He could still recall the look on the man's face. That million-watt smile turning the other way.

"Seems fair, wouldn't you say—considering the actual value I brought to the company. What's your personal portfolio now worth with where our stock is? Four billion and rising? And what was it I saved the company's clients again? Was it three hundred billion? I forget. All those zeroes seem to run together."

That had felt good. Not that James thought the guy would actually pony up. He had no intention of talking to the press. But he'd had it with being short changed. It was time he stood up for himself.

He was no longer afraid. He had options. He didn't have to just take what they gave him.

The FBI had even offered him a job as well. The pay was better. Which was funny, he'd always heard the government didn't pay much. He'd be working for their Cyber Warfare Unit.

Options. It was a nice feeling. But James had his sights on something else.

They were called dreams.

"Honey, if you're looking for me I'll be at Best Buy. I've got to pick up another router for the computer."

He picked up his car keys to his new Porsche and walked out the door.

Epilogue

HE emptied from the taxi and walked up the steps of the hotel. In his breast pocket was a passport he'd paid dearly for. Just shy of ten thousand dollars was hidden inside his bag's liner.

Pocket money. But it would do for the next twenty-four hours. He'd make a more substantial withdrawal from the *Banco Bilbao Vizcaya Argenteria* tomorrow. Seventeen million he'd squirreled away in various offshore banks. Not exactly the billions he'd been counting on, but considering the lemons he'd been given, he was lucky to have that surfeit of lemonade.

Three months living on the run had not been easy. It had cramped his style. Nick Paulson was looking forward to getting back…

His thoughts were interrupted.

"Sir?" It was the hotel's concierge.

"What is it?"

"There is a package for you."

Paulson frowned. "Give me a second. I've got to hit the john." He touched his stomach and grimaced. *"Baño. Entiende?"*

"Si, señor."

Paulson headed towards the men's room. *Fuck, how had they found him?* He quickly walked down the corridor and continued past the dual doors for *Senoritas* and *Hombres*.

There was another door that said *No Admittance / Porhibida La Entrada*. He pushed it open and quickly went inside. Less than a minute later, he

386

was walking out a rear door into a service dock area.

"Going somewhere?"

Paulson turned. There were several men by a van. Two of them walked over to him. A short and tall one. Paulson considered trying to run, but he was boxed in.

"You're a hard man to find." The tall one was wearing a cheap knockoff *Tommy Bahamas* shirt, jeans and flip flops. He had Fed stamped all over his forehead.

Paulson raised his hands. "You got me."

"Looks like it." The man took out his gun. "Drop the bag. Hands behind your back. You know the drill."

Paulson let the other man, who was short and stocky, put the cuffs on him.

The men by the van came over. They were dressed differently. Probably the local scouts who'd spied him at the airport. Paulson was thinking about the extradition process. It was one of the reasons he'd picked Venezuela. He just had to get hold of his lawyer.

"I want a phone call."

"Sure," said the Fed. The man took a drag of his cigarette and flicked it on the ground. "Tell it to these guys."

Paulson frowned. "What do you mean?"

"Hold on," said the man. He spoke rapid-fire Spanish to the men. An envelope was exchanged and he waved his hand.

"See you later, Nick."

The men grabbed hold of him. "What's going on?" Paulson said.

One of the guys threw a canvas bag over his head. Paulson tried to yell and was hit in the gut. *Umphh.*

Lights out.

"GOT the bag?"

Denis mumbled an affirmative.

Peter lit another cigarette. "Stiff us for twenty-five thou. What a tool." He started counting the cash in the envelope. It wasn't exactly twenty-five thousand, but it would make the trip worthwhile. Pay for their expenses with a little extra on the side.

They watched the van drive away. Some mutual friends had given them the contact. Guys specialized in organs. Livers mostly. But they took everything, down to the eyes.

"I wonder how that stuff works? You think they kill him first?"

"Beats me," Denis said.

"Ready for a beer?"

"Sure, but none of that *Cuba Libre* this time, I got the shits."

ACKNOWLEDGMENTS

TWENTY years, seven books, and countless half-done projects ago, the loss of one of my best friends, Jeff Cudlip, prompted me to start writing. We all have books in us. While I couldn't find meaning in why Jeff left us so early, I thank him for the gift he left me. He turned me on to writing.

Jeff touched many lives. Thank you, Jeff, for touching mine.

In addition to Jeff, this book is dedicated to those below:

For my dad. I miss you.

For my wife, Kristi. For believing in me, for reading all my other works that preceded this one and never once telling me I shouldn't shoot for my dream.

For my readers: Nicole Mazzola, Janelle Selembo, Sam Bloom and Jeff Wilson. Thank you for giving me your time and letting me know you enjoyed the read. Your praise and helpful critiques, while you may not know it, kept me thinking I can do this.

For my technical advisers: Jeff Robison and Jeff Dittrich. Both of you really helped make this book better. Much of the technical aspects are not far from reality. Some are a stretch. You pointed those out to me, and I took some liberties. Any technical gaffes contained in this work are my own.

For John Talbot, a fine literary agent and an amazing editor. Thank you for seeing this book's potential and teaching me to be a better writer.

For Pat LoBrutto. Thank you for your editorial input; you helped me see what I was missing and improved the read.

Made in the USA
Columbia, SC
10 April 2020

91476283R00236